WRITERS
AND LIARS

WRITERS AND LIARS

A Novel

CAROL GOODMAN

WM
WILLIAM MORROW
An Imprint of HarperCollins*Publishers*

WRITERS AND LIARS. Copyright © 2025 by Carol Goodman. All rights reserved. Printed in the United States of America. No part of this book may be used or reproduced in any manner whatsoever without written permission except in the case of brief quotations embodied in critical articles and reviews. For information, address HarperCollins Publishers, 195 Broadway, New York, NY 10007.

HarperCollins books may be purchased for educational, business, or sales promotional use. For information, please email the Special Markets Department at SPsales@harpercollins.com.

FIRST EDITION

Designed by Diahann Sturge

Olive tree illustration © AK082/Stock.Adobe.com

Library of Congress Cataloging-in-Publication Data

Names: Goodman, Carol, author.
Title: Writers and liars : a novel / Carol Goodman.
Description: First edition. | New York : William Morrow Paperbacks, 2025.
Identifiers: LCCN 2024047253 (print) | LCCN 2024047254 (ebook) | ISBN 9780063398733 (paperback) | ISBN 9780063398771 (hardcover) | ISBN 9780063441354 | ISBN 9780063398740 (ebook)
Subjects: LCGFT: Novels. | Thrillers (Fiction)
Classification: LCC PS3607.O566 W75 2025 (print) | LCC PS3607.O566 (ebook) | DDC 813/.6—dc23/eng/20241021
LC record available at https://lccn.loc.gov/2024047253
LC ebook record available at https://lccn.loc.gov/2024047254

ISBN 978-0-06-339873-3
ISBN 978-0-06-339877-1 (simultaneous hardcover edition)

25 26 27 28 29 LBC 5 4 3 2 1

To my daughter, Maggie

WRITERS AND LIARS

CHAPTER ONE

The envelope lands with a thud on my desk along with the rest of the day's mail. "Oh. My. God," my work-study assistant, Jenner, gasps. "Is that an invitation from Argos Alexander?"

I glance at the heavy, cream-colored envelope. My name is handwritten in calligraphy across the front and there's a Greek postage stamp with an image of a marble goddess in the right-hand corner but there's no return address. I turn it over, my fingers lingering on the heavy, expensive paper, which feels like the pelt of a pampered animal. Looking back up at me is an eye, blue as the Aegean—the *mati*—a charm to ward off jealousy. *Beware*, it warns, *of envy*. But I'm long past envy. I stepped out of the chase years ago.

"It's just like the one Annika Greer posted on TikTok!" Jenner squeals.

I look up at Jenner and see she's already got her phone out and is scrolling to a recent post that she shoves in front of my face before I have a chance to tell her, *No, I don't want to see Annika Greer doing* anything *on TikTok. Or anywhere. Ever.* I'm too late. There she is, Annika, beautiful as ever, the same long red hair and eyebrow-grazing bangs, the same wide blue eyes, holding up the twin to my envelope, waving it at the camera. She performs a little dance with a decorative letter opener that she slides under the envelope's fold and slices up with a decisive thrust as if she's performing a ritual sacrifice. For a moment I imagine Annika slicing her own hand and blood spurting out.

Not so past envy, after all, a little voice says inside my head.

The TikTok ends before the contents of the envelope are revealed. The caption, in cerulean blue, reads: *#Blessed to be offered this opportunity. #Grateful to the Great Goddess!* Followed by a string of emojis: namaste hands, moons, suns, and a lot of multicolored hearts.

"It must be an invitation to his island, Eros!" Jenner says, clapping her hands. "Didn't you go there once? Back when you were a writer?"

Back when I was a writer. I smile up at Jenner, who has an unfamiliar expression on her face. She's been my work-study assistant since last September and has been fairly reliable except for a few bouts of the flu and a weepy period when some boy broke up with her. She's shown a polite interest in the workings of the college museum that I supervise even though she's a digital media major and we here at the Museum of Ancient Antiquities are decidedly low-tech, and enough interest in me to learn how I like my coffee (drip, no flavoring, whole real milk) and that, yes, I really do care about spelling and grammar in our outgoing emails. I have never seen her looking at me like this, though, like I might actually be someone *important*. Like I might actually be someone worthy of envy.

"The island isn't called Eros," I correct. "That's the god of love. Eris is the goddess of discord. She's the one who threw the golden apple into the wedding of Peleus and Thetis—" Noticing that Jenner's eyes are glazing over I resort to a visual aid and point to a poster on the wall behind her. It features the museum's prize object, the seventh-century BCE black-figure Wedding Vase. "See that scary winged woman holding an apple? That's Eris. She was angry that she wasn't invited to the wedding of Peleus and Thetis so she tossed a golden apple marked 'To the fairest' into the party. Hera, Athena, and Aphrodite fought over it so they asked Paris to judge who was the fairest and Aphrodite bribed him by offering him Helen, which is what started the Trojan War—" Seeing that I've lost her again, I sigh and add, "Yes, I went to the residency on Eris but it was a long time ago—fifteen years ago. I wrote my first book there." *Back when I was a writer.* Is that why Argos invited me and Annika, because it's our anniversary? Does that mean he's inviting *all* the residents who were there that summer?

"Then he's definitely inviting you back to Eros!" Jenner enthuses, ignoring my lesson on Greek mythology. "I read that he invites artists and writers he thinks have a great work in them. Wasn't Annika Greer there the same time you were? And that classics mystery writer you're so into? Aren't you going to open it?"

I stare down at the blue eye, picturing Annika's blue eyes, the way they'd widen when she was impressed, or moved, or surprised. Would she be surprised to learn that I have received an invitation, too? Would she be a little . . . *jealous?*

"Not now. And no—" I add, holding up my hand before Jenner can make the request I can see is on the tip of her tongue. "I don't want you to make a video of me opening it. Really, it's like your generation doesn't remember what it was like to get mail! Besides, even if it *is* an invitation, I'd have no reason to go. Because I'm not a writer anymore."

Jenner gapes at me. "But if Argos Alexander is inviting you to his island, then he must think you still are! Besides, isn't his villa, like, *gorgeous*?"

Images of whitewashed walls against blue sky, terraces dripping with bougainvillea and jasmine, silver olive groves shivering in the sea breeze, and aquamarine grottos scroll through my mind like a travel video. Like something Annika might post on TikTok. "Yes," I tell Jenner, "it's the most beautiful place on earth. Now would you please get me the end-of-year budget report? I need to have that to President Hubert before four today."

I spend the rest of the afternoon shuffling around expenses, trying to find ways to keep the Museum of Ancient Antiquities running on a shoestring budget. I send in the report and half an hour later the president shows up at my office. Not a good sign, but perhaps not surprising. Donations to the museum are down and operating costs are up. Interest in the classics is declining. Five years ago, the Classics Department was folded into Comp Lit. Digital Media has been angling for the space the museum occupies on the top floor of Old Main and the administration has been suggesting we store our collection in a subbasement of the library.

"If this is about the budget," I say, reaching for the report, "I have some ideas of cuts we could make."

"I didn't come to talk about the budget, Maia," he says, sitting down in the old leather armchair across from my desk.

"What did you come to talk about?" I ask, shifting in my chair, which lets out an angry squeak. It's as ancient as some of our artifacts but I haven't dared request a replacement.

"I hear Argos Alexander is calling his lambs home—"

"To the slaughter," I can't help adding.

"You didn't end up so badly the last time," he says. "Didn't he launch your career?"

"Like Helen's face, Argos Alexander has launched a thousand careers." I could add that he takes even less responsibility than Helen for the trajectory of those careers once he's cast them adrift on the sea, but don't want to sound as if I'm blaming him for how I foundered on the rocks in the years after my residency on Eris when I know no one's to blame for that other than myself.

"I'm always reminded of the benefits of a classical education when I'm in your company, Maia. Your father would be proud."

My father, a classics professor and former head of this museum, would say that the Helen simile was low-hanging fruit and surely I could have come up with something more original.

"So," he goes on, compliment delivered, "you must have received an invitation." He leans forward and props his elbows on my desk, rumpling the pages of the budget report. "I saw your old friend Annika Greer was invited—"

"Et tu, Philip? I wouldn't have pegged you for an avid TikTok fan."

"I have a Google News alert set for Argos Alexander and all our most generous donors," he says, "and besides, I liked that book Annika wrote—"

"I got an invitation," I say abruptly, determined not to be upstaged by Annika in my own office. Especially not by Annika's first book, which featured an unlikable character named Freya who was dominated by her Medieval Studies professor father—an obvious stand-in for me.

"Ah," he says, leaning back and steepling his fingers as if I've just exposed my queen in a game of chess. *Never let yourself be provoked*, my father always said, *least of all by vanity.* "When do you go? I can arrange a travel grant if that's necessary and I'm sure the museum can spare you—"

"What makes you think I've accepted? Why would I drop everything at his summons?"

"And what exactly would you be dropping?"

Blood rushes to my face. "I'm working on a book," I say, thinking guiltily of the manuscript collecting dust on my desk at home. *Working on* is perhaps an exaggeration.

"Write it there," he says. "Isn't the island supposed to be the seat of the Muses?"

"No," I snap, tired of everybody getting this wrong, "that's Mount Parnassus. Eris is the goddess of discord, a mean-spirited bitch who likes to stir up the worst in people. Her island is not a happy place." I picture for a moment that white-walled room with its view of the sea, the olive-wood desk scattered with seashells. "So why in the world would I go back there?"

"Because," Philip says, uncowed by my mythology lesson and taking a crisp envelope stamped with the *mati* from his pocket, "Argos Alexander has written to say he's considering making a substantial bequest to the Museum of Ancient Antiquities. He says he looks forward to discussing it with you when you come to the island."

Philip knew all along I'd been invited. "We have other donors," I say, "and there are a few more cuts I could make."

He shrugs and gets to his feet. "If that's what you prefer, but if you don't have the funds to support the museum by the end of the summer, I'll have to recommend that we consider closing up shop."

He stops at the door and looks back over his shoulder. "And

frankly, Maia, mightn't that be the best outcome for you? When your father got ill and you stepped in to help out here, we were all grateful, but it was only meant to be temporary. I can't help feeling that the museum has gotten in the way of your writing. Maybe a trip to Eris is just what you need."

He leaves before I can respond, which is just as well. While it's tempting to go along with the story he's spun—dutiful daughter puts career on hold to nurse ailing father and carry on his legacy—I know it's a lie.

AFTER PHILIP LEAVES, I spend half an hour clearing my desk and tending to end-of-semester chores. Jenner has asked for a recommendation for an internship in the fall that I write with genuine enthusiasm, sure she'll be better suited working for an advertising firm in New York City than among the dusty artifacts of the museum. I'm surprised to feel a pang as I send it off, but I chalk that up to the work I'll have training another Gen-Z student to write grammatical emails and remember how I take my coffee.

Jenner's left already to take a final so I'm alone in the museum. I usually enjoy these last moments in the galleries but today the late-afternoon sun slanting through the tall windows throws long shadows across the old hardwood floors, and the bars of sunlight trapped between the shadows are filled with dust motes, like flies in amber. Passing through them on my way out I feel as if *I* am preserved in amber, too, one of the museum's relics. The little clay Tanagra figures tip their dreidel-shaped hats at me, and the archaic Persephone statue smiles slyly as if to say, *You're one of us. Watch out or you'll end up in the subbasement, too.*

I stop at the Attic black-figure amphora, known as the Wedding Vase because it depicts the wedding of Peleus, a mortal man,

to the sea nymph Thetis, and look closer at the winged figure of
Eris getting ready to lob the apple marked "To the fairest" into the
crowd. Already Hera, Aphrodite, and Athena are gazing up, ready
to fight for the honor—*Like housewives squabbling over the sales
rack at Loehmann's*, my father used to say to get a laugh when he
lectured on the vase. Then, sobering, he would add, *But there is
a kind of strife that Hesiod tells us "stirs up even the shiftless to toil"
and is "wholesome for men."* Then he would tell the story of how
he found the first shard of the vase on his honeymoon in Switzerland and how he searched the world to find the other pieces, determined to bring together the Wedding Vase before anyone else
could, as a testament to his beloved, departed wife. *Sometimes*,
he would conclude his lecture, *a little competition spurs us on to
do great things*.

A slant of light lands on the vase, catching the arrow gripped
in Eris's hand, and I see Annika dancing with that letter opener.

Or sometimes, I think, turning my back on the goddess, a little
competition spurs us on to do *terrible* things.

CHAPTER TWO

When I get home, I toss the invitation on my desk, right on top of the typescript of my last unfinished novel, where it sits among a scattering of objects—a Murano paperweight, assorted seashells, a lump of marble—like the exhibits in a museum of a lost civilization. Eventually, I figure, it will lose its power as everything else that touches my desk does.

I spend the rest of the weekend sitting on the screened-in porch reading the new Detective Pythagoras book—*Pythagoras Walks the Labyrinth*—by Clive Davies, *that classics mystery writer you're so into*, only Jenner had it wrong. The author of Detective Pythagoras wasn't on the island when I was there; it was his son, Ian Davies. But she was right that I love the books. This one is set on a Greek island at a Mycenaean palace built over an intricate labyrinth. By the end of chapter one, a young woman is shot through the heart by an arrow on an altar while surrounded by onlookers. Pythagoras is tasked with discovering the killer through calculating what angle the arrow was shot from. It's a pleasantly engaging puzzle, complete with diagrams, maps, a cast of suspicious characters, and vivid local scenery.

Who needs to travel to a Greek island when I've got one right here in my head?

But then my agent, Diane, calls.

I call her my agent although she hasn't represented a book of mine in years. Mostly she's assumed the role of friend and scold. "Did you get one in the mail?" she asks in that raspy voice of hers that always makes me think of forties movie stars.

"You'll have to be more specific," I tell her. "I'm drowning in mail—an L.L.Bean catalog, this week's *New Yorker*, a jury summons—"

"An invitation to Eris," she says, breaking into my sad list. "Annika Greer posted hers on TikTok."

"You know I stopped doing social media years ago," I say, feeling a stab of betrayal that Diane follows Annika on TikTok, "and I've been a happier person since."

"It's a hellscape," Diane agrees, "but it's *our* hellscape, Maia. I know that things didn't end perfectly last time but this would be a chance to get back on track. You might even get a blurb from your friend—"

"I got something from Argos," I say to forestall Diane's suggestion that I beg Annika for a blurb. "It's sitting right here on my desk."

I pick up the envelope to prove to myself that I'm not making it up. I don't tell Diane that the cream-colored stock has acquired a coffee ring and a splash of red wine over the two days it has sat on my desk.

"You have! I knew it! What does it say? Annika was coy but I gather it's an invitation from Argos Alexander to come to the island this summer along with a select group of authors for a writing retreat."

A select group. I feel a spike of dopamine at the joy of being *chosen*, which I quickly squelch. I know from experience how addictive that rush is, and how brutal the withdrawal. "I haven't opened it."

The silence that follows is ominous. Diane is rarely silenced. When I told her I wanted to set my second novel in 11,000 BCE she managed to gulp out, *Like something by Mary Renault?* When my editor passed on it, she called me right up to say, *The news isn't good, kid.* Finally, after about thirty seconds she manages, "Do you think maybe you could open it now? For me?"

I sigh. "I can't go back there."

"You don't even know—"

"It will be an invitation. He likes to gather his disciples around him, like Jesus."

"He wields a lot of power in the publishing world, Maia. A word from him and—"

"What? Someone will want to publish my last one? Or are you hoping that if I go to Eris I'll be touched by the hand of the muse and write something salable?"

I instantly regret my tone. Diane has stood by me while most agents would have stopped answering my calls. Luckily, she has a thick skin.

"Salable would be nice, Maia, but frankly, I'd just like to see you working on something that makes you happy."

"I don't think anything *happy* has ever come out of that god-forsaken island. Remember it's named for the goddess of discord. That's, like, literally, the goddess of unhappiness."

"So, you weren't happy writing your first book there?"

It's the worst question she could ask. For a moment I see myself in a white room cool as a cave, seated at an olive-wood desk beneath a window framing blue sky and bluer sea, loose pages rustling in the thyme- and salt-scented breeze, words spilling onto the paper like water from a fountain.

"Happy?" I echo. "I'm not even sure I was myself when I wrote it."

After I end the call with Diane I stare at the envelope. It stares back with the still, unblinking gaze of a Gorgon. Only Argos would send an invitation with a *mati* on the envelope, daring the recipient to open it. But that, after all, was how his generosity worked. *Come to my island, set like a jewel in the Aegean Sea. I will give you beauty—Homer's wine-dark sea, thyme-scented paths, grottos carved from limestone, and silvered olive groves where the faces of the ancient gods beckon from their marble shrines. I will give you the time and space and leisure in which to become your truest self and realize your heart's desire: to write the masterpiece you were born to create. But like all gifts granted by the gods, this one comes with a curse.*

I hadn't been able to resist at twenty-two, but then I hadn't known the price for such inspiration. What it cost to step outside of yourself. What you might find when you looked into the eyes of your *truest self.* Surely nothing inside this envelope will have power over me now.

To hell with it.

I claw at the envelope with my fingers instead of using the decorative letter opener I received when I won the Golden Dagger award for my first book. A single card slides out like a mollusk from its shell. A black-and-white block design of a labyrinth is pressed into the thick paper like an ancient inscription carved in marble. Looking at it, I find myself following the maze until I grow dizzy. I turn the card over quickly, the edges so sharp I slice

my finger on it. Already the island is exacting its tribute. I suck
the blood while reading.

You are invited to the Villa of Lavyrinthos
On the island of Eris
For a select gathering of artists
To commune with the Muses,
To become your truest self,
And create the work you were born to create.

To become your truest self. I would laugh at the claim if I didn't
know that it was accurate.

After all, that's what I'd been looking for when I applied to the
Eris Writers Residency. I thought it was my last chance at becoming a writer before I followed my father's wishes into graduate
school in classics to become a college professor like him. How
could I tell him I wanted to be a writer when being an artist had
practically killed my mother? All I'd wanted to do since she died
when I was nine was assuage his grief and make him proud. But
there was a story in me that was struggling to get out. I wrote a
short piece called "The Professor's Daughter" and sent it to the
Eris Residency. How mad could my father be, I reasoned, when
the residency was in his beloved Greece and he even knew the
director from his days at the American Archeological School in
Athens? When I got in, I thought it was a sign from the gods, like
the omens Roman augurs read in the entrails of birds.

My father wasn't angry as I'd feared; worse, he looked scared.
Afraid I'd end up like my mother and go up in flames in pursuit
of my art, no doubt.

It's just a summer, I told him. *If I'm not cut out to be a writer I'll apply to graduate school in the fall.*

But it wasn't just a summer; it was another world. From the minute I set foot on Eris I felt as if I were in the place where myths were born and I was metamorphosizing like Daphne sprouting leaves from her fingertips and Arethusa melting into water. I found a best friend—beautiful, talented Annika Greer, unlike any girl I'd ever met (or who ever had time for me)—who made me feel like my funniest, smartest self. I fell in love with Ian Davies, who knew what it was like to live in the shadow of an overbearing father. They made me feel like I could be the person I wanted to be—a writer, a best friend, beloved. They gave me the courage to sit at that desk and write the novel that had been struggling to get out.

When I read it aloud at night on the terrace, overlooked by the statues of Greek gods who seemed to be listening, Argos said I had tapped into the sacred font of the Muses. Ian had simply declared: *You are a writer!* Even one of the older mystery writers there, Olivia Knox, had grudgingly told me that I had *chops*. And one of the other residents, a shy girl whose name I've forgotten, had looked at me with such envy I almost felt bad. But when I saw the spark of jealousy in Annika's eyes, I'd exulted. *Beautiful, talented Annika Greer is jealous of me!*

I should have taken that look as a warning.

On the last night, as I sat at my desk putting the finishing touches on my novel, a little drunk from our farewell dinner, a little full of myself from what Argos had told me in our last conference—that I had a great work inside me—I'd heard voices coming from the balcony below my window.

We have to tell her. Annika's voice, followed by Ian's.

Can't it wait until we're off the island? It will kill her.

Were they talking about me? What did they think would kill me?

I'd gotten up from my desk and carefully crept out onto my balcony. My room was on the lowest floor of the villa facing the sea. Below me, stairs led up from the dock and branched off to small, whitewashed balconies carved out of the cliffside below the villa. The balcony directly below mine was Annika's favorite spot for sunbathing because it contained a little grotto scooped out of the rock and was fitted out with Turkish carpets and embroidered cushions. *Like a pasha's seraglio*, Annika had pronounced when we discovered it. *The grotto of the Muses*, Ian had christened it because of a marble statue of a woman holding a lyre.

What were Annika and Ian doing there now? I wondered. When I'd left them on the terrace after my conference with Argos—glowing and a little unsteady from the praise he had heaped on me—they'd both been waiting for their conferences and Annika had said they would come get me when they were done. Why had they gone to the grotto instead? And what were they afraid would kill me?

I leaned over the edge to shout at them but then I saw them in the moonlight move closer to each other until their lips met. I stared, frozen to the spot, until they moved inside into the grotto—with all those rugs and cushions—and disappeared.

I'd gone back inside and numbly sat back down at my desk, where I'd sat all summer, so immersed in the spell of the Muses that Annika had taken her revenge and stolen Ian from me. Because she could. Because she couldn't let me have the book *and* true love.

Which hadn't turned out to be *true* at all.

Then I'd looked down at the rough draft of my novel and realized what I had to do.

Now I look down at the invitation, which sits on top of my un-finished manuscript. Superstition has kept me from moving the manuscript off my desk even though I haven't even tried to work on it in years. Tossing it would mean admitting that I was never going to finish it. It would mean it was time to start something new. But what? I haven't had a single idea worth writing since the one I had on Eris—

Maybe if you go back there, a seductive voice whispers in my ear.

"It's not the island of the Muses," I say aloud. "It's the island of that nasty bitch who inspires envy in our hearts and makes your supposed best friend steal your boyfriend."

I drop the invitation and the envelope in my wastepaper basket and go to bed. When I close my eyes, though, I see the blazing blue Aegean Sea and Annika, gorgeous in a red bikini, diving into the water, her blue eyes when she surfaces the same color as the sea. I'm treated to a whole travel reel of Annika on the island— hiking along the ridge trail to the ruins of a temple with Ian trail-ing behind her, picking poppies and threading one behind Ian's ear, beckoning to Ian to swim with her in the blue grotto of the island's east cove, twining herself in between me and Ian at din-ner, lying on the villa rooftop late at night between us as I pointed out the constellations above.

Whenever I look at the stars from now on I'll be right back here with you two, Annika had said.

I open my eyes and find I am looking up at the night sky, the stars spinning overhead. Maybe I *have* gone back, I think. Maybe I can change what happened.

Then I blink my eyes and the stars dim. I am in my child-hood bedroom and the stars are the ones my mother painted for me. The glow-in-the-dark paint has been steadily fading. One day they'll be gone entirely, but for now, like stars that have died a million years ago but still shine, they carry my dead mother's voice. *Whenever you are lost, follow the stars*, she had told me, holding up her hand to show me the ring she always wore. It was made from an ancient Greek intaglio carved with a pattern of stars. It had been set into an earring, my mother told me, but my father had it made into their wedding ring—*a constellation to always guide them to each other*. After my mother died, my father gave the ring to me. I rub my thumb over the pattern of stars now, hoping it will calm me, but remembering that it hadn't kept her from becoming lost inside her own troubled mind any more than it will lead me back to who I was before I went to the island.

Finally, unable to sleep, I give in to the siren call of social media (I'd fibbed when I told Diane I didn't follow it) and go onto Annika's Instagram to see what she's posting about her upcoming trip to the island and who's liked it. And there, like her feed is hot-wired to my brain, are all the images that have been haunting me. She's posted a dozen photographs from that summer . . . and not just pictures of her, but pictures of me and Ian, too. I pause on one of Ian—grinning, skin bronzed, tousled brown hair gold in the Mediterranean sun—with Annika and me on either side of him, an arm around each of us.

I made the best friends on the island last time! Annika has written in the caption. *I can't wait to see who's coming now! If you've gotten an invitation don't be shy, let me know!*

She's tagged me and Ian. So, she's still in touch with him. Over the years I've combed Annika's social media for any sign of him but he's either been camera shy or they weren't together anymore.

Maybe she's trying to find out if he's coming. Maybe she's wondering if I am.

Maybe, I think, *she's afraid that I will.*

A spark flares in my chest, like that dopamine rush I'd felt earlier from being *chosen*, but this flame burns steadier and fills my heart with a dark craving to see that confident look in Annika's blue eyes waver. To let her know that she's not the only one who's been chosen. *I bet it would really drive her crazy to know I've been invited, too.*

What an ugly thought, I rebuke myself. It's the island. I haven't even set foot on it but already it's exerting its dark force from across the sea.

I am past envy, I tell myself. *I have stepped out of the chase.*

Then why do you still follow Annika? And why is that manuscript still on your desk?

I'll unfollow Annika and throw out the manuscript tomorrow, I reply. I've worked hard these last fifteen years to put my life back on track, taken over the museum my father ran at the college, risen to Rank IV in the university staff hierarchy, complete with benefits and a retirement plan. I don't need to go halfway around the world chasing some ridiculous notion of inspiration and creation. I don't need to be a writer.

As I'm putting down my phone, I notice I've got a private message on Instagram. When I open it, I see it's from Annika. *Hey, I suppose you've heard that I'm going back to the island. I hope it didn't upset you to know I'd been invited back. I know that things ended badly between us, but I understand that you weren't really yourself. Maybe none of us were. I just want you to know that I have no hard feelings and that I'd really love to see you again. xoxoAnnika*

I stare at the text so long the letters swim and dissolve, like foam in the surf. *I just want you to know that I have no hard feelings?* As if I'm the one who had betrayed our friendship!

Instead of answering her message, I reply directly to her post on Instagram. *I wouldn't miss it for the world. I'll see you there.*

CHAPTER THREE

Ten days later I'm at the portside taverna in Volos where I've been instructed to wait for Argos's yacht. When I RSVP'd by email an automatic reply from Despina Outis, Mr. Alexander's secretary, had directed me to a travel agent in Athens who had been instructed to make all my travel arrangements. A private limo had picked me up at my house and driven me to the airport, where I was whisked through check-in and security by the grace of my first-class ticket. The last time I had flown, for an antiquities conference in Minneapolis, I'd been shoehorned into economy between a businessman who elbowed me every time he moved and a sulky preteen playing a video game without headphones. This time, I'm greeted by name at the gate, escorted to a seat that looks like my own private cabin, and given a glass of champagne and a pair of silky pajamas should I want to nap on the eleven-hour flight. Everyone was so nice! Apparently, all it takes to have people treat you well is to have a ton of money. By the time I reached Athens I felt like I belonged to an Olympian class of beings and that kindness and hot towels were my due. Already Argos and the island were working their magic on me.

I sit down and order a Mythos, the Greek beer I learned to love more for its name than its taste, and immediately feel a prickle up and down my back, as if someone is watching me. I look up and my gaze snags on a man at the next table, fortyish, in khakis and a loose white shirt, an open Moleskine notebook on the table in front of him, fountain pen in hand, a bottle of Mythos at his elbow, battered felt fedora shading his face as he writes. When I meet his gaze, his deep brown eyes take me back fifteen years—

Are you going to Eris, too? Don't you feel as if we're sailing off with the Argonauts?

Ian.

I'd watched Annika's Instagram all week to see if he'd comment on the post we were both tagged in, but he hadn't. He must not be coming, I'd concluded, remembering what he'd said during our last week on the island: *I never want to see this godforsaken, cursed rock again.*

And yet, here he is.

Is it too late to pretend I don't see him? Is it too late to take the train back to Athens and max out my credit cards on airfare home? No, he's already rising and heading over, knapsack in hand as if he plans to stay awhile. He sits down at my table without asking permission—when did he ever?—and does the worst thing he could do. He says my name the way he used to.

"*Maia.* I wasn't sure you'd really come."

"I was sure you *wouldn't,*" I counter, taking a long sip of my beer. "As I recall, you were pretty pissed off at Argos at the end— you called him a monster and the rest of us fools and enablers."

He winces. "Ouch. Was I really that much of an asshole—don't answer that! I'm sorry. I was still in my angry young man phase."

"Oh, was that a phase?" I ask, falling so quickly into vitriol it's like falling into a warm bath—the kind Seneca took to slit his wrists. "What phase are you in now?"

He studies my face for a moment as if to recall the girl who'd have gone easier on him, but when he can't find her, he replies, "The repentant old man phase. When I saw you were coming, I hoped I would get a chance to talk to you and clear things up."

For a moment those warm brown eyes soften me, but then what he said sinks in. "When you saw I was coming? Where was that?"

He flinches but then tries to pass it off as a shrug. "Somewhere on social media."

"I don't post on social media—" I begin, but then I recall the comment I left on Annika's post. So committed Luddite Ian Davies with his analog notebook and fancy fountain pen follows Annika on Instagram, like everybody else I know. There'd be some satisfaction in catching him out if he hadn't just caught me at the same thing. We haven't even gotten to the island yet and already Annika is sitting between us.

He must be thinking about her, too. He looks around the taverna and asks, with studied nonchalance, "Is she here with you? Did you travel together?"

"Ha! Not likely," I scoff, but already I'm also scanning the tables for the flash of red hair and blue eyes. Instead, my eyes fall on an elegant older woman in white capris, a sailor's shirt, and an Hermès scarf tied around her hair. Her eyes are shielded by oversized sunglasses in which my reflection is perfectly framed. I feel as if I've been caught looking into Medusa's face and been turned to stone.

"Is that—?" I begin as the woman rises and approaches us, wheeling an enormous silver roller bag that appears to be made out of some space-age material and clutching a full-to-overflowing

Louis Vuitton tote to her side. She looks as if she just landed here from another planet or a 1950s Fellini film.

"Mia Gould?" she asks, lowering her sunglasses down her nose in my direction. And then turning toward Ian, "And Ian Davies?"

Of course she gets Ian's name right. "Maia Gold," Ian corrects her, standing to pull out a chair for her. "It's good to see you, Olivia." Olivia offers her cheek to Ian and then leans down to kiss me on the cheek. Instead, her designer tote bag whacks me in the ear with what feels like a ream of paper. She must be carrying the manuscript of her next book with her.

"Of course—*Maia*—I remember now. You came out with that debut everyone made such a fuss over the year after we were all here . . . what was it called? *The Dean's Wife?*"

"*The Professor's Daughter*," Ian corrects.

"Oh yes, there were a lot of wife/daughter/sister books that year. It made the *Times*' Notable list, didn't it? I remember being surprised that such a sweet young thing like you wrote something so . . . *edgy*. I'm afraid I must have lost track of what you wrote next."

"I didn't," I tell her, looking around for a waiter to order another beer. "That was my one and only."

"Oh!" she says, as if unable to imagine such a paltry production. Olivia Knox is a legend in the world of mystery fiction. Her Detective Moreau series is in its twenty-fifth year, each book eagerly welcomed by her fans—although lately the reviews have been lukewarm and I personally stopped reading them a few years ago because they'd become repetitive. Still, you had to admire her stamina, producing a book a year for twenty-five years.

She leans across the table and rests the tips of her fingernails on the back of my hand. "Was it the pressure of all the attention your debut got? I remember worrying you might have a problem. I'm sure Argos *thought* he was doing you a favor by pulling strings at the *Times* but sometimes it's worse to have a big success right out of the gate. It can make it so intimidating to write that second book."

Did she just suggest that Argos finagled that review in the *Times* for me?

"Yes, poor Maia," Ian says, flagging down a waiter and ordering us all refills—Mythos for me and him, an Aperol Spritz for Olivia. "I felt positively terrible for you when I saw that glowing review in the *Times*. I guess you never had that problem, Olivia."

"What?" I can't see her eyes behind those reflective glasses but I do see her jaw muscles twitching at the suspected insult. "I've gotten excellent reviews in the *Times*—"

"No, I meant you've never had a problem churning out the next book. What is it now? Twenty-five? Thirty?"

"I've just finished my twenty-fifth Detective Moreau," she says, sighing. "My wonderful team at Paulson Pratchett gave me an anniversary edition with silver-tipped pages—you know, for the silver anniversary? So thoughtful of them. And you, Ian, you write that quaint historical series, don't you? Detective Aristotle—"

"Pythagoras," he says. "Detective Pythagoras. And that's my father. I'm afraid that like Maia I've produced an only child—and I can't blame the lack of a second sibling on my overwhelming debut. My publisher released my freshman effort as if it were a confidential, top-secret document."

I laugh in spite of myself and before I can put up my guard—*if only I had Olivia's sunglasses!*—Ian gives me a look that takes me straight back fifteen years ago and turns me not to stone, but molten lava.

"Oh, look," I dimly hear Olivia saying. Out of the corner of my eye, I see she's pointing to the waterfront as if warning us of a coming tsunami, but it's only when she says, "There she is. Your friend Annika," that Ian and I break our gaze. I'm not really sure who looks away first.

What does it matter? I tell myself. We're only the chorus providing the *parode*, the entrance ode to the first act. And what an entrance it is! A sleek, teak-hulled yacht is motoring into the harbor, two wide blue eyes painted on either side of its prow. Standing at the tip of the prow, leaning forward like an ancient figurehead, is a woman whose red hair streams backward in the wind. Annika. The hero of the play has arrived.

CHAPTER FOUR

As we make our way down the dock, we're joined by a short, middle-aged man with a fringe of frizzy hair framing a receding hairline, wearing a yellow windbreaker, and carrying a large duffel and a canvas tote bag with the insignia of the Society for Classical Studies.

"Sydney?" Ian says, clapping the man so hard on his back that he staggers a little. I wonder if it was intentional—I remember there was some bad blood between Ian and Sydney—but if it was, Ian covers it up with an enthusiastic greeting. "Good to see you, man! I saw your essay in the *New York Review of Books* last winter. Way to go!"

Sydney Norton turns bright red, as if Ian has accused him of an indecency rather than publishing in a prestigious journal, and simpers, "Thank you. Unfortunately, the editors butchered it."

"The nerve!" Ian says. "No respect for the author. But, wait . . . didn't you argue in that piece that the author was dead?"

"I said the novel—specifically the *mystery novel*—was dead," he corrects as Ian catches my eye and, in spite of myself, I smile. It's at just that moment—Ian and me sharing a joke at someone else's expense as if the last fifteen years had evaporated in the pitiless Mediterranean sun—that Annika saunters down the dock in a long blue and white gauze caftan, regal as a Greek goddess. She stops and lowers her sunglasses and gazes at me with a force that feels as ancient and weighted as the *mati* painted on the prow of Argos's yacht. "Maia," she says, her voice husky, her eyes shining. Are those actually tears? Is she actually going to cry here in front of everybody? And why, I wonder, is she on the boat before the rest of us, as if *she* were our host and not Argos?

But all my suspicions are momentarily hushed when she holds out her arms and crushes me to her ample bosom. *Has she had implants?* I wonder meanly.

"I'm so glad you came," she whispers in my ear, as if she had been the one who invited me. As if I am here for *her.* "I couldn't have borne being here without you." Then she steps back and holds up one arm, rattling a macramé and shell bracelet on her right wrist. "See," she says, "I'm still wearing it. Remember? When we made these on the beach on Eris, we swore we'd only come back to the island together."

Before I can think of anything to say to that, perhaps telling her that I shredded my frenemy bracelet on the boat back to Volos fifteen years ago and fed the fragments to the sea, she lets me go and moves to greet the rest of the guests—as if they really were *her* guests, first stooping to kiss Olivia. "Olivia! It's so great to see you again! How long has it been? Bouchercon? The Authors Guild gala? I loved the last Detective Moreau! I bought two copies, one for me and one for my mother, who's such a big fan."

Olivia twists her mouth at being put in the my-mother's-a-fan group (*the kiss of death*, she'd informed us fifteen years ago), but returns Annika's air kiss and thanks her for giving her a blurb.

I'd be surprised that Annika and Olivia are so friendly—Annika couldn't stand her fifteen years ago—but I've seen them liking each other's posts and promoting each other's books online.

Annika gives a cooler greeting to Sydney, cryptically commenting on his latest *jeremiad*, and then turns to Ian. I wait to see what their greeting is like. Will Annika embrace him, too, and recall all the good times they've had on Mystery Writers of America panels and at PEN galas over the years? Have they been seeing each other? But instead, she glances at him guardedly.

"Ian, I'm really glad you decided to come." Then her eyes swivel between me and Ian like we're tennis players on opposite sides of a court and she stage-whispers: "I told you it would be worth it." Is she suggesting that Ian came *for me*? Because that's absurd; Ian Davies hasn't spoken to me in fifteen years.

Even Ian looks embarrassed at the suggestion. "Is this all of us?" he asks. "I kind of imagined it would be ten, like in the Agatha Christie novel."

"I think so," Annika says, turning to escort us all to the boat and lowering her voice. "Our ship's captain doesn't exactly speak much English."

"You mean you haven't been to the island yet?" I ask.

She shakes her head, long red hair flashing in the sun. "Oh no! I was on Skiathos visiting a film producer who's interested in optioning my latest novel. Argos was kind enough to send the boat for me but I insisted we come pick the rest of you up before going to the island." She turns back and beams at me. "I wanted to return together."

She spins away again quickly, greeting the ship's captain, who's lounging on the boat smoking a cigarette, with an enthusiastic *"Kalispera!"* and then directing everyone in stowing their luggage.

There's something off about this explanation, I think. Skiathos is the island of the Sporades closest to Eris. Why come all the way to Volos and then back again? Why not take the opportunity to spend some time alone with Argos and then greet us when we arrived? And why is *she* the one directing everyone?

Despite her waving me toward the front of the boat along with Olivia Knox, I find a seat in the stern, where I think I'll be alone. Sydney Norton has retreated down below, where he is probably, given how green he looked the minute he stepped on board, being sick, but then Ian joins me. I see Annika glance back at us from the bow as we motor out of the harbor and I wonder if she's regretting her seating choice. I know I am.

"Olivia hasn't changed much," he says after we have motored out of the harbor. "Suggesting Argos got you that review in the *Times*. Talk about sour grapes."

"What does she have to be sour about?" I ask, drawn into the gossip in spite of myself. "She's a bestselling author."

"Maybe she's tired of that pompous ass Detective Moreau," Ian says, "and wants to do something new."

"Then why doesn't she?" I ask.

"Her publisher probably wants her to keep doing the same thing as long as it's making money," Ian says. "My father wanted to write something else a few years ago and the publisher wasn't having it. *I'll be writing Detective Pythagoras until I'm in the grave*, he told me."

"I, for one, am glad he's still writing them. I love those books."

"Really?" he asks, tilting his head to the side as if he thinks I'm having him on. "I know you said your father liked them—I was sorry, by the way, when he died. I wrote—"

"After my father had his stroke," I say, quickly eliding over the letter that Ian had sent after my father's death, which I had thrown in the garbage without reading, "when he couldn't read, I read aloud to him and the only books he wanted to hear were your father's. I read the whole series to him and got to like them so much I kept reading them. I think this last one was his best," I add, taking a perverse satisfaction in praising Ian's father's books. Fifteen years ago, he told me he despised them. *My biggest fear*, he'd confided, *is that I'll end up writing the same sort of popular pablum. I'd rather write nothing.*

"That's . . ." He clears his throat. "I read your book, too," he continues, lowering his voice an octave into a register that vibrates deep in my core. Or maybe that's just the boat's engine. "It was . . ." He pauses and I find myself leaning forward, eager to catch a crumb of his praise. How quickly I've fallen into his orbit. ". . . *devastating.*"

I laugh so loudly that Annika and Olivia both turn their heads back to look at us. "Remind me not to ever ask you for a blurb."

"I meant it in the best possible way. It gutted me. Especially the end with what happened to the lovers—"

"You mean when the man betrays the woman by sleeping with her best friend?" I ask.

"Maia," he says, turning bright pink, "let me explain—"

Before he can continue—and really, how could he possibly explain what he did fifteen years ago?—a curved scimitar of silver cleaves the blue water off the starboard bow and we both gasp. We've just rounded the Pelion peninsula, where the Pagasetic Gulf becomes the Aegean, and just as they had the last time we made this journey, a pair of dolphins has come alongside our boat, their mercury-slick backs breaching the waves.

"Remember what you said when we saw them last time?" he asks.

I do, but I don't give him the satisfaction of saying the words.

"We're entering the land of myth," he quotes, as if he'd memorized my words from fifteen years ago, *"traveling the route the Greek ships sailed to wage war on Troy and the passage they took to return, laden with their spoils."*

"At which point I believe that girl—what was her name?" I say, recalling that there'd been someone else with us on the boat. A girl who it turned out was nearly the same age as me and Annika but who had seemed much younger because she was still in college. She was so shy and withdrawing that when I try to summon her face it seems to fade into the sea spray.

"Gena," he says.

"That's right, Gena. She pointed up to that chapel on top of that cliff and said, *Look! That's where* Mamma Mia *was filmed. That's my mother's favorite movie!"*

"And Olivia snorted at her and she was so mortified she barely spoke the rest of the time on the island."

"I wonder what happened to her," I say, "and why she's not here."

Ian shrugs. "I don't think she ever published anything after she left here. You know, you were right."

"About what?" I ask.

"That we were entering the land of myth, following the path of gods and heroes."

"I suppose I was," I say. "You remember what happened to Agamemnon when he came home from Troy—"

"He was cut down in his bath by his wife, Clytemnestra," he supplies.

"Because Agamemnon had betrayed her by sacrificing their daughter Iphigenia and then bringing Cassandra back as his slave-mistress. And then, of course, their son Orestes had to kill her to avenge his father. That's the thing about betrayal," I say, turning to him and looking straight into those brown eyes that seem to glow gold as the sun lowers over the Aegean. "It's never over. It sets up a chain reaction that rolls down through the ages and destroys everything in its path."

And then I turn away from him and look out at the sea. We travel the rest of the way in silence, heading east, the sun setting behind us and turning the sea gold, then crimson, then violet—Homer's wine-dark sea—until a smudge appears on the horizon. A crescent-shaped island, so slender it might be a mirage, floats between the purple sea and lavender sky—Circe's island under a veil of invisibility. But then the setting sun hits the limestone cliffs, and the whole island blazes like the watchtower signal fires that brought news of Troy's fall back to Clytemnestra.

"Eris," I say, as if I were saying the name of a long-lost loved one. I touch my mother's star intaglio ring, recalling she was here once, too. It's where my parents met and, I once figured out, where I was conceived. Perhaps that's why I felt that I was coming home the first time I set foot on the island.

I steal a brief look at Ian and see he's staring at me but then he quickly looks away, as if he's as embarrassed by the emotion that was in my voice as I am. I look back toward the island, where I make out the ruin of an ancient temple and then, as we round the headland and approach the western harbor, the long white length of Argos's villa. The sight of it makes my heart squeeze, as if it were, indeed, the face of a long-lost loved one.

A long colonnade echoes the columns of the ancient temple. Behind it a grove of pines stretches across the next ridge. Stone steps spring from the harbor and climb up to the terrace, branching off to small, whitewashed balconies like blossoms on a flowering tree. My eye goes straight to the balcony of my old room and then to the one directly below it, where a drift of jasmine and bougainvillea stirs in the breeze—the grotto of the Muses, where I'd seen Ian and Annika on the last night. Beneath the scent of jasmine, I catch a whiff of pine that seems to travel straight from the heart of the island as if the forest is stirring at our arrival. I feel an answering stir deep inside. Maybe the island will work its magic on me again, I think, maybe I'll be able to write again.

As we come into the harbor the cliffs on either side close around us like curtains dropping between us and the outside world, and the salt air carries another scent on it—sulfur and something ferrous—blood—and that spark of hope is chilled by fear. This island changed me when I was here last time. It gave me the gift of inspiration to write but, like one of those ancient two-sided blessings—eternal life without eternal youth or the gift of prophecy without ever being believed—it took away something, too. *The gods give and the gods take away*, my father was wont to say. *Look at how they gave me your mother and then took her away.*

It had seemed a cruel way of looking at the world but after Annika stole Ian and destroyed our friendship, after Ian betrayed me, after I'd taken the book the island had given me and turned it into an instrument of revenge, I understood what he meant. It was more than not being able to trust in a friend or a lover; I haven't really trusted myself since then. After all, how could I have been so wrong about them? Argos had said it himself during our conference on the last night. *Your friend Annika will be very successful but there will always be something missing in her books because there's something missing in her. I'd watch out for her if I were you.*

I hadn't wanted to believe it. I'd made excuses for her—she'd had a bad experience in college that made it hard for her to trust people—but he'd only tapped his nose and told me to wait and see.

I hadn't had to wait long.

I should have known that the gift I'd received on Eris would come with a price. Now I wonder what Eris has left to offer me. Forgiveness? No. No matter how Ian and Annika try to explain their kiss—and really, how can they?—it won't change what happened. And no matter how much Annika pretends that she's happy to see me I know it's a show. A performance for the other guests—and ultimately for Argos. Maybe that's why she didn't want to come here by herself first. She wanted to arrive with me so she could show Argos that she was the bigger person and that she had mended fences between us. No. I haven't come here to forgive Annika or Ian.

So, what have I really come for?

As we come alongside the dock, Annika is the first to jump across and secure the line to a cleat. Ian follows, carrying with him a line at the rear of the boat to tie us off. Our captain tosses our bags onto the dock unceremoniously as if he's eager to be rid of us. Sydney Norton comes up from below looking pale and sweaty. Olivia shrieks when she steps over the gap onto the floating dock and teeters until Ian grabs her elbow and steadies her. When I step over, Annika reaches out a hand to help me but I ignore it. She may think we're a team but I didn't come here to make friends.

"I wonder why there's no one here to greet us," Olivia says, looking balefully up the long flight of stairs. I remember that fifteen years ago she complained about the stairs. Now she must be in her sixties. Had she thought that Argos would have installed a gondola up to the villa in the intervening years? She starts up them with a grim resolve.

"Argos will be waiting for us on the terrace," Annika says, following Olivia. She turns back to look at me. "Do you remember, Maia?"

Mixed with the hope in her eyes, I see a hint of fear. Of what? I was right that she didn't want to come here alone. I pull back a memory of our arrival on the island fifteen years ago. The stairs and terraces had been lined with votive candles as they are now, casting flickering shadows over the design of the labyrinth carved into each stone step and our faces as we climbed the stairs, whispering like children on Christmas morning at the spectacle before us. Annika had led the way then and Ian after her—he was always trailing her; why hadn't I seen that?—and then me and Olivia . . . who else? Sydney must have been here and that girl Gena—and hadn't there been a cozy mystery writer?—but they're all shadowy in my memory, incorporeal shades like the pale ghosts Odysseus describes on his trip to the underworld who cannot speak until they've drunken the sacrificial blood. None of us, it had seemed, had substance until we reached the terrace and Argos, standing between two monumental ancient statues of Greek goddesses (genuine antiquities, I'd realized, awestruck, like something in the Metropolitan Museum), had welcomed us with bronze goblets of red wine as if we were ancient warriors back from the sack of Troy.

Kalós órises! he'd greeted us. *Welcome to Lavyrinthos. Here, if you are brave and honest enough to walk the labyrinth, you will know your true self at last. But first you must pass between the daughters of Night, who guard the threshold of the underworld.*

The statues are there now, at the head of the stairs, but Argos is not. I see Annika hesitate before them. A sudden gust of sea breeze molds the gauze of her caftan to her body and for a moment she looks like she could be the third goddess, another daughter of Night. When she turns around her face is pale as marble in the candlelight and she's still as a statue. She doesn't want to go alone, I think, climbing the last steps; she needs me, which means I have power over her. I'll just have to figure out what she needs from me and then I can take it from her just as she took Ian from me. Because that's why I'm here, I admit to myself as I step in between the two statues myself. On my right, Eris holds her golden apple and on my left the second goddess holds a pair of scales and a golden dagger. She is Nemesis, Night's most awful daughter, the goddess of retribution. That's what I've come for: revenge.

CHAPTER FIVE

Once I'm next to her, Annika threads her arm through mine and propels us both in between the statues of Eris and Nemesis. Although her face is serene and confident as an archaic kore's, Annika is trembling as we step onto the terrace and her tremor (*fear? excitement?*) transmits itself to me. It feels as if we're walking onto a stage set for a Greek tragedy. The terrace itself is paved in a geometric black-and-white pattern that leads the eye to the long table, which gleams with stainless-steel cutlery, bronze goblets filled with bloodred wine, and bone-white china, all cast in frantic shadows by flickering candles in candelabras made from the twisting arms of coral. A sputtering torch stands between each column, painting the scene with flickering light. The terrace feels so full that I don't notice at first the one glaring absence. Argos is not here. Annika's hand tightens on my arm. She's put on this show for an empty theater.

Well, not quite empty. A woman in a black uniform, hair pulled severely back from her deeply furrowed brow, steps from the shadows and clears her throat. "Mr. Alexander welcomes you to Lavyrinthos and begs your forgiveness for his absence. He has been unavoidably detained but hopes to be with you tomorrow.

In the meantime, he has left instructions for your comfort and entertainment."

She makes a stiff quarter turn and holds her hand out to the table, where a man in a white chef's uniform has appeared holding a tray of small, gilt-rimmed glasses. The whole speech has been delivered in flawless English with only the slightest of Greek accents, but stiltedly as if memorized. She looks familiar to me but I can't place where I know her from. Beside me I hear Olivia Knox huff.

"Are you Des—" She abandons her attempt to remember the unfamiliar Greek name. "The secretary who sent us our invitations?"

"Ms. Outis is also detained with Mr. Alexander. I am Eleni, Mr. Alexander's housekeeper."

"Eleni," I say, embarrassed I hadn't recognized her right away. "You were here fifteen years ago, the last time we were all here."

The ghost of a smile appears on her face and then vanishes, perhaps only an effect of the torchlight playing over her still, immobile features. I can see why I didn't recognize her. Her hair, which used to be black, is ash gray now and her face is etched with deep lines. The last fifteen years have not been kind to her. It's much easier to recognize the chef, who is delivering glasses to each of us. As I take the small glass of clear liquid from him, he winks at me.

"You were here, too," I say, remembering the cozy mystery writer from last time. "Phil?"

"Bill," he corrects. "Bill Collins. I was a guest, but Mr. Alexander liked my food so much he invited me this year as chef."

"From writer to chef," Ian says, holding up his glass. "I'd call that a promotion."

Bill turns pink in the torchlight. "I was a chef before I was a writer. Mr. Alexander admired my food mysteries and challenged me to produce a menu based on one of my books, *No Pita for the Dead*."

I hear Sydney Norton mutter under his breath, "Puns are the lowest form of humor," while Olivia says more loudly, "I hope no one gets poisoned in it."

"Well, let's find out," Ian says, holding up his glass.

"Stop!" Eleni says, holding her hand out as if the drink really were poisoned. "It is traditional to add a drop of water. Chef . . ."

Bill retrieves a small silver pitcher from the table and pours a drop of water in each of our glasses. The clear liquid turns a milky white that quivers like captured moonlight and the scent of licorice perfumes the air. Ouzo, I guess, or perhaps some rare elixir prepared only for Argos. I recall that Argos had his own private reserve, which he only took out on special occasions. When all of our drinks have been transformed, Eleni holds up her glass. "Mr. Alexander extends his welcome," she says as if reciting from a cue card. "*Kalós órises*, welcome to Lavyrinthos. Here, if you are brave and honest enough to walk the labyrinth, you will know your true self at last. But first you must pass through the daughters of Night, who guard the labyrinth. Eris"—she holds her drink up to the goddess of discord—"because without the goad of strife we never achieve our best. And Nemesis"—as she turns to the second goddess her hand trembles, and the silver drink shivers like liquid mercury—"for who among us does not create without a desire to right the wrongs we have suffered and punish the wicked."

I sense an uneasy shifting among the other guests. When I look around, each of their faces looks naked in the flickering torchlight, like a Greek chorus at the end of a play where justice has been brutally delivered. Annika looks warily at me as if she's guessed my desire for vengeance against her.

"May we achieve our best," Eleni concludes, "without drawing the jealousy of the gods." She raises her glass and tips it between her lips, drinking its contents in one long quaff. We all wait a second and then only when we are sure no god has taken their vengeance do we all take a drink.

THE SHOT OF OUZO may not loosen the tension, but it loosens our tongues as we move to the table.

"It seems a bit macabre," Olivia says as she sits down at the table, "to drink to the goddess of revenge."

"Actually," Sydney Norton says, seating himself unselfconsciously at the head of the table, where I remember Argos always sat, "I've written quite extensively on the role of revenge as one of the prime motivators of art."

"I think the toast meant that writers write to right wrongs," Ian says. "Think of Dickens writing about the orphanages and poorhouses—"

"Dickens was trying to keep himself out of the poorhouse after seeing his father end up in one," Olivia Knox cuts in. "I'd say that making a living is the governing force of literary ambition."

"Surely there's a better way to make money," Ian says. "Just about any trade is more reliable."

"So why do you write, Ian?" I ask.

It's the first time I've addressed him directly since he tried to apologize on the boat and he looks at me warily, as if I'm trying to trap him.

"I don't much anymore," he says, snapping his napkin open to punctuate his comment, "but when I did, I'd say it was to keep dark thoughts at bay. How about you, Maia?"

"I've given it up," I tell him.

"That's such a shame," Annika says. "Your novel was so powerful. I especially liked the part at the end where the evil best friend plunges to her death over a cliff."

"You didn't find that a bit melodramatic and overwrought?" Sydney asks, as if the writer of the book they're discussing isn't right here . . . also, something about the phrasing sounds familiar . . .

"So why do you write, Annika?" Ian asks, perhaps to stop Sydney from going into a further dissection of my first and only novel.

"Immortality," she says, gesturing toward one of the marble statues guarding the terrace. "Isn't that why we all write? To avoid death and gain immortality? As Shakespeare said, *So long as men can breathe or eyes can see—*"

"*—so long lives this, and gives life to thee,*" I finish the line for her. "But Shakespeare's talking about giving immortality to his lover, not to himself."

"So, are you saying that love is why writers write, Maia?" Ian asks.

It's not what I meant at all but before I can protest, Bill and Eleni arrive with trays of *mezze*—small dishes of olives and goat cheese, tiny fishes and marinated meatballs, fried potatoes drizzled with lemon, crisp, savory phyllo pastries filled with cheese and spinach, wedges of pita with tzatziki and taramosalata. The last dish is in a copper pan, which Bill holds a lighter to, igniting a blue dancing flame.

"*Opa!*" he cries and we all dutifully echo him.

As Bill serves the hot, melting cheese to each of us he says, "I couldn't help but overhear your discussion. Personally, I think you all have overlooked the best motivator for writing—food."

"I believe that falls under the heading of making a living, mate," Ian says, helping himself to a stuffed grape leaf.

"I don't mean brute sustenance, *mate*," Bill retorts archly, pointing at Ian with his lighter. I feel a little sizzle of competition in the air along with the smell of lighter fluid. "I mean the lust for life—"

"That comes under *love*," Annika points out.

"Or *sex*," I add.

"Sure," Bill says, standing back, his eyes roaming over all of us, "sex, love, food, and all the appetites that are satisfied on the page. Haven't you ever read something that made you hungry—or horny—or just made you laugh or cry? That's why *I* write—to make my reader really feel. It's like getting to live twice."

"And that," Ian says, holding up his goblet of red wine, "falls under the heading of *immortality*. So let's raise a glass to the immortal gods, may they grant us long lives—or at least lives long enough for us to write our best work."

What if we've already written our best work? I wonder, lifting my glass. The goblet is heavier than I expected. I wouldn't put it past Argos to use real ancient artifacts. These are stamped with the labyrinth design, the pattern adding to the dizzying effect of the alcohol. When I look around, I see on all our faces the reflection of the polished bronze goblets, revealing the naked hope that somehow, against all odds, we will trick death and truly live forever—or at least our words will. For a moment I think I see Argos himself sitting in the shadows, the gleam of his shaved head and his white teeth reflected in the torchlight, his hooded, reptilian eyes lowered as he watches us all. A master puppeteer watching the play he's set in motion.

But then I blink and the illusion vanishes.

It makes me realize again, though, that there's someone else missing from our gathering.

"There was another writer when we were all here together," I say. "Gena . . . I forget her last name—"

"Gena Wilson," Ian says. "She was very shy."

"Not so shy she didn't ask me for my agent's name," Olivia says.

"She was working on that retelling of the Trojan War," Annika says. "Remember, Maia, she wanted you to read it, but you were too busy working on your own novel."

"It sounded quite derivative," Sydney says.

I snort. "Yes, technically, since it was literally derived from the *Iliad*. But that's like saying the *Aeneid* is derivative—or James Joyce's *Ulysses*."

Sydney looks up from his plate, which is littered with the heads and bones of tiny fishes, and pats his mouth with his napkin before answering. "I hardly think that girl can be compared to Virgil or Joyce, but you do have a point," he says, holding up his hand as I sputter that I hadn't been comparing Gena to those authors. "Everything has been done already. So why go on writing novels? As I argued in my essay, the novel form—and most especially the mystery novel—is dead. I don't really understand why all of you go on—"

"If we didn't, you'd be out of a job," Bill says. "At least your gig at *Circus Weekly* would be over."

Sydney colors, as if embarrassed that he writes for the industry magazine—and suddenly I know where I've heard the words *overwrought and melodramatic* applied to my book—in the *Circus Weekly* review. Sydney must have written it. *Jerk.* My ears burning, I reach for my water glass and meet Eleni's gaze. She's standing a few feet from the table, hands clasped behind her back and rigid as one of the statues, waiting on us like a servant in an English country house drama. Something in her stance, the way it echoes the marble statues behind her, makes it feel as if she's standing in judgment. I feel ashamed suddenly of how we're all dissecting the fate of this girl who was once one of us. Why wasn't she invited, I wonder. Just because her book wasn't published? I remember she was on the early boat I took back to Volos on the last day, huddled belowdecks in a hoodie and sunglasses being sick. Hungover, I'd thought, from all we'd drunk at our farewell dinner, but now I wonder if something hadn't happened to upset her that last night.

I lose track of the conversation as there are more toasts, often made by Annika, who seems to glow brighter as the evening progresses, as if the silvery ouzo has lit her up from within. Just as she was last time, Annika is the center of attention; even the statues guarding the terrace seem to look on her with envy. Bill brings all the plates to her first for her approval. When he brings her a plate of grilled octopi, though, she shudders and declares she can't possibly eat them because they're too smart. This occasions a discussion on whether it is more immoral to eat an intelligent animal than an unintelligent one, which in turn leads to a debate on who makes the best victim in a mystery novel.

"Kill only the bad people," Annika says, looking straight at me as if she's planning to kill me in her next novel.

"Too obvious," Olivia says.

"And untrue to life," Ian concurs, "as if only bad people fall victim to evil."

"Why should the reader care," I ask, "if only the bad people die?"

"I've written an essay on this," Sydney says for about the twelfth time tonight. I notice that whenever he's about to make a particularly pompous statement he fidgets with his gold monogrammed cuff links as if reassuring himself that he's the important kind of man who wears cuff links. I remember the gesture from fifteen years ago but then the cuff links had been silver. He's come up in the world. "'On the Killing of Beautiful Women in Modern Crime Fiction.'"

I notice that when he says *beautiful*, he looks straight at Annika.

"*Fridging*, in other words," Annika says. "Kill a beautiful young woman so the wounded male detective can feel all mopey and avenge her. That's why beautiful women are always the victims."

She glances at me and I feel a stab of remorse recalling that Annika had told me in confidence that she had been assaulted her junior year of college. But then I remind myself that it didn't make it all right to steal my boyfriend.

"It's interesting," I say, "that we all write about murder. Even you, Bill"—I smile at Bill, who is delivering a tray of pastries and fruit to the table—"write cozy mysteries; Olivia writes detective novels—"

"You killed off the duplicitous frenemy in your book," Annika says.

"And you write psychological suspense novels about socio-paths," I counter.

"I didn't kill anyone in my novel," Ian points out.

"But your father writes detective novels," Sydney says, stroking one of his gold cuff links, "Maia makes an interesting point. One might even say that murder is our muse. Of course, I don't kill anyone in my reviews—"

"Only the author's presales," I hear Olivia mutter under her breath, too low for Sydney to hear. Or at least he pretends not to.

"But I have studied the form and I think I know a thing or two about it. Our situation, for instance"—he looks around the table, pausing for effect—"is straight out of the Golden Age tradition."

"A group of guests are invited to an island, you mean?" Olivia says.

"Their host is absent," Ian adds.

"Each of them has a reason to want someone dead," Annika says.

"I thought of that, too," I say. "You think we were invited here to reenact Agatha Christie's *And Then There Were None*?"

"Argos loves games," Sydney says. "I wondered if he might have invited us here and staged his absence as part of the game."

The idea instantly makes me uncomfortable. *Argos likes to play games with human beings as his chess pieces*, my father told me when he was trying to convince me not to come to the residency fifteen years ago. I don't want to be part of one of Argos's games. "Do you know, Eleni?" I ask as Eleni brings out the coffeepot. "Did Argos say anything to you about this summer's retreat being mystery themed?"

"Gawd," Olivia Knox says, "you make it sound like one of those awful dinner theater events."

"Mr. Alexander has told me nothing about that," Eleni says carefully, "but he has left written instructions for each of you." She begins handing out envelopes to us. When I get mine, I see it has my name written on it in the same calligraphic script as on my invitation. Argos's handwriting, I wonder, or Despina Outis's? Or does he employ a calligrapher especially for these missives?

"Are we supposed to open them now?" Sydney asks.

"He must have known he wouldn't be here," Olivia Knox huffs, getting out a pair of reading glasses, "if he prepared these in advance."

Annika glances at me as if waiting to see what I'll do. I take the sharp-edged knife we'd been given to debone our fish and hook its blade under the fold of the thick paper—what a lot of money Argos must spend on stationery!—and thrust upward. I hear the rest of the guests tearing into their envelopes as I retrieve the card inside.

"I feel like we're in an episode of *Survivor*," Annika says, "and one of us is about to be voted off the island."

"Look for a black spot," Ian says. "That's how the ancient Greeks exiled people, right, Maia? With marked pottery shards."

"Ostraca," I say, following the black lines of the labyrinth printed on the card, "which is where we get the word *ostracize*." As I turn over the card, Sydney Norton takes it upon himself to read aloud in his prissy voice.

"I hope you are enjoying the hospitality of Eris thus far and that it is already working its magic on you. In the spirit of healthy strife and to give the Muses a little push, I propose a contest. You'll have noticed that you are in the company of murderers—or at least those who write about murder—"

"So I was right," Sydney interrupts himself to gloat, adjusting his cuff links and clearing his throat before continuing. *"What better contest, then, than to see who can plot the best murder? And what better setting? A secluded island, an absent host, a cast of mysterious guests, and a chorus of Greek demigods watching. Here, then, is your assignment: Write the opening chapter of a murder mystery set on this very island. Feel free to use your fellow guests— and staff—for your dramatis personae. After all, that is what you writers do, use the people around you as grist for the mill. Bring your first chapter to breakfast tomorrow and we will see who the winner is and we will see—"* Sydney's voice falters, as if he doesn't want to read the last sentence. When he summons the nerve, we all join in as if *we* have become the chorus.

"—who among you is the Nemesis out for revenge and who is their first victim."

CHAPTER SIX

s this some kind of a joke?" Olivia Knox demands. "I didn't agree to be part of some *amateur* contest." Her lip curls on *amateur* and she looks directly at me. I suppose from her great height the author of a single book might qualify as an amateur.

"Afraid your Detective Moreau isn't up to the challenge?" Ian asks, glancing at me as if I'll join in with the joke. I quickly look away before he can see the smile that flits across my face.

"It's as I deduced," Sydney says. "I'm not sure about writing a chapter, though. I'm not a novelist, after all," he adds, as if talking about a disreputable trade.

"Ah, so you can critique mystery novels," Ian says, "but not write them. I guess you're out of the competition."

"I'm sure I can churn out something adequate." He turns to Eleni. "How much prize money are we talking about anyway?"

Eleni, who has remained still, her face frozen as a statue's, shakes her head. "I do not know the details. Mr. Alexander left instructions for me to hand out the envelopes. I do not know any more than you do."

Sydney rounds on Bill, who has begun to clear the plates. "And what about you? You were here before us. Do you know anything else?"

"Only what's on the card," he says, pulling an envelope out of his pocket.

"*You* have been invited to participate as well?" Olivia asks. "A writer of . . . *cozies?*"

"I bet Bill here knows how to murder the lot of us," Ian says, holding up his coffee cup toward the chef. "I, for one, will not be killing him off after this excellent meal."

"I think it sounds like fun," Annika says, smiling at me. "I always find a challenge inspiring. What about you, Maia, who are you going to kill? You killed the evil best friend in your last book so you may not want to repeat yourself."

"That would be spoiling the surprise," I say, getting to my feet, "but if we're supposed to have a chapter by the morning, I'd like to go to my room now." I look toward Eleni. "If you could just let me know where my bags and room are. . ."

"The boat's captain has brought up your luggage and left it in your rooms. If you are all ready to retire, I will show you to them."

"In other words," Ian says, getting up, "we're all supposed to stay together? Are you going to tell us to lock our doors as well?"

"That is up to you," Eleni says, refusing to play along.

"Do we have a word limit?" Sydney asks, clearly getting into the spirit of the competition despite his declaration that the mystery novel is dead. "Are we supposed to bring a printed copy of our chapter to breakfast? Or email it—"

"No email," Olivia Knox says, looking up from her phone. "Or cell phone service. Unless . . ." She looks at Eleni. "I assume there's some kind of access to the outside world. Argos Alexander must surely have a way of conducting business from his own island."

"There is a telephone, fax machine, and shortwave radio in the library, all of which are at your disposal," Eleni says. "I will take you there after I have shown the others to their rooms."

Olivia opens her mouth—no doubt to demand she be taken to the library immediately—but then she looks around at the rest of us. We've all gotten to our feet. I sense a nervous energy in the air. Perhaps it's only the hectic light of the guttering torches, but I imagine that everyone feels anxious to get to their desks to write. Annika's right: a challenge *is* inspiring.

Apparently Olivia sees that, too, and she's not about to let the rest of us get a head start. "I'll do it in the morning," she says, tossing her napkin onto the table like a medieval knight throwing down a gauntlet to challenge their foe, "after I've won this silly contest."

WE FOLLOW ELENI into the interior of the villa, down a long hallway softly lit by shell sconces. The temperature drops five degrees. The walls are made of thick whitewashed limestone that insulates the villa from the heat of the day. It's like entering a cave.

"My quarters and Chef's are on this floor," Eleni says, leading the way down the hall, "to be close to the offices and kitchen. Mr. Alexander specified that you were all to have the rooms you had the last time you were here. I imagine that you may have forgotten your way around the villa in the intervening years, so please follow me closely, the layout can be very confusing."

"Remember how we used to joke that Argos had designed his villa on the ruins of King Minos's labyrinth," Annika says, walking beside me, "and that if we weren't careful we'd be eaten by the Minotaur?"

"King Minos's palace is on Crete," I say.

She is right, though, that the layout of the villa is labyrinthine and unusual in that it is built into the cliff with two floors below ground level. I remember that Argos said he had the villa designed that way to blend in with the landscape. I always suspected, though, that he enjoyed watching his guests get lost in the subterranean mazelike corridors and surprising them with grotesque statues—one of which I come across now as I turn a corner: a bronze mask of a Gorgon, turned green with age, whose fierce stare freezes me in my tracks.

"Miss Gold? Can you please stay with the group? I don't want you to get lost."

Eleni's voice frees me from the Gorgon's spell.

"Oh, I'm sorry, I didn't mean to hold us up. I was just startled by this mask. It's . . ."

Eleni's gaze shifts from me to the ancient mask and her eyes harden. "Grotesque? Yes, Mr. Alexander enjoys his little games."

Then she moves briskly on until she reaches a room at the end of the hall and opens the door. It's an elegant room—whitewashed walls, blue-tiled floor, olive-wood four-poster bed, crisp blue and white linens, a vase of wildflowers on the desk below the window.

"I believe this is where you stayed last time, Miss Knox."

"Yes," Olivia says, lingering on the threshold. "But I'd written Argos asking for a room with an en suite bathroom so I wouldn't have to go traipsing down the hall in a robe like a college coed."

"I wasn't informed of that request," Eleni says, sniffing. "And the only en suite bathrooms are on the lowest floor. Perhaps Mr. Alexander didn't think you could manage all those stairs."

Olivia looks affronted at the suggestion she's too old for the stairs, but then she glances back at the steep winding staircase leading to the lower floors and seems to reconsider. "I suppose this will be all right. I don't have to share the bathroom with anyone, do I?"

When Eleni assures her that she's the only one using the bathroom across the hall, Olivia gives us all a hard stare worthy of a Gorgon, as if daring us to try to use her private bathroom. Then she closes her door without saying good night to any of us.

I fall in next to Sydney as he follows Eleni down the stairs to the next level, leaving Annika and Ian trailing behind us. *That didn't take long,* I think. *Even if they haven't been in touch all these years it's clear that they're happy to take up where they left off.*

"They're thick as thieves, aren't they," Sydney says, as if reading my invidious thoughts. "And yet I seem to remember that you and Ian Davies were an item when we were here last."

I glance at him and notice that his small, close-set eyes are regarding me eagerly. *He's enjoying this,* I think. I look down at his Classical Society tote bag and remember suddenly that I ran into Sydney once a couple of years after the residency at the yearly conference for the Classical Society. I'd been asked to speak on a panel about classics and contemporary fiction that he was moderating. He'd pointedly snubbed me on the panel, directing all his questions to its more illustrious members, and he'd even quoted that damned *Circus Weekly* review in my introduction with an insufferably smug look almost as if—

"You wrote that review of my book in *Circus Weekly*, didn't you? I remember that line—*melodramatic and overwrought.*"

I expect him to look at least a little embarrassed to be caught out, but instead he stretches his scrawny neck like a preening peacock. "The reviews are *supposed* to be anonymous to protect the integrity of the reviewer—but yes, I did."

"*Integrity*?" I echo. "Shouldn't you have recused yourself because you knew me?"

"Did I really know you, though?" he asks, arching one eyebrow. "As I recall we didn't spend much time together here. You were too busy with your friends Annika and Ian." He looks toward the stairs, where they have failed to appear. "And, of course, showing off for our host."

"What's that supposed to mean?"

"Oh, I think you know. Argos had a taste for pretty young girls and you and your friend Annika were not above courting his attention for your own benefit."

"What an ugly and sexist idea!" I say, narrowing my eyes at him. His skin has gone all blotchy but whether from shame or too much sun on the boat today, I can't tell. "You were jealous, weren't you, because *you* wanted Argos's attention."

He smirks. "I got Argos's attention soon enough—with my brain, not my body."

"How? With your nasty reviews—you wrote that review of my book out of spite."

"It was a fair review," he says. "I even gave you a few phrases your publisher could pull for quotes."

To my horror, I realize he's right.

"*An ambitious debut . . . a promising premise . . .*" he quotes. "And it *was* promising—daughter of an overbearing classics professor goes to Greece to find her muse—albeit a bit autofiction for my tastes. But then you ruined it with that ridiculous melodramatic ending with the best-friend-turned-mustache-twirling-villain." He barks a harsh laugh. "Not only was it overwrought, but it was also clearly wish fulfillment. I wonder what your dear friend Annika did to deserve such ire?" At my expression he scoffs, "You called her Monica, for heaven's sake! You sacrificed your art on the altar of revenge."

"I thought you said revenge was one of the prime motivators of art."

"Yes," he says, smirking, "but I didn't say it always worked. If you're going to write for revenge you have to fully embrace the spirit of Nemesis. Your attempt was half-hearted at best, so don't blame me for your failed career. I'm not surprised you never wrote anything else. You clearly don't have the stomach for it. And now, if you'll excuse me, I have some writing to do. It's a ridiculous assignment but I've studied the Golden Age locked-room mysteries enough to nail it and perhaps do something interesting in the metafictional line. Ah, and here is my room. Good night, Ms. Gold."

He turns and leaves me standing in the hallway, alone save for another of the Gorgon masks that leers at me as if he's agreeing with Sydney. He's right, I think, aghast that a worm like Sydney Norton has so accurately assessed me. I did ruin my book in a spiteful gesture of petty jealousy.

Not that it hurt sales. It was probably what sold it—what Olivia called edgy was really just meanness.

I look back up the stairs but Ian and Annika are nowhere to be seen. A prickle of unease stings the back of my neck as I wonder what Annika is saying about me. Is she telling Ian how hurt she'd been by my depiction of her? Monica! I hadn't even tried very hard to disguise her in my book. My suspicion is confirmed by the laughter that precedes them when they finally come down the stairs and their guilty expressions when they see me waiting for them.

"Better keep up," I say, "or you'll get eaten by the Minotaur."

I turn to catch up with Eleni, who is waiting for us at the end of the hall. "Here is Mr. Davies's room," Eleni says, opening a door.

"Oooh, I remember this room from last time," Annika says. "It has one of the nicest balconies."

"I would not advise using it," Eleni cautions. "The stone is crumbling."

"Uh oh," Ian says, saluting us from his doorway, "that makes me the first victim. *Morituri te salutant!*"

Annika giggles. "If you keep quoting Latin, you'll certainly be *my* first victim, but Maia here probably knows exactly what you mean."

"Of course, I do," I say, turning away. "It's what the gladiators said in the Colosseum before a battle. It means *Those of us who are about to die salute you.*"

"Wait," Annika says, hurrying to catch up with me. We've taken another staircase and turned twice down two corridors. Eleni is out of sight ahead of us. But I don't need her. I know where we're going. The layout isn't really that confusing once you know it; each level is basically a loop with a few wrong turns. I learned last time that if you followed the diamond pattern on the mosaic floor you won't get lost. I do that now and find Eleni standing at the end of a corridor between two open adjacent doors.

"Argos wanted you both to have your old rooms," she says, gesturing to each. Annika swans into hers but I hesitate on the threshold of mine.

"Thank you, Eleni," I say. "I remember you from back then. Only . . . you weren't the housekeeper . . ."

"I was Mr. Alexander's personal secretary," she says. And then before I can ask how she went from secretary to housekeeper she says, "I am surprised you remember me at all. You were so busy with your writing." She pauses, letting the comment hang in the air, not clarifying whether she means it as praise or blame. Then she says, "I hope you are as productive this time," and turns to leave. I watch her go and then as I'm turning into my room Annika pops out of hers.

"Isn't it great we've got our old rooms? Remember how we left our windows open and talked across our balconies?"

"After what I saw last time from my balcony, I'll be keeping my window shut, Annika, and locked," I say.

"What are you talking about?" Annika asks, grabbing my wrist before I can retreat into my room.

"You know what I mean," I snap, yanking my hand out of her grasp and pointing into my room to the window overlooking the balcony. She follows my gaze and looks puzzled.

"Saw what?" she asks, sounding genuinely confused—only I've seen her put on that look before. She's a consummate actress.

"You and Ian in each other's arms moaning about how hard it was going to be to break it to me that you were together. *We have to tell her,*" I mimic. "*Can't it wait until we're off the island? It will kill her.*"

Annika stares at me blankly and then a veil of pink washes over her pale skin like dawn lighting up the morning sky. I don't think I've ever seen a more literal demonstration of an idea *dawning* on someone. "*That's* what this has all been about? Jesus, Maia, I can explain—"

"Aren't you afraid it might kill me? Or is that what you were hoping for? Well, it didn't kill me. It just made me a bit more realistic in my expectations of human nature. Now, if you don't mind, I'll say good night. I have some writing to do."

I step into my room and shut the door in her face, then close my eyes and lean my back against it as if I expect her to try to break it down. Explain? How could she ever explain what I saw? Anger pulses through me, but something else, too—*satisfaction*. She did come here to beg for my forgiveness, which means I have the power to deny her. My blood fizzes with that knowledge.

I open my eyes.

The room is dark save for a wedge of moonlight coming through the half-opened drapes, which stir restlessly in the breeze as if invisible fingers are plucking at them, trying to get in. I cross the room and push them aside and the moonlight pours into the room thick as cream. Stepping out onto the balcony, I see the steps winding down to the harbor. Directly below me is the balcony where I saw Ian and Annika on our last night on the island. The moon had been full that night as well, casting sharp black shadows over the white stone. For a moment, they take the shape of two people standing close together, as if the shadows Ian and Annika cast that night had been seared into the stone and the ancient rock had kept an imprint of their betrayal. But then a cloud moves over the moon and the shadows vanish. The illusion, I see now, comes from the statues that stand on the terrace above. I look up, making out the statues of Nemesis and Eris. My balcony is directly below them. I shiver at the thought that Eris and Nemesis, those two destructive daughters of Night, are watching over me, but then I hear my father's voice.

A little competition spurs us on to do great things.

And then I hear what Argos said to me on our last night fifteen years ago: *It is the thirst for revenge that will spur you on to the great work I know you have inside you. Revenge will be your muse.*

The clouds blow away and the moon shines once again, tracing a path across the sea. I feel as if I am on the prow of a ship setting sail. Jason off to find the Golden Fleece. Odysseus sailing through the enchanted isles. Agamemnon embarking to Troy to avenge the abduction of Helen. On the olive-wood desk below the window, white pages rustle like sails filling with wind. All I have to do is tighten the line to rein them in. I sink down to the waiting chair, pick up a pen, and begin to write.

CHAPTER SEVEN

The sun wakes me the next morning, tinting the room as pink as Homer's rosy-fingered dawn. Loose pages litter the desk and bed, crackling like kindling as I turn them over. I remember the way the moon had come as a visitation last night but this looks like the aftermath of something violent—the bloodied feathers of the swan that ravished Leda. That's how I feel, as if I have been *taken* and *used* by some force outside myself. Or maybe I just drank too much ouzo last night.

I gather the pages, praying they're not gibberish, and sit down at the olive-wood desk to read them. When I'm done, I look out the window. There is that view of sea and sky, a flawless stretch of blue that's haunted me all these years with its promise—*if I could just go back*—I could write. And I have. I'm not entirely sure yet what it is I'm writing. There's a bit of Argos's prompt in it—the gathering of writers on a beautiful island, none of them, including the narrator, quite what they seem, a competition that sparks strife between them, and then a death . . .

That part had been easy. It was obvious who had to die first.

I look down at the harbor and see Eleni standing on the dock with the ship's captain, making wide gestures with her hands while he remains still, slouched and smoking. Finally, he tosses his cigarette in the water and says something to Eleni that makes her step back. Then he unties the line, hops in the boat, and revs the engine. Eleni stands, hands on her hips, watching him speed out of the harbor. I wonder what their argument was about and how soon he'll be returning and whether he'll bring Argos with him.

I take the last page in the pile—no need to share all of it—and leave the rest weighed down by shells and rounded stones arrayed like a tribute to the gods.

A BUFFET HAS been set up on the terrace offering hot coffee, fresh-baked rolls, thick Greek yogurt, fruit, and honey. Ian and Annika are seated at the end of the long table, heads leaning so close together that Annika's red hair hangs over their faces like a bloody veil.

"Good morning," I say brightly, taking satisfaction in how Ian and Annika spring apart. Do they really think they have anything left to hide? "Glad to see you both survived the night. You must have heeded Eleni's warning to avoid midnight assignations on crumbling balconies."

"Annika told me about what you saw that night," Ian says. "I can explain—"

"It's really not necessary," I say, taking a sip of the scalding black coffee. "As I explained to Annika last night, nothing I saw or heard *killed* me as you feared it would. You'll have to try harder if you want to get rid of me—perhaps you can practice in your story for the contest. I know I had great fun plotting a murder last night. Who did you kill off, Annika? Or don't you want to give it away?"

Annika shrugs at Ian as if to say it's pointless to make me see reason while I'm in this mood. "I decided to go with someone who argued with everyone so that suspicion would fall on a number of the guests."

"Good thinking," I say. "So . . . Olivia?"

She shakes her head and mouths, *Sydney*.

"Even better," I say. "Put me down as suspect number one. I realized last night that he's the one who wrote that *Circus Weekly* review of my book."

"He gave the last Detective Pythagoras a tongue-lashing, so you won't be the only suspect," Ian says.

"Oh, he trashed my latest, too," Annika adds. "Maybe we should go full *Orient Express* and *all* kill him. We could call it *Death of a Reviewer*—speak of the devil—" She gestures toward the kitchen door, where Bill has appeared with a tray of fresh-baked bougatsa, a Greek breakfast pastry, with Sydney trailing close after him.

"I am sure I wrote to the secretary about my food allergies—no dairy, no gluten—"

"I'll make you some eggs," Bill says.

"I'm vegan," Sydney tells him. "I generally have millet soaked in almond milk with dried fruit."

"Got it," Bill barks, putting down the tray of fragrant pastries. He catches my eye and winks. "I'll go milk some almonds directly. In the meantime, there's plenty of fruit and homemade granola."

Bill makes his escape only to run into Olivia, who asks for a pot of hot water—*very hot*—so she can make her own tea from a special blend she's brought with her. She looks askance at the rich custard pastry and carries a banana and plum back to the table.

"Good morning," she says to the rest of us. "Was anyone else kept up all night by that god-awful screeching?"

"I slept the sleep of the dead," Ian replies.

"I'm on the sea side," I tell Olivia. "If you're on the forest side on the ground floor you're probably hearing owls."

"*Athene noctua*," Eleni says as she comes onto the terrace. "The little owl of Athena. The island is full of them. I find their calls soothing."

"They sound like cats mating," Olivia says distastefully. "As soon as Argos arrives, I'll speak with him about a better room. I remember from last time that girl Gena had quite a nice one on the first level and since she isn't here—"

"That room is no longer available," Eleni snaps. "Mr. Alexander uses it for . . . storage."

Olivia visibly blanches at Eleni's peremptory tone but recovers her sense of wounded dignity quickly. "I'll take that up with Argos when he arrives. Surely he'll be here to judge our contest. I have my solution right here." She removes a gilt-edged leather portfolio from her tote bag and takes out a sheaf of handwritten pages, which she brandishes at the rest of us as if shaming us for our inferior word count. I take out my folded sheet of paper from my pocket. Sydney pulls a Post-it note from his wallet and slaps it on the table as if he were dealing a hand of blackjack. From the looks of it, he's written his solution in haiku form. Ian takes out his Moleskine notebook and Annika lays her phone down on the table.

"So when *is* Argos coming?" Olivia demands of Eleni. "I saw you talking to the captain before he left this morning. Was he going to get Argos?"

Eleni colors, unnerved perhaps that someone had witnessed her argument with the captain. After a short pause she recovers herself and answers.

"The captain's instructions were to return to the port of Volos and await a call from Mr. Alexander. I imagine he will be with us by tonight but his presence is not necessary to judge the first stage of the contest. I have instructions to escort you all to the place where the answer awaits you."

"A field trip?" Annika says. "I'm dying to explore the island again." In a bikini top, very short shorts, and flip-flops, she looks more ready for a day at the beach.

"As soon as you finish your breakfast," Eleni says, and then, glancing at her feet, adds, "You may want to wear sturdier shoes."

"Where are we going?" Olivia demands, looking down at her own flimsy espadrilles.

"It's a mile hike along the ridge," Eleni says, "to the Temple of Eris."

"The Temple of Eris," Annika repeats, sounding surprised and a bit displeased.

"Ah," I say, "that makes sense."

"Why?" Olivia asks.

"Because Eris is who started this contest; she should end it."

A HALF HOUR later we gather on the terrace in sturdier shoes and hiking gear. Bill, outfitted in Bermuda shorts, high-top sneakers, and a canvas bucket hat, hands out water bottles.

"Are you coming, too?" Sydney asks. In his khaki cargo shorts, yellow windbreaker, and clunky hiking boots, he looks like an overgrown Boy Scout.

"You betcha," Bill replies, holding up a folded sheet of paper. "I've got skin in this game."

"I'll collect those," Eleni says, taking the sheet from Bill. "If you would all hand over your solution to the first challenge— you needn't give me everything you wrote, just the page with the identity of who dies first." She collects pages from everyone but Annika, who holds up her phone.

"Mine's on my Notes app," she says. "Can I text it to you?"

"There's no cell phone service on the island," Eleni reminds her, handing her a sheet of paper. "Please write down your solution here."

While Annika studiously applies herself to pen and paper, Olivia rolls her eyes at me. "It's a wonder this generation is even literate. I despair for the readership of tomorrow."

As if I weren't the exact same generation as Annika! I wonder why she's chosen me as a confidante. I'm hardly the same age as her, but then, as Annika once told me, having been brought up by a classics professor, I was *old before my time*. Or perhaps Olivia thinks I have experience with Gen Z because I work at a college.

"Unless you count TikTok as reading," I say, thinking of my assistant, Jenner. I deliberately say it loudly enough so that Annika will hear what I think of her TikTok posts and she rewards me with a reproachful look over her shoulder as she follows Eleni off the terrace and up the path behind the villa.

The path climbs steeply through scrubby pines toward the ridge and is only wide enough to allow us to walk two abreast. Sydney attaches himself to Eleni with a list of dietary complaints. Bill lags behind, no doubt to avoid hearing his cooking critiqued, and tries to latch on to Annika, who ignores him and hangs back to talk to Ian. I end up with Olivia, who has decided I am in league with her against Gen Z—even though I'm closer in age to them than I am to her—and treats me to a litany of complaints about the decreasing age of the personnel at her publishing house.

"Would you believe," she demands, clutching her heavy tote bag to her side—*why on earth she has brought it with her, I can't imagine*—and struggling in her thin-soled espadrilles on the rocky path, "that my new editor had the nerve to suggest that my Detective Moreau might be out of date and that I should consider giving him a younger assistant so as to reach a more modern audience?"

It doesn't sound like such a bad idea to me but when I try to say so Olivia interrupts to start another diatribe against all the new technology she has been forced to learn just to read her editor's notes. "It used to all be in blue pencil," she bemoans, "and now it's in *text bubbles* like the Sunday funny pages! And I swear I can see my editor rolling her eyes when I get some teensy little detail wrong, as if I'm losing my faculties."

"Maybe you should hire an assistant," I suggest but she shakes her head.

"Argos could fix all of it with a word."

"Why Argos?" I ask. "What can he do about your publishing situation?"

"Didn't you know?" she asks, looking at me as if I'm dim-witted. "He bought my publisher, Paulson Pratchett, six months ago. Why do you think I'm here? Certainly not because I need inspiration. A word from Argos and my publisher would stop harassing me. And I'm sure once I explain all that to him . . . if he'd only get here . . ."

He wields a lot of power in the publishing world, my agent Diane had said. Of course, I realize now, she'd have known that Argos bought Paulson Pratchett. No wonder she'd been so anxious for me to come here. If I hadn't snapped at her she might have had a chance to tell me.

I pause so Olivia can catch her breath, seeing that the rest of the group, having reached the ridge, has stopped above us. From here their dark shapes silhouetted against the bright sky, their hands performing cryptic gestures, look like figures on a vase enacting some ancient, mysterious rite. I'm reminded of the procession of gods and goddesses on the Wedding Vase, with spiteful Eris flying overhead, which makes me wonder who the uninvited guest is here. Is it Argos with his challenge? But he can hardly be the uninvited guest since he owns the island. Maybe it's Gena, the missing guest, but I can hardly imagine that shy, awkward girl suddenly arriving and causing trouble.

As we get closer, I see that Eleni and Annika are standing a little apart, both gesturing at the horizon as if in disagreement about which direction to go, while the others shade their eyes from the glaring sun, drink from their water bottles, and take pictures with their phones.

"What is it now?" Olivia mutters under her breath. "I know she's your friend but Annika is quite the drama queen."

"She's no friend of mine," I snap, tired of Olivia's constant carping, but when I turn around, I see that she's sweating, red in the face, and wincing at every step. She's older than she looks, I realize, probably in her late sixties, and the climb has taken a toll on her. I offer her a hand to scale the last stone outcropping and then a drink from my water bottle and move closer to hear what Eleni and Annika are arguing about. They're perched on the ridge that runs north to south along the spine of the ancient volcano that formed Eris, pointing down to the caldera, the crater of the volcano that collapsed in its last eruption and filled with water. When I peer over the side of the ridge it's like looking into the eye of some vast leviathan of the deep. I remember that although it appears to be a peaceful cove, the rocks below the water make it treacherous for boating or swimming, which is what Eleni is telling Annika.

"The terrain on the east side of the island is quite dangerous. I advise you not to go there."

"But we went swimming there last time," Annika says. "Remember, Maia? We hiked down to the beach and swam to the blue grotto—"

"The grotto is very dangerous," Eleni repeats. "The currents in the cove are unpredictable and if you are caught inside at high tide, you could easily drown. There are also stories about the grotto . . ."

"What kind of stories?" Ian asks.

Eleni turns to him. With the sun at her back I can't read her expression but there is something in the stiffness of her pose that makes me think she doesn't like Ian's question. I remember that Argos told us that the locals were very superstitious about the island, which made it difficult to keep reliable staff. Eleni's voice when she answers, though, is cool and level as if she were a docent in a museum.

"There is an old superstition among the fishermen in these islands that the blue grotto is the entrance to the underworld." Eleni turns and looks down at the pitiless blue eye of the cove. "And that on nights of the full moon the unsettled dead rise from below and drag sailors and swimmers down to the underworld." Eleni turns back to us, her face still as a statue's. "And so, as I was saying, it is best to avoid the east side of the island. We will be making our way along the ridge to the Temple of Eris"—she points northeast along the curving arm of the cove where a few columns are framed against the blue sky—"where the solution to today's challenge will be found."

She turns to continue north along the ridge path, which is now only wide enough to accommodate one. As the group reassembles itself into a single file, I take one backward glance at Olivia and, with only a small twinge of guilt, abandon her. What she's told me has raised a lot of questions in my mind and I know who can answer them.

I edge myself behind Annika, cutting off Bill. He gives me a surprised look and then, glancing between me and Annika, nods knowingly. I bet Annika told him about our spat and he thinks we're mending fences. *Fine.* I hold her back while Bill helps Olivia over a fallen tree and let them get ahead of us so they won't hear us as we continue walking.

"Thank goodness," Annika says, glancing over her shoulder at me. "Are you finally willing to listen to reason? I can explain about what happened—"

Refusing to take the bait, I ask: "Did you know Argos had bought Paulson Pratchett? They're your publisher, too."

"It's not exactly a secret, Maia, unless you've been living in the second century BCE—oh wait, I guess you have. It's been all over social media for months. Everyone's wondering what he's going to do when the sale goes through—who he's going to let go, what direction he'll take the company in, whose books will rise and whose will fall. Honestly, I thought it might be why you came—to get a contract for your next book."

"Would he really have that power?" I ask. "Surely Paulson Pratchett wouldn't have agreed to the sale without an assurance of editorial independence."

Annika laughs out loud. "Wow! You really have been living in the dark ages, which I guess are practically modern for you. Of course he would have made assurances—no massive layoffs for the first year, editorial independence, yada, yada, but everyone knows that won't last very long."

"Is that why you came?" I ask. "Because you're worried about getting your next contract?"

"Actually, they're not even my publisher anymore. They dropped me right after Argos bought it."

"Oh," I say, taken aback. "Really? But your books—"

"Have been trending down," Annika says. "Honestly, I thought you might have had something to do with it."

"Me?" I ask, appalled. "Why would I do that?"

"You wrote that horrible version of me in your book."

"I only showed what you were capable of," I say defensively.

"Because you thought I had stolen Ian from you?"

"I *know* you betrayed me with Ian. I *saw* you in each other's arms."

"I was upset and Ian was comforting me . . . and it got a little out of hand. But I swear, we only kissed."

"Only?" I snort. "And what were you so upset about?"

"My conference with Argos, if you must know. Not all of us came out of our conferences all starry-eyed and glowy with the master's praise. And then afterward I overheard something . . . about your father."

"My father?" I snap, grabbing her arm and spinning her around to face me. We've come to the path that slopes down to the Temple of Eris. The rest of the group has vanished into the woods. We're alone on top of this high promontory, inches from a precipitous drop to the rocks below. "What are you talking about? You don't know the first damn thing about my father."

"You see, this is why I was afraid to tell you about it. You clearly worshipped your father—"

"That's ridiculous," I say. "Yes, I loved my father, but I didn't worship him. I came here fifteen years ago, didn't I, even though he didn't want me to."

"And why do you think that was, Maia?" she asks, stepping toward me and reaching her hand out to touch my arm.

"You know why," I snarl, slapping her hand away. "I told you about my mother, how unstable she was, especially when she painted—" An image of my mother standing in front of her easel, face and hands so splattered with red paint she appears to be covered in blood, blooms inside my head and I instantly banish it. "He was afraid I might end up like her."

Annika was the first friend I told about my mother's episodes of paranoid delusion, extreme claustrophobia, and pathological fear of getting lost. *It sounds like she had PTSD*, she said as we lay on the roof looking up at the stars. *I was the same after what happened to me junior year.* She had told me then that a man had sexually assaulted her at a party in college. She'd had symptoms of PTSD afterward, which she thought sounded like the ones my mother had. *Maybe your mother was assaulted*, she'd suggested, *maybe when she painted, she was trying to deal with what happened to her.*

It was a relief to talk to someone who seemed to understand, who didn't act like my mother had been some kind of freak, who didn't think that I was destined to follow in her footsteps. But then she had used it all against me. When her book came out there was a character named Freya who had a domineering academic father (a medievalist instead of a classicist) and an artistic mother (opera singer instead of painter) who had gone insane and killed herself.

"You used what I told you in your book," I say now.

"Only after you depicted me as a monster in *your* book," she snarls back. "And I'm not the only one who betrays confidences. I told you about what happened to me in college and you told Argos."

"I didn't—" I begin, but then I remember that when Argos told me that there was something wrong with Annika, I *had* told him that she'd been assaulted in college. "I might have said something but I was only trying to defend you and explain why you acted the way you did—"

"Aha!" she says, as if I've just proven her point.

She steps forward so fast I stumble backward toward the edge of the ridge. "So you did tell him—"

I can feel the ground beneath my feet crumbling and Annika reaches for me—but whether to rescue me or push me I'm not sure. Before I can find out, a scream splits the air and we both freeze, clutching each other on the precipice and looking over the edge. Below us, in a cleft of rock overlooking the east cove, is the ruin of an ancient shrine—a couple of columns, a broken, headless statue of a winged goddess, and a long marble altar along which a recumbent statue reclines—a sacrifice to Eris, the goddess of discord and strife. Eleni is standing above it, one hand over her mouth. She looks like she's part of the tableau, as frozen as the statue on the altar—

But then I remember. There's no statue on the altar of Eris.

I leave Annika and hurry down the steep path, dirt and pebbles tumbling in my wake. Ian is comforting a sobbing Olivia, Sydney is being sick over the side of the cliff, Eleni is leaning over the prone figure. Bill takes off his bucket hat and stands like a mourner at a grave.

Which is what the altar has become.

The figure lying on the ancient altar is pale and lifeless as a statue. But it's not a statue; it's Argos Alexander. Our illustrious host is dead.

CHAPTER EIGHT

Eleni is the first to approach Argos's body. She presses two fingers to the side of his neck although it's obvious that he's dead. She turns to the rest of us and shakes her head.

"When did this happen?" Annika cries, glaring at Eleni accusingly. "When did you see him last?"

Eleni stares at her as if she doesn't understand the question, then looks back at the body as if it will answer for her. "Fifteen years ago," she says at last. "I haven't seen Argos Alexander since I left this island fifteen years ago."

Annika shakes her head as if trying to clear water from her ears. I don't blame her. I feel as if I've been plunged into the icy sea. "What do you mean? Didn't he hire you?"

"I received an email from Argos two weeks ago offering me the job of housekeeper for the duration of the retreat. All my communication since then has been through his lawyer and a travel agent in Athens. When I arrived, I found all my instructions, along with the letters for each of you, in my room."

"Then we have no way of knowing how long he's been dead," Annika says.

"There are ways of knowing," Olivia says, coming closer to the body. "Is he stiff?"

"Just because you write mysteries doesn't mean you're a medi-
cal examiner," Annika snaps. I glance up at her, surprised at how
angry she sounds. What's Olivia done to her? Maybe she's still
angry at me and just taking it out on Olivia.

Ignoring her, Olivia points to the back of Argos's legs. "Look at
the color of the skin where the flesh presses against the stone."

I move closer to see what Olivia means, bracing myself for
an odor, but all I can smell is the thyme and lavender under my
feet. The breeze stirs his clothes—khaki shorts and a loose white
shirt. There are greenish patches where his flesh touches the stone
and, when I look closer, *movement*. I rear back, bile rising in my
throat.

"Maggots," Olivia says, confirming my fear. "I'd say the body's
been here for a couple of days at least—maybe longer."

"Well, it's clear what killed him," Ian says, pointing to the back
of Argos's head. "It looks like he hit his head against the corner
of the altar and bled out right here. There are traces of blood beneath his head, but they've been washed away elsewhere. It must
have rained since he was killed, but it hasn't rained in the islands
for over ten days, has it, Eleni?"

She's shaking her head but it's Sydney, returned from being
sick in the bushes, who speaks up. "How do you know that? How
long have *you* been in the area?"

"I've been in the islands doing some research for my father,"
Ian says, ignoring the accusatory tone in Sydney's voice. "I heard
locals complaining that it's been a dry summer and that the last
rain was over ten days ago. Is that right, Eleni?"

"Yes," Eleni says. "It's been so dry on the mainland that there
have been many forest fires. There was a brief storm that moved
across the islands ten days ago but that was the last of the rain."

"We need to notify the police," Ian says, getting to his feet and turning to Eleni. "What's the nearest island with a police station?"

"There's one on Skiathos, we can call from the house," Eleni says. "But what should we do with Mr. Alexander? We can't just leave him here . . . *alone.*"

"He's been alone here for at least ten days. A couple of hours more won't make any difference," Olivia says. "We shouldn't disturb the body."

"I'll stay with him," Bill offers. "The man hired me—"

"Did he?" I ask. "In person? By phone? Or by email like Eleni?"

Bill shakes his head. "I received his request with the invitation ten days ago. When I wrote back I got an automatic reply instructing me to contact a travel agent in Athens to make my travel arrangements."

"That's what happened when I RSVP'd," I say.

"Me too," Ian says, "so we don't really know if it was Argos who hired Bill or you, Eleni." Then, looking around at the rest of us, he adds, "And if Argos died more than ten days ago, we don't really know if he invited any of us. We might all have been invited by his murderer."

BILL STILL WANTS to stay behind and Sydney, surprisingly, offers to stay with him. He looks pale and sweaty from being sick so maybe he's just not up to the hike. Eleni's not looking too well, either. Ian hangs back with her, lending her a hand on the steep parts of the path.

"Do you believe her?" Olivia asks me when they're too far behind to overhear. "Do you think Eleni really hasn't seen Argos in fifteen years?"

She's addressed the question to me but it's Annika who answers.

"It seems fishy to me. Who takes a job without at least a Zoom call?"

"We all came here on the basis of a paper invitation and a few emails with a travel agent," I say. "Unless—" I turn toward Annika. "You said that Argos sent the boat to Skiathos for you. Had you talked to him?"

"I tried," she admits, looking embarrassed. "I wrote to him saying I was going to be in the islands earlier and I wanted to talk to him."

"About your publishing situation?" I ask.

"What publishing situation?" Olivia asks eagerly, no doubt looking for someone else to join in with her complaints.

Annika glares at me, clearly unhappy that I've given this information away to Olivia. "That doesn't matter now. He wrote back that business matters prevented him from seeing me."

"What about you, Olivia? Any communication with Argos? You said you wanted to talk to him after he bought Paulson Pratchett to ask him to help sort out things with the publisher."

Olivia shoots me a daggered look, as clearly displeased as Annika was that I'm revealing her professional woes.

"I wrote to congratulate him on the purchase of Paulson Pratchett six months ago," she says, "and to offer him some information about the publisher I thought he'd find valuable, but he said the same thing—business matters prevented him from discussing the matter right then, but he looked forward to hearing my insights and talking about my future at Paulson Pratchett at a later date. When I got the invitation, I thought he was ready to talk. It was really the whole reason I came. But when I RSVP'd I got that same automatic reply."

"Someone has lured us here with false promises, only to kill Argos and dash our hopes," Annika says.

"I hardly think someone cares enough about making you unhappy to kill Argos," I say.

"Not even you, Maia?" Annika asks archly. "You're clearly angry at me because you think I stole your boyfriend fifteen years ago."

Olivia raises her eyebrows at this information and flicks her eyes toward me, eager to see my response.

"I just got to Greece yesterday!" I cry. "I could hardly have sneaked onto the island, killed Argos, and magically made his body decay in that time."

"You could have gotten someone to do it," Annika points out. "Your father had many contacts in Greece and you do, too, since you run that museum."

I laugh. "Most of my contacts in Greece are octogenarian archeologists and classics professors—hardly the trained assassins to send on a *hit*. Besides, why would I want to kill Argos? He was one of my father's dearest friends and one of the museum's biggest donors. In fact, he just wrote to my college's president offering a donation—"

"So, you were lured here, too," Annika says. "You would have been angry if he'd changed his mind when you got here—or maybe you were angry at him already because he dragged your father into that looting scandal."

"What looting scandal?" Olivia asks, her interest piqued again. "You didn't mention that."

"It was years ago," I say. "Argos arranged a sale of some pottery shards that he recognized as matching some fragments my father had of a seventh-ccentury black figure amphora known as the Wedding Vase. Reassembling it was my father's lifework. The accusation that the fragments were looted was totally ungrounded."

"I recall that case in the *Times*," Olivia says. "Was Julius

Gold your father? He was accused of knowingly acquiring looted antiquities—"

"It was an outrageous claim," I snap, furious that Annika has brought up this old wound in front of Olivia. "My father had no idea."

"And didn't your father have a heart attack after someone confronted him about it at a conference?" Olivia asks.

She's right. It was just after my panel at the Classical Society conference. I remember looking through the crowds afterward for my father, hopeful that he'd be proud of how I'd merged writing and classics, but instead I'd spotted him red-faced and sweaty in an argument with a reporter. By the time I reached him, he'd collapsed.

"I remember you saying that the scandal killed him," Annika says.

"Why, you must have hated Argos!" Olivia says. "I'm surprised you would still come here—unless you hoped for revenge." She lifts one eyebrow, clearly delighted to have found my Achilles' heel after I revealed hers in front of Annika.

We've reached the ridge trail, which makes it necessary to go single file. "After you," I say stepping aside to let Annika and Olivia walk in front of me. I no longer want either of them walking behind me.

I WALK SLOWLY to put some distance between me and the two other women. They'll probably talk about me when they see I'm out of earshot but I'm past caring.

It killed him.

I had said that to Annika but I didn't think she'd remember it. It was over thirteen years ago, just after my father died. She called with her condolences, all sympathy and concern as if I would for-give her because she felt bad for my father. She'd seen the article in the *Times* questioning the provenance of the Wedding Vase, which was ridiculous, and then the article about my father dying at the conference—*Classicist has fatal heart attack after confron-tation at classics conference.* My father had been collecting pieces of that vase since he had come across a fragment at an antiquities dealer in Switzerland while on honeymoon with my mother. He had spent years hunting down fragments in private collections, regional museums, and university holdings. How could that be looting?

Unless my father had lied about where he found that first frag-ment. I'd overheard him arguing with Argos on the phone and I knew the relationship between them had become strained, after which my father had a stroke, brought on, I've always believed, by the humiliation of that article. The stroke had rendered him aphasic—my father, who had always known the right word and exactly where it came from!—for the short remainder of his life and I'd never learned the source of their argument. He was just getting better when he accompanied me to that conference and died of a heart attack.

When my father died, Argos sent flowers and condolences. By then the dispute over the Wedding Vase had died down. There were higher-profile cases—the Euphronios Krater at the Met, the Elgin Marbles—to occupy the media. Yes, of course, get-ting the invitation from Argos had brought it all up again but the idea that I'd come here looking to avenge my father against Argos was even more absurd than thinking I'd kill him to make Annika unhappy.

But someone *has* killed him.

I stop on the path above Argos's villa. *Lavyrinthos*, the labyrinth. I feel as if I have been walking a labyrinth in my head. From here I can see the flat roof above the library where Annika and I used to stargaze at night. I remember pointing out the constellations I knew so well from the ones my mother painted on the ceiling and feeling somehow close to her because the stars felt closer here on this island in the Aegean—as if the gods and goddesses for which they were named might alight beside us. I remember telling Annika about my mother and thinking she understood because of her own struggles with PTSD. But then she betrayed me—first by stealing Ian and then by using those confidences in her book. As I start down the path, I see the two statues guarding the stairs down to the dock. Eris, the goddess of discord, holds her golden apple up to the sun, tempting us to vie for favor and fame, while Nemesis yields her golden dagger to punish those who commit crimes to achieve those ends. What a narrow path, I think as I head down to the villa, there is to tread between the two.

WHEN I REACH the terrace, Olivia and Annika fall silent, confirming my suspicion that they spent the rest of the walk talking about me. Ian and Eleni are conferring together when they arrive.

"You can all wait here while I go to the library to call the police," Eleni says.

"Not bloody likely," Olivia says, following Eleni into the villa. "I have a few calls to make myself."

"I bet she wants to call her agent," Annika murmurs to me as we all follow Eleni to the library door, "to complain about the treatment she has received here."

I snicker before I can stop myself and cover my mouth, horrified both that I can laugh so soon after seeing Argos's body and that Annika can still make me laugh. It's too late, though. I can see from Annika's eyes that she's remembering the two of us standing in front of the door to Argos's library—the *sanctum sanctorum*, we called it—afraid to go into our weekly conferences, daring each other to go first.

Argos was an intimidating man. Even now, having just seen his lifeless body, it's hard to believe he's not waiting inside for us. When Eleni opens the door and I step inside it feels like he's everywhere. He's in the floor-to-ceiling bookcases lined with books in all the languages he mastered—ancient and modern Greek, Russian, English, Italian, German, French—and the signed first editions from twentieth-century masters he personally knew. He's in the busts of Greek philosophers—Socrates, Plato, Aristotle, Pythagoras—silhouetted against the wide south-facing windows. Perhaps most of all, he's in the large framed architect's rendering of the villa, which hangs on the wall opposite his desk. I remember that when I asked my father once if Argos had ever tried his hand at writing himself, he said Lavyrinthos was his opus. When I sat in front of him at his desk, his eyes would sometimes drift over my shoulder and I knew he was looking at that drawing. I'm almost afraid now to look toward the long desk, sure I'll find him sitting behind it like a priest at his altar . . .

But here the illusion of his presence ends. The desk, which I remember as a vast pristine expanse of polished teak punctuated by a few choice objets d'art—a marble faun, a bronze letter opener with the word *NEMESIS* inscribed on the blade, a fifth-century bowl filled with shells and sea glass—is now a scene of chaos, the faun toppled on its side, the bowl reduced to shards, a bottle of black ink spilled across the satiny wood, papers scattered everywhere. More than the elegant tableau at the shrine, *this* looks like a murder scene.

"Was it like this last night?" Ian asks, scanning the wreckage on the desk.

"I-I didn't check," Eleni stammers. "I only arrived yesterday morning and there was so much to do. Mr. Alexander never liked anyone to interfere with his private papers."

"Someone has certainly *interfered* with them now," Olivia says, pushing past Ian to scan the desk. "Is that the phone?" She points to a pile of plastic and wires on the floor behind the desk. I recall the old-fashioned landline that once sat there. It looks like someone has taken a hammer to it.

"Where's the radio?" Ian asks.

Eleni points to a cabinet behind the desk. I remember the two-way radio that crackled and dispatched cryptic messages in Greek, Turkish, Russian, Italian, and French. Argos said he could follow the progress of his ships throughout the Mediterranean and Adriatic Seas—even across the Atlantic—and see that they were staying on schedule. When a ship was behind schedule, he would radio the captain himself to demand an explanation and urge him to go faster.

Ian crouches in front of the radio console, flicks a switch, and adjusts a dial but no sound comes out. When he removes the front grille it's clear why—the wires inside have been cut. I feel the sinews in my legs buckle as if they've been cut as well. Annika must, too, because she sinks down into the desk chair, her face as white as the marble faun.

"Is this the only radio?" Ian asks, his voice tight. It occurs to me that he looked calmer when examining Argos's body.

"Yes," Eleni says. "There used to be one in the kitchen but I noticed yesterday it had been removed."

"And you didn't think to mention that or check that this one was working before you let the boat leave?" Olivia demands in a shrill voice.

"There's no point yelling at Eleni," Annika says, looking up from her seat. "Can't you see she's upset and as surprised by all of this as the rest of us?"

"That could be an act," Olivia says. "We have only her word that she just arrived yesterday. She could have been here for weeks, murdering Argos, sending us those invitations—"

"Why would I do any of that?" Eleni cries. "I never even wanted to come here again! I only did because I needed the money."

"Ah, so you needed money. Murdering a billionaire would be one way of getting it."

"In which case," I say, "why wouldn't she just take the money and go?"

"Exactly," says Annika, pulling open a bottom drawer and taking out a metal box. She puts it on the desk and opens it. It's full of cash.

"How did you know that was there?" Olivia asks, her suspicions swinging to Annika as swiftly as a pendulum.

"Everyone knew this was where Argos kept his 'petty cash.' If Eleni murdered Argos for money, she could have taken this and half a dozen other valuables"—she waves her hand over the wreckage of the desk—"and been long gone before we got here. Why bother to invite witnesses to her crime to the island?"

"Why would anyone," Olivia pleads, her hectoring tone turned now to terror, "unless they had a reason to want us all dead? I've written this kind of book before. It's a Golden Age chestnut—a rich and powerful man with lots of enemies is murdered, the suspects are limited in number and unable to leave, which should make it easy to solve. The real challenge"—she laughs suddenly, her terror now verging on hysteria—"is finding the murderer before becoming their next victim."

CHAPTER NINE

O livia," Ian says, laying a hand on her arm. "We don't even know if the person who killed Argos is still on the island—"

"You're probably the one behind it!" she cries, swatting Ian's hand away. "This is exactly the kind of book your father writes."

Ian's mouth twists and I can see that he's trying hard not to laugh. He once told me that he hated being the son of a popular mystery writer but he's probably never been accused of murder as a result.

"Instead of accusing each other of murder," I say, "we should look at what the murderer was looking for. These papers—" I wave my hand over the mess on the desk. "It looks like someone was looking for something." I pick up one of the crumpled sheets. "I recognize this—it's the letter I wrote Argos when I applied to the residency fifteen years ago."

Ian, taking my cue, sorts through the papers and picks up another page. "Here's my application letter." He winces. "God, I was a pretentious jerk." At the suggestion that the papers spread around the room might have something interesting—and possibly embarrassing—in them, Olivia's focus narrows and she picks up one of the scattered pages. "This looks like a recommendation letter for you, Annika, from someone named Hilary Pond."

Annika turns bright pink and grabs for the paper. "Let me see that!"

Olivia hands over the page to Annika, pulls a chair over to the desk, and dumps her overflowing tote bag on top of the mess. With one hand she begins sifting through the papers on the desk while her other hand rummages around her bag. She pulls out a water bottle and takes a drink from it, but not before slipping something into her mouth. A pill, I think, that she's trying to keep anyone from seeing.

Ian turns to Eleni. "Where would these pages come from? Did Argos keep files on all his guests?"

"Yes," she says, "at least he did when I was his secretary. In addition to the application and references, he requested extensive background searches for everyone who came to the island—not just the writers but the staff as well—" Color drains from her face like a veil dropping and she hurriedly scans the pages on the desk. She must be worried there's something about her. What, I wonder, is she afraid of us discovering?

"Where would those files be kept?" Ian asks.

She drags her eyes away from the desk and turns to a row of file cabinets behind the desk. "They were kept in here when I worked for Argos, but I don't know if my replacement kept the same filing system. And the cabinets were always locked."

Annika swivels her chair around and easily opens the cabinet nearest to her. "It looks like the lock was broken—these cover the nineties." She shuts the cabinet and then runs her fingers along the label cards on the outside of each cabinet until she finds one with the dates she's looking for and opens that easily as well; all the locks must be broken. "Here are the residency files for 2008, 2009 . . . but the files for 2010 seem to be missing."

"I think we'll find them scattered around the office," Ian says. "We should check what's here and what's missing. It's too big a coincidence that we were all here together—even you, Eleni, and—"

"Bill," I say. "We're forgetting about Bill and Sydney. They're still at the shrine with Argos's body." An image of Argos's body laid out on the altar flashes through my mind. There's something about the scene that pricks at my memory but I can't think what. "We need to tell them to come back."

Ian nods. "You're right. There's no point preserving the murder scene since the police won't be coming any time soon. I'll go—"

"You shouldn't go alone," Olivia says, looking up from the pile of paper in her lap. She seems perfectly calm now, the hysteria of a few minutes ago gone. Whatever she took must have done the trick—or maybe it's having a task that has helped her regain her equilibrium. I wonder how often she has employed the habits of research and writing to keep fear and anxiety at bay. "The first rule of a locked-room mystery is that no one should be alone."

"I'll go with you," I offer. As much as I don't want to see Argos's body again—or be alone with Ian—there's something about the scene that feels familiar. Maybe if I see it again I'll figure out what.

We leave Annika, Olivia, and Eleni combing through the files. Ian stops in the kitchen to fill water bottles for the hike and we leave by the back door. As soon as we're far enough from the villa not to be overheard he stops and turns to me.

"Annika told me what you think you heard and saw that last night."

"Wow, talk about condescending," I say, walking past him up the trail. "Are you going to mansplain what I saw with my own eyes and heard with my own ears? Don't you think we have bigger things to worry about right now?"

"Maybe what's happening now has something to do with what happened then," he says, catching up with me. "Tell me exactly what you heard me say and do. It's the least you can do after cutting me off without a word of explanation fifteen years ago."

"I heard Annika say that *we have to tell Maia* and then you said it would kill me and then I saw you"—I come to a stop, gasping for breath in the hot, dusty air, the moonlit scene playing out before me like a sunstruck mirage—"kiss Annika, so don't tell me I misunderstood that. You were both so carried away that you felt the need to retire inside the grotto."

"Where we both instantly realized we were making a mistake," he says.

I snort. "How convenient that you realized the error of your ways as soon as you were out of sight. Am I supposed to believe that? Clearly, you'd both been lusting after each other all summer."

"It wasn't like that," he says. "Annika was upset. Not everybody's conference with Argos went as well as yours did."

I laugh. "Was that it? You were jealous that my conference went better than yours? How do you even know mine went well?"

"Please," he says, rolling his eyes. "We could all hear what Argos said as you left the library. And then your face—you looked like the cat that swallowed the canary."

I laugh at the old-fashioned phrase, but it's made me relive the moment. As I was walking out of the library, preoccupied by what Argos had said to me (not all of which was pleasant), he said something I couldn't quite make out. I'd turned on the threshold and asked what he said and he'd shouted it in his booming voice. *I said that your mother would be proud of you!*

It had felt like a benediction.

When I turned toward the terrace I must have been beaming. They were all there. Annika and Ian were sitting next to each other, Bill and Sydney were huddled together on the edge of the terrace, Gena, as usual, was alone, Eleni hovering in the background. Olivia, sitting near Ian and Annika, snarked: *Well, we don't have to ask how that went. It must be nice to be the favorite.* The animosity had caught me by surprise. I'd turned to Annika for support but I saw instead what Argos had predicted: *There's something missing in her. I'd watch out for her if I were you.* And when I turned to Ian I had seen the same spark of envy.

"You were jealous," I say now. "Is that why you decided to punish me by sleeping with Annika?"

"I didn't—"

"If you didn't sleep with her, why didn't you tell me that?"

"How could I?" he asks, holding his arms open wide as if he's beseeching the heavens. We've come to the top of the ridge and he's silhouetted against the pitiless blue glare of sea and sky. "You wouldn't answer my calls or emails. You dumped me! And then you came out with that book—"

"You read it?"

"Of course I read it! I thought it would help me understand what went wrong. And there I was—*Sean*, the whiny wannabe writer cowed by his famous father's legacy, so weak he steals his girlfriend's manuscript—something I would never, *ever* have done."

"It was an objective correlative," I say prissily, "for stealing my heart and cheating on me, which I think was worse."

"But I hadn't done that, either! The only thing I could figure out had happened was that you were auditioning me for a starring role in your precious book—" He takes a step forward, his face so contorted with hurt and rage that I step back—and find myself teetering on the edge of the cliff. It occurs to me that the first rule of locked-room mysteries isn't *never be alone*; it's never be alone with *one* person who could be the murderer. I had never thought about how angry Ian might have been when I cut off contact with him. Why should he be? *I* was the injured party, the betrayed one. But if what he's saying is true, *if he hadn't slept with Annika*, I can see why he'd be angry. So angry he might, fifteen years later, want to get his revenge. Which would be easy to do here on this remote cliff on a Greek island.

"Was it you?" My voice comes out a hoarse croak. "Did you invite us all here to get your revenge?"

He stares at me for a moment as if he doesn't understand what I'm suggesting, and then all the color leaches from his face as if he has been turned to stone, as if I am the Medusa who slays heroes. "If you really think that of me, why don't you go back to the villa. I won't stop you. In fact—" He takes a few steps to the edge of the ridge and turns his back to me, his hands held high over his head. "If you think I'm the murderer you can end this all now with one firm shove."

I wonder if he knows that was what I was picturing him doing to me before. "That's hardly convincing," I say. "I'd have to explain to everyone what happened and they'd think *I* was the murderer."

He turns and smiles. "Exactly. We're in the same boat, so to speak. Mutually assured destruction. So shall we?" He waves toward the ridge trail. I return the gesture.

"After you," I say.

WE WALK IN silence along the ridge path, Ian's tensed back muscles an eloquent reproach of my accusation. Did I really believe

Ian orchestrated this whole thing because he's angry at me for dumping him fifteen years ago? No. I can't flatter myself that I meant that much to him. It was just a flirtation, after all, a summer fling made glossier by a romantic setting. At least, that's what I've told myself all these years. Sure, there'd been the connection that had sparked between us almost immediately. We had a lot in common, after all. Our fathers knew each other, although as far as we both knew they hadn't seen each other since their days at the American School in Athens. Still, Clive Davies sent my father a signed copy of the latest Pythagoras book every year and my father read each one with pleasure. Even though I soon realized that Ian didn't like talking about his father much, he did love the mythology and literature his father had raised him on. We got each other's references because we had both been brought up on the same bedtime stories of heroes and monsters.

It's like you belonged to the same dorky club in high school, Annika had snarked one night.

Latin club! we'd both simultaneously cried and then gone on a nostalgia-fest of classics tournaments and Certamen matches, which we had to explain to Annika was a sort of *Jeopardy!* for classical knowledge.

What nerds! she'd shouted. *Did you wear togas?*

Please, I'd scoffed, *women don't wear togas—*

They wore stolae, Ian had finished for me. *I wore a toga. I had one made out of Power Ranger sheets.*

Even more than our love of the ancient world, though, we shared the burden of our fathers' expectations. I thought his father at least would have been happy Ian wanted to be a writer but it turned out he was even more dead set against it than mine. *Are you kidding?* he told me and Annika one night over ouzo and smuggled hashish in the grotto of the Muses. *He says it's the worst way to make a living in the world. If I can't be a professor I ought to be an accountant or a civil servant. Something with a pension.*

The two of you should write your own series about the Greek gods, Annika told us.

Rick Riordan already has, we'd answered at the same time.

But we had spun out stories on those long sunstruck days and moonlit nights of gods and goddesses, nymphs and fauns, who seemed to roam the woods and groves and swim beside us in the secluded coves. It felt as if the gods were with us, as if our love story were part of the ancient landscape—

I come to a sudden halt as if awakening from a dream and look around. We've strayed from the ridge path into a glade ringed by olive trees, their smooth, tawny boughs forming a perfect circle. The ground is covered in white, star-shaped flowers. Half hidden beneath them a marble girl crouches above a spring, cupping water in one hand. Persephone, we'd thought, because the flowers in the glade were asphodels, which were associated with the underworld as Persephone was. This had been our favorite place to come together.

"I sometimes thought I'd dreamed this place," Ian says, his voice hushed as if he is in a church.

I turn to him and for a moment, in the shivering silver-green shade of the olives, he is the boy I met here fifteen years ago. *Maybe we did dream this place*, I start to tell him, *maybe we can go back to it—*

But before I can finish, a startled cry comes from below us. Ian whips his head around to peer through the trees. "I think that's Bill," he says.

He plunges into the woods, heading down the steep slope. I follow, my feet slipping on the dry pine needles and loose earth—*no rain in ten days*, Ian had said. Did he really know that because he'd been on another island? And does he really remember this path from fifteen years ago? Or has he been here more recently? It also occurs to me as I spy glimpses of the sea below, that if I fell here and slid off this slope into the sea, he could easily explain that I died racing to help Bill and Sydney.

I don't fall. But when we come out on a rise above the shrine, I see that another sacrifice has been made in the Temple of Eris. Bill is lying face down on the ground. Ian reaches him first and turns him over. I'm relieved to hear a groan come from him and see his eyes blink open.

"What happened, mate?" Ian asks, helping Bill to sit up while gingerly inspecting the back of his head. "And where's Sydney?"

I kneel down and offer him my water bottle.

" . . . must have hit me," Bill manages between gulps of water. "We were arguing. He said this was a classic Golden Age murder mystery setup and he had it all figured out, including who the secretary Despina Outis really was and that we were all going to die if we didn't get off the island. He wanted to go down to the cove to search for a boat because he said there'd been one in the caves the last time we were here. I said we should wait for the police and he said, *Don't be an idiot, the police aren't coming.*" His eyes flick between me and Ian. "*Are* they coming?"

Ian shakes his head. "The phone and radio have been trashed. We're on our own."

"How did Sydney know that?" I ask.

"He said it was Locked-Room Mystery 101," Bill says, touching the back of his head and wincing. "And then he pointed out to sea and said, *Look!* and when I did, like an idiot, he conked me over the head."

I get up and approach the edge of the cliff. As I do, I feel a tingle up and down my spine, aware of how vulnerable I am. But when I glance over my shoulder, I see Ian busily wiping blood from Bill's head, neither of them paying any attention to me. I turn back to the cliff and look over the edge to the east cove below us and make out a small rowboat only fifty or so feet from shore, rowed by someone in a yellow windbreaker. "Where does he think he's going?" I ask. "The nearest island is twenty miles away. He'll never get there in a rowboat."

"Especially not that one," Ian says. "Look at how low it's riding. It's taking on water."

I turn to tell him he's right but Ian is already scrambling down the hill to the cove below. His plan, I assume, is to be waiting to grab Sydney when he comes to shore. For surely that's what Sydney will do when he realizes that his boat is sinking. And yet, when I reach the cove and look up, his boat appears farther away from shore and lower in the water. "Doesn't he realize it's sinking?" I ask, joining Ian at the edge of the water.

"No more than he realized that taking a boat most probably left by a killer wasn't a good idea. It's just the kind of behavior he'd have ridiculed in one of his reviews," Ian says. "The boat must have been sabotaged. Look, he's stopped rowing. He must see he's taking on water."

I cup my hands around my mouth and shout, "Sydney! Come back! You're sinking!"

His head jerks up and he looks toward me. "You!" he yells. "It's you." Then instead of rowing to shore he continues heading out to open sea, beyond the protection of the cove, where the waves swell higher and break against the jagged rocks at the mouth of the cove. I remember what Eleni said about the submerged rocks and tricky currents in the east cove.

"What the hell is he doing?" Ian swears. "And what does he mean, *it's you*?"

"I have no idea," I say, yet something about his words combined with the scene—a figure on a shore shouting to another out to sea—feels familiar. Before I can retrieve the memory, though, I watch in horror as a wave swamps the sinking boat and flips it over. Sydney's head pops up, his arms thrashing in the air.

"Oh crap," Ian says, shucking off his sneakers. "I bet he can't swim. I'm going to have to swim out to get him."

He's in the water before I can object—and how can I? Ian's right. From his frantic thrashing it's clear Sydney can't swim. He'll drown if Ian doesn't get to him. He might drown anyway and take Ian with him.

"Shit!" I curse, shucking off my own shoes and wading into the water. It's colder than I expected and I remember it's early in the season. I remember, too, as I wade out, Eleni's warnings about the treacherous currents in the cove and the legends that creatures from the underworld lurk beneath the water waiting to drag unsuspecting swimmers back with them to hell. I try not to think of those stories as I swim toward Ian. He's reached Sydney now and is trying to get him in an overhead lifeguard hold but Sydney is thrashing too hard.

As if some horrible creature has him in its grip and is pulling him down.

"Sydney!" I scream as I come closer. "We're trying to save you. Let Ian help you."

"You!" he shouts, although it sounds more like *Ooo!* as he gargles water. "Ooo it's ooo it's—"

He suddenly lunges at me and flings his arms around my neck. His weight pulls both of us down below the water. I don't have time to close my mouth. I take in a gulp of salt water that burns my throat. I open my eyes and see Sydney's face inches from mine, mouth open wide, still screaming, "Ooo it's ooo it's ooo it's—"

Like some horrible curse.

Only, no, that's not exactly what he's saying. As my vision blurs and darkens, I hear my father's voice—*Ooo tis, ooo tis*—and I struggle for the translation as if it's the key to releasing me from the monster's grip. With his hair waving around his face like sea snakes Sydney looks like Medusa—

A hand grabs those snakes and yanks his face away from me. His arms lose their grip around my neck and I struggle toward the surface, which looks like a shining disk floating above me—too far to reach. The bright disk of sun on the water seems to shrink, contracting like the eye of some one-eyed monster. Of course, I think as everything turns dark, the Cyclops—

I feel something grab my hair. I fight against it, sure it's the monster, but then my head breaks the surface of the water and I hear Ian calling my name. "Don't make me knock you out, too, Maia Gold."

I relax my muscles and let him put his arm over my head and swim us both to shore, where he drags me up onto the shingle and turns me on my side so I can cough up seawater and bile. Then Bill is there, handing me my water bottle and thumping me on my back.

"You okay?" he asks. Only it sounds like *ooo okay.*

"I know what he was shouting," I say, looking around for Sydney. Only there's no Sydney.

Ian is crouched beside me, his face wet with seawater or tears. "I had to leave him," he says. "He was going to kill you."

I nod. "He was shouting *You-tis* only he meant *Outis*."

"The secretary?" Bill asks, looking at me as if I've lost my mind. "Why would he be calling you the secretary's name?"

"There's no secretary," I say. "Odysseus tells the Cyclops that his name is Outis so when the Cyclops tells his brothers who blinded him—"

"They'll think it was no one," Ian finishes for me.

Bill looks at us as if we've both lost our minds.

"It means *no one*," Ian says. "The person who invited us to this goddamned island is no one."

CHAPTER TEN

We go back to the villa, leaving Argos rotting in the sun and Sydney drowned in the sea. It feels wrong abandoning our fallen comrades. In Greek mythology the dead are restless without a proper burial. They haunt the living and demand vengeance. But we have no way of carrying Argos's decomposing body over a mile in the hot sun while also helping wounded Bill, and Sydney may have already been washed out to sea or been dragged down to the underworld by hungry ghosts. We have to deal with the living avenger first.

We bring Bill in the back door and head toward the kitchen but Eleni pops her head out of a pantry before we reach it and cries out when she sees the blood spattered on Bill's shirt and the makeshift bandage wrapped around his head. "Take him out on the terrace and I'll bring water and bandages," she says, shooing us past the kitchen, where, I guess from the clutter on the counters, she's been preparing our lunch in Bill's absence.

We take Bill out onto the terrace and settle him in the most comfortable chair—the one at the head of the table that Argos used to sit in and where Sydney sat last night. Something about him taking the place where two dead men have sat makes me shiver despite the hot sun.

"What happened?" Eleni asks, coming back with a basin of water and a first aid kit. She scans the terrace and then asks, "Was it that awful man Sydney Norton? I never liked him."

I almost echo the sentiment before remembering that we're speaking ill of the dead. "Where are Annika and Olivia?" I ask, not wanting to tell the story twice. "We should all be here together."

"Still in the library," she says. "I came out to make us some more coffee and see what we had for lunch since our chef was not here. And to check on our supplies . . . in case we have to remain here for some time."

"Good thinking," I say, wondering how long we can survive here if the boat doesn't come back for us. "Did the captain say when he'd be back if Argos *didn't* contact him?"

Eleni shakes her head. "He said he was hired by Mr. Alexander and took his orders from him. He wouldn't even do a simple errand for me in Volos."

From her tone I guess that's what they were arguing about this morning. "Is it likely that any other boat would come here?" I ask. "Local fishermen, perhaps?"

She shakes her head. "Mr. Alexander strictly prohibits fishing anywhere near his island. Not that he has to. The local fishermen don't like to come here. As I told you, the locals believe that Eris is cursed. It's unlikely any boat will come by chance."

I LEAVE IAN and Eleni attending to Bill on the terrace and go to the library to get Annika and Olivia. None of the commotion—even Eleni's startled cry—has drawn them out. For a moment, as I push the door open, I'm afraid I may find another scene of horror—Olivia and Annika murdered in the library as in a game of Clue. Instead, the previous chaos of the library has been tamed into order. Annika and Olivia are seated on either side of Argos's long teak desk sorting through neatly arrayed stacks of paper and file folders. They both look up at me—Olivia in reading glasses, Annika's unruly red hair neatly coiled on top of her head—like two scholars interrupted from their archival research. Olivia shows no sign of the hysterics she'd displayed earlier.

"There have been some . . . *developments*," I say, reduced to deference. I feel like I did as a child when I would be sent to my father's study to tell him dinner was ready. "You should come out on the terrace." They look at each other and I feel a pang at the familiarity of the glance—*Annika has a new friend*—and then a flash of annoyance. "I know who Outis is—"

"No one," Annika says. "Olivia and I figured that out, too. And we think we know why they've called us here."

I look down at the page in her hand and recognize the stylized Greek amphora from the Museum of Ancient Antiquities stationery. I recognize the handwriting, too. It's my father's. Before I can read it, Annika slips it into a folder and gets to her feet.

"But our *developments* can wait until we've heard yours," Annika says. "Shall we?"

IAN IS WRAPPING a new bandage around Bill's head while Eleni lays out coffee cups and food on the table. It's a strange scene—our chef crowned with a white headdress at the head of the table while lunch is spread out before him. It's a simple meal of bread, feta cheese, tomatoes, cucumbers, olives, and plums, which makes it look all the more like a ritualistic offering to a god—or to a sacrificial victim. *Maybe we should be pouring libations and searing burnt offerings.* Anything to halt this tide of death.

When we're all gathered, Bill relates his argument with Sydney that preceded his attack and then Ian picks up with us finding the unconscious Bill and spotting Sydney rowing out to sea right before he capsized.

"We tried to save him," Ian says, "but he struggled and tried to drag Maia down. I had no choice but to hit him to save Maia." He glances at me and I realize that he saved my life—even after I practically accused him of being a murderer—and how close I came to dying. I'm suddenly back in the water, struggling with Sydney, his face a mask of terror.

"He was afraid of me," I say. "He acted like he thought I was trying to kill him and he kept saying *Outis*."

"He did seem to be shouting that name at you," Bill says. "Maybe he thought you were the one who had killed Argos and invited the rest of us for revenge."

"Why would Sydney think it was me?" I ask, wounded that Bill would suggest I'm the murderer after Ian and I practically carried him all the way back here. "Why would I kill Argos?"

"Maybe because Argos ruined your father," Annika says.

I glare at her, "I already told you that the looting accusations were false, so why should my father blame Argos for them?"

Looking almost sorry for me, Annika takes a page out of her folder and lays it down on the table. It's the one with the museum logo I'd glimpsed in the library. I pick it up, instantly recognizing the large shaky hand my father wrote in after his stroke. *Dear Argos*, it reads, *I received your last letter asking after my health, which you already know has not been at its best. Please don't concern yourself, however, Maia is taking excellent care of me. And as for the matter of the vase, rest assured that I will say nothing. It is not my wont to cast blame when I have been equally at fault. No one need know—*

I turn over the page to see if the letter continues, but that side is blank. It wasn't my father's habit to write on both sides of the page. "Is there another page?" I ask.

"We didn't find one," Annika says. "In fact, we didn't find any files relating to the vase or other antiquities at all, which isn't all that surprising. If Argos was involved in the illegal sale of Greek antiquities, he'd hardly leave the evidence lying around. But it's clear from this that Argos was involved in the acquisition of the Wedding Vase and your father knew it was looted—"

"I don't think that's clear at all," I say, fighting back tears.

Ian and Annika exchange a look that makes my skin prickle. "I overheard Argos talking about your father on our last night here," she says, "and it was clear he was involved in the antiquities looting with Argos. That's what I was afraid to tell you—"

"I don't believe you," I interrupt, not interested in hearing her excuses about what happened that night, "and even if it were true, do you think I would come all the way here and murder Argos thirteen years after my father's death?"

"You *were* unusually attached to your father," Olivia says. "Argos mentioned it—"

"That's right," I say, turning on Olivia, "you and Argos were such good friends that you thought he could solve your publishing problems." An image blooms in my mind of Olivia sitting beside Argos at the dinner table, leaning forward eagerly to catch his every word, the candlelight catching on the sequins of her embroidered, low-cut blouse. "More than friends, I seem to recall," I add crassly. "But what if you had already come here and asked for his help with your publisher and he, no longer so taken by you, had turned you down? I can picture you giving him a nice hard shove."

Olivia narrows her eyes at me and, without saying a word,

reaches into her ever-present tote bag and produces her passport. "Here's my entry stamp into Greece three days ago. Do the rest of you have your passports handy to show us when you arrived in Greece?"

"You could have had an accomplice," Bill says quietly.

Olivia glares at him. "Says the man who was demoted from writer to chef. Don't tell me you're not jealous of my career, Bill Collins—"

"This is getting us nowhere," Ian says, getting up so suddenly his chair topples over backward. "We all have reasons why we might be angry at Argos—"

"Why would you be angry at him—" I begin, but then I realize what it was about the scene at the temple that bothered me. "The body laid out on the altar," I say. "It's exactly like a scene from one of the Detective Pythagoras books. Did Argos do something to *your* father, Ian?"

Ian turns on me with a wounded look that makes me want to take back the accusation but before I can, Olivia says, "There was that awful review Sydney gave of your father's last book. And the fact that Argos encouraged him to do so."

"What?" Ian gapes at her, the wounded look turning to utter confusion. "What are you talking about?"

"We found a file of Sydney's reviews for *Circus Weekly*," she says, picking up a sheaf of paper. "They were in Sydney's file. Apparently, he sent them to Argos as writing samples! Here's one for your father's latest book: *Detective Pythagoras has gotten so dreary that I would suggest he emulate his namesake and drink hemlock.*"

"That's not even the right philosopher," Ian complains, looking to me for verification, but I'm done playing the classics game with him.

"To be fair, he slammed all of us," Annika says. "He said my first novel, *Exile from Cythera*, should be exiled from any reputable bookstore."

"He called my Detective Moreau *Ersatz Poirot*," Olivia says.

"He gave me a terrible review, too," I say, "but I'd hardly kill Sydney over it."

"Because it didn't really hurt your book," Annika points out. "You got a starred review in *Publishers Weekly* and then that great review in the *Times*." She looks away from me as if embarrassed to admit that she'd read my reviews. "And it didn't really hurt you two, either," she says, looking from Olivia to Ian. "But remember what Sydney said last night about Gena's book being derivative?"

"I have a feeling that Sydney thinks every contemporary novel is derivative, but what of it? Sydney didn't even get a chance to pan Gena's book in *Circus Weekly* because it was never published."

"No," Annika says, "but apparently he read the manuscript and told her it was no good. We found this—" She holds up a file folder. "Sydney wrote a reader's report on Gena's manuscript for Argos. Her book was a modern retelling of the play *Agamemnon* with a tyrannical Greek billionaire named Atreus—"

"Agamemnon's father," Ian and I both say at the same time. Annika goes on without even bothering to roll her eyes.

"— who sacrifices his daughter Jeannie in pursuit of his fortune."

"Yikes," I say. "It sounds like she had a beef with Argos. And you say Sydney gave this report to Argos?"

"Yes," Annika replies. "It was in his files along with a copy of a letter Argos wrote to Gena telling her that she had abused his trust and hospitality and that he would personally make sure her book was never published."

"So Gena would have good reason to want revenge on Sydney

and Argos, but why the rest of us?" I ask. "I don't remember doing anything terrible to her."

"Do you remember much about her at all?" Annika asks.

I shake my head. "Not really. She was kind of quiet and shy—and she seemed younger, but I think that was because she was still in college. I remember wondering how she got into the residency."

"I asked her point-blank how she got in," Annika says, "and she looked like I'd asked her how she lost her virginity."

I suddenly recall the moment. We were on the terrace after dinner, drinking ouzo as usual. Ian and I had made a drinking game out of all the Certamen questions we could remember from those classics tournaments and Annika, bored and restless, had turned to Gena for distraction.

How'd you get in here, Gena? she had asked. *I didn't think the residency was open to college students. Did someone pull some strings for you?*

Gena had stuttered something about her advisor recommending her, and then Ian, trying to help her save face, I think, said, *Don't feel bad. I'm pretty sure half the reason I got in was because Argos is an old friend of my father's and loves his Pythagoras books.*

And Maia's father is also an old friend of Argos's, Annika had supplied. *They were at the American Archeological School in Athens together.*

I hadn't been thrilled that Annika was implying that I'd only gotten in because my father knew Argos. I noticed that she hadn't offered up any reason why she'd gotten in other than her own talent and writing ability. Maybe, it occurred to me, she'd deliberately asked Gena how she got in to expose how I got in.

I remember I felt something tugging at me, as if someone had stolen up beside me on the terrace to pull on my sleeve, but there was no one by my side, only the wind, which had picked up after dinner, stirring restlessly around the terrace, plucking at table-cloths and flinging napkins around like a bored, spiteful child.

And Annika, I said, the words spilling out of my mouth like a magician's scarf, *must have sent her picture.*

Olivia had laughed, I remember, which made it worse. Annika had turned bright pink and then Olivia had said, *Argos does have an eye for beautiful women. Perhaps that's your secret, Gena, you're Argos's love child.*

"You suggested Gena was Argos's illegitimate child," I say now to Olivia.

Olivia grimaces. "That was unpleasant of me—and totally un-grounded; she looked nothing like Argos! But I felt rather pro-voked. All you *young people* were always ganging up together like a flock of vultures. No one suggested *I* had been invited for my looks. And it was just a joke. Your generation is so sensitive."

"Gena looked like you had slapped her," Annika says. "She got up and left the terrace and she never hung out with us again."

"Who can blame her?" Ian asks. "We were all pretty self-absorbed and full of ourselves. But where does that leave us? Gena isn't here. Does anyone know what happened to her?"

"I remember that she was on the first boat leaving the island the last day," I say. "But we didn't talk. She was belowdecks being sick the whole time and she took off for the train station the min-ute we got to Volos. I didn't see her on the train to Athens." And I hadn't looked. I was too sunk in my own bad mood. "Is there anything in her file?"

Annika shakes her head. "That's the thing—there's no file for her. No application letter, no writing sample, no copy of her passport—he kept all that for us, you know—or record of what happened to her except for that letter of Sydney's and Argos's letter to her. Someone's gotten rid of all her paperwork."

"Which might be the case if she had been here and didn't want us to know too much about her," Olivia says.

"Do you remember anything about her, Eleni?" I ask.

Eleni startles. She's been quiet throughout, not adding to our confessional accounts. Maybe she's embarrassed for us, I think, or tired of the antics of Argos's guests. "Me?" she asks. "All I remember is that she was a quiet girl who made no trouble."

"But what about her file?" Olivia asks. "You were the secretary then. You must have seen her file."

Eleni shrugs. "All of your files seemed much the same to me. Always long lists of your accomplishments and flowery letters about how inspiring it would be to write in the birthplace of the Muses."

I blush, recalling I'd written something very much like that.

"And what about Olivia's idea that she could be Argos's love child?" Bill asks, the first question he's posed. He looks so bleary-eyed from his head injury that I'm surprised he's followed the conversation at all. "Do you think it's possible?"

Eleni pales and sits up very straight. "I did not concern myself with my employer's personal life," she says with cool dignity. But then suddenly all that dignity crumbles. "That poor girl! I saw she was suffering but I couldn't do anything to help her."

"We were all awful to her," I say, squeezing Eleni's hand.

"We all put our ambitions ahead of this girl's welfare," Ian says, looking around the table. "We're all potential targets of this Nemesis. The question, then, is who among us *is* the Nemesis?"

CHAPTER ELEVEN

H ow do we know the murderer is still here on the island with us?" Annika asks. "Whoever killed Argos could have left already and Sydney got himself killed."

"Whoever sent the invitations certainly wanted to see us suffer," Olivia says.

"But why does it have to be one of us?" Annika asks. "There could be someone else hiding on the island. Down in those sea caves in the east cove, for instance, where Sydney found that boat." She turns to Eleni. "Have you been on the east side of the island since you got here?"

Eleni shakes her head. "No, I was too busy getting everything ready for your arrival."

"Wouldn't anyone on the island have had to leave a boat at the dock?" Olivia asks, pointing toward the dock.

"Despite all Argos's warnings about how dangerous it was, a boat could moor in the east cove," Annika says, turning to me. "Remember, Maia, that time we were sunbathing and those French tourists motored in on their yacht and gave us champagne and foie gras and peppered us with questions about Argos?"

"They wanted to swim in the famous blue grotto," I say, recalling how Annika had offered to show them how to swim through the underwater entrance even though we hadn't done it yet. "I guess they hadn't heard the local ghost stories. Do you really think someone could be hiding in there?"

"There's only one way to find out," Ian says, getting to his feet. "I'll go and check it out while there's enough daylight. I don't fancy spending another night on this island without knowing if there's a predator hunting us down."

"The grotto is very dangerous," Eleni says. "The *local ghost stories,* as you call them"—she gives me a reproachful look—"are not just superstition. Many people have died in the grotto over the years—" Her voice quivers and I wonder if someone close to her had been one of the casualties. Is that why she's aged so much in the last fifteen years? Grief, I know from watching my father after my mother died, can age a person faster than time.

"Those of us who live here," Eleni goes on, "know to stay away from it."

"Which would make it a perfect place for our Nemesis to hide," Ian says.

"Maia and I went there once," Annika says, glancing at me nervously as if she expects me to deny it. Or maybe she's just remembering how frightening the place really was. I know I am. I have no desire to go back there—least of all with Annika, who may plan to do away with me by pushing me into one of the bottomless underwater caverns. But as usual, Annika's challenge provokes me.

"I'll go," I say. "We should stay in groups of threes in case one of us is the Nemesis."

"I think I'd prefer looking through the library than spelunking in your underworld caves," Olivia says. "And Bill, of course, is in no condition to go anywhere."

"And I have no wish to go to that cursed place," Eleni says.

"So it's settled," Annika says, a spark in her eyes as she looks at me. "Me, Ian, and Maia—what did Argos call us that summer? The Three Graces?"

"I think it was the Three Furies," I say.

"Exactly," Annika says, beaming. "It will be just like old times!"

BEFORE WE LEAVE, Olivia suggests that we all hand in our passports.

"Do you think we're going to take off on a Jet Ski stashed in the grotto?" Annika scoffs.

"I should think it would be obvious to anyone who has ever even *read* a mystery," Olivia says with elaborate patience, "that we should all establish our whereabouts over the last ten days to rule out who had the opportunity to kill Argos."

"Fine," Annika snaps, "but I've already told you all that I was on Skiathos for the last two weeks so my passport won't establish anything."

She storms off down the stairs to her room and I follow her. Halfway down the second flight of stairs she rounds on me. "Why are you following me?"

I roll my eyes. "I'm going to my room for my passport."

"Which I suppose will prove that you've been neatly tucked away on a shelf in your father's museum all year—for the last fifteen years, in fact."

"Why does that bother you so much?" I ask, genuinely curious. "I mean, I get that you're angry I cut you off after we left here and, if Ian's telling the truth that you two really weren't involved, I can see why you'd be angry about how I portrayed you in my novel. I admit that was a little petty and I do regret it. Not just because I hurt your and Ian's feelings but because I think I ruined the book and spoiled my ability to write the next one. So I get all of that," I say, before she can chime in with an opinion on my writer's block. "But why does my job at the museum piss you off so much?"

"Because you're wasting your life!" she cries. "You had so much talent—more than I'll ever have—but you gave into your father's plans for you and immured yourself in his dusty old museum like one of his precious relics, which were stolen in the first place! He and Argos stole your life just like they looted and stole everything they dug up here."

I stare at her. She's delivered this speech with the same impassioned intensity she uses to tear through life—hers and that of whoever's in her way—certain that she knows what's right for everybody else. But she has no idea what it was like watching my mother get lost inside her mind or seeing what that did to my father. She has no idea what it takes to live with that. I don't have the time or patience to explain it, so I only shake my head. "Even if all that's true," I say, walking by her, "what's it to you? I don't see why you care."

I PUT ON a bathing suit under my shorts and T-shirt and then go back to the library. I pause at the door and hear Bill, apparently delivering his passport to Olivia.

"Here you go," he says. "You can see I arrived in Greece four days ago."

"From Switzerland," she says. "I do love Switzerland. Where were you?"

"Geneva," he replies.

"Oooh, posh."

"Yeah, I was cooking for a tech-startup billionaire for a couple weeks—look, this is his estate on the lake, pretty nice, eh?"

"Gorgeous. I was reading something about Geneva recently," Olivia remarks. "Where was it? It will come to me—probably some bit of research for a book. I've written so many I can't keep track of them all."

Bill rolls his eyes as he passes me in the hall and whispers in a high falsetto, "*I've written so many books I can't keep track of them all!* I don't think that's why she's having trouble staying on track. Check out the bottle in her bag." He winks at me and goes into the kitchen.

Olivia looks distracted when I go into the library. I hand her my passport, held open to the stamp I received in the Athens airport two days ago.

"Thank you," she says, barely glancing at it. She has the same absent-minded look on her face my father would get when he was trying to recall a Greek word or the name of a book. Or maybe she's reliving some delightful memory of Geneva. I glance at her tote bag, which gapes open on the table next to her, and see the same vial of pills I noticed earlier. Was that the bottle Bill meant? Does it look emptier than it was before? I try to make out the label on it but it's turned away from me.

I meet Ian and Annika in the kitchen filling water bottles, and then we leave by the back door and head up to the ridge trail. I look back once to the villa and see Bill stretched out on a lounge chair and Eleni clearing dishes. Olivia must still be in the library. What if *she's* our Nemesis? I can't help wondering. She's certainly angry enough at everyone—Argos most of all. She could do away with Bill and Eleni while we're away. Or what if it's Eleni? She was probably in Greece when Argos died. But why would she kill

Argos? And what could she have against the rest of us? After all, she's the only one among us who isn't a writer. What reason does she have to resent us?

"Are you thinking about who the Nemesis is?" Annika asks.

I look up the path to where Ian is walking ahead. Maybe he's had enough of both me and Annika today.

"Of course I am," I say. "I can't help it. But it's an awful thing, mistrusting everyone around you."

Annika clutches her heart as if I've delivered a fatal blow. "Touché, Maia. Is that how you've felt all these years, because of me?"

"Don't give yourself so much credit," I say, although it's true that in the years since I saw my friend and boyfriend together on that balcony and assumed they were sleeping together I've made no really good friends or dated anyone longer than a few months. I'd blamed my lack of close relationships on the burden of caring for my father and then the work of keeping the museum going after his death, but maybe Annika and Ian's betrayal had more to do with it than I was willing to admit. "But to answer your first question—I would have thought it was Sydney. And maybe it was. Maybe he killed Argos and then tried to make his escape before any of us figured it out."

"In a leaky boat?"

I shrug. "My second choice would be Olivia."

"Why her?"

"She seems pretty bitter. She has a lot of complaints about her publisher, which Argos bought, and how young everyone is and that they make her use Track Changes."

"She's lucky she's got an editor who checks her work so carefully. I have a feeling her books wouldn't make much sense if she didn't."

"What do you mean?" I ask.

"She told me the same story twice, forgot where her glasses were when they were on top of her head, and at one point called me Jacqueline and seemed to think I was her publicist."

"She's under a lot of stress," I say. "We all are."

"I think her failing memory has been a problem for a while. I found a letter she wrote to Argos complaining about how she was being treated at her publisher and asking him to intervene. Apparently he tried because there was a letter back from her editor explaining to Argos all the challenges of working with her and that they've had to hire a ghostwriter and rewrite the last three of her books."

"That's—"

"Sad?" Annika asks. "Yeah. Even sadder that she came here to get Argos to exert pressure on her publisher and he's not here to help her."

"Or," I suggest, "she got here early, asked Argos for his help, and he told her what her editor said. Maybe she was so angry at Argos when he refused her that she pushed him and then decided to invite the rest of us because she resents all of us *young* writers."

"But her passport is stamped three days ago," Annika reminds me.

"Convenient," I say "since she's the one who asked us all to deliver ours. What if she faked that stamp? Olivia's spent her life plotting mystery novels; it's just the sort of thing one of her culprits would do."

A small smile creeps over Annika's face. "You sound like you've read them."

"I have," I admit. "They were actually pretty good—not as good as the Detective Pythagoras books, but well plotted and ingenious until they started getting repetitive. I think she even wrote one about an aggrieved killer gathering their enemies on an island to dispose of them. Of all of us, she has the skills to pull something like this together even with her failing memory. And if she *is* losing her mind, it might be just the kind of crazy thing she would do."

"Good theory, Sherlock, but she'd have had to fake all the time-stamped photos on her phone as well."

"How do you know what's on her phone?"

"I looked when she went to the bathroom."

"Sneaky," I say, impressed in spite of myself. "What did you find?"

"Besides a ton of tags on Instagram and X—she *really* has a devoted fan base—there were dozens of dated pictures at libraries, book clubs, and bookstore events over the last six months. She might be losing her memory but she still works like a Trojan. She was at a library book event in West Palm Beach last week. There are, like, a million selfies with fans. There's no way she could have flown to Greece and back."

"Well, it's not Bill, either," I say. "I just overheard him giving his passport to Olivia and he was in Geneva for the last couple of weeks. He showed her a picture of the billionaire's estate where he was working. You, on the other hand, admit that you were in Greece last week, as was Ian."

"So you think the two of us came here together to kill Argos? Why would we do that? I haven't even seen Ian in fifteen years."

"He follows you on social media," I say.

She smiles. "As do you, apparently. Honestly, I think he lurks around my posts hoping to catch some sign of you." She glances up to the ridge where Ian has paused, waiting for us to catch up. He lifts his hand to wave, the sleeve of his worn white shirt falling to his elbow, revealing a tan and muscular forearm, the sun turning his hair golden. His face, shaded by the tilt of his hat, is unreadable.

"I think you're the real reason he's here. Why would he want to kill Argos and punish the rest of us?" Annika asks.

"Don't you remember how much he hated Argos at the end?" I say, recalling that a few days before the end of the residency Ian had come back from his weekly conference with Argos angry and upset. "He called Argos a monster and said we were all fools and enablers for listening to him."

"He was right," Annika says. "You couldn't see it because you were Argos's favorite, but he said terrible things to Ian in his conference on his last night. He told him he'd always be in his father's shadow. He told me I'd be successful—"

"Poor you," I say.

"—but that I'd be stuck writing the same damned book over and over again like that stupid guy with the rock and he was right."

I'm surprised to see tears in her eyes but then I remember that she once admitted to me that she was able to cry on demand.

"Maybe it was a self-fulfilling prophecy," I said. "You let him get under your skin. It's been easier not to try to write anything new because Argos said you wouldn't."

She glares at me but instead of refuting what I've said she nods. "You're right. Just like it was easier for you to play the betrayed girlfriend."

"What?" I scoff. "You think I wanted to see my new best friend and boyfriend making out?"

"It gave you a reason to scamper on home back to your father and not try very hard to be a writer afterward. It gave you an excuse to live the safe life your father wanted for you—"

"My father had a stroke," I say coldly. "I stayed home to take care of him."

"Yes, very admirable, but you could have kept writing. You didn't have to take over the museum or stay on after he died. You didn't have to shut Ian and me out."

"So why do you think I did all those things, Dr. Freud?"

"Because you were scared of turning into your mother. Being here on the island and writing about your mother exposed something in you. It scared you. The book you published turned into something else—a revenge drama about a woman who's punished for daring to want to really live. And you haven't been able to write anything else because you won't face the truth."

"And what's the truth, Annika? What could you possibly know about why my mother killed herself or what it felt like to find her, or what kind of life I should lead after that? Maybe living a quiet, orderly life running a museum is the best, safest thing for me."

Before she can say anything else, I turn and stomp up the path. *What hubris, to think she knows anything about my life!* When I reach Ian, he tells me he thinks we should approach the cove from the temple instead of from here. "The path here is pretty steep—" he begins.

"We always took this path the last time we were here," I say, and walk past him so carelessly that I skid on the steep decline. Ian grabs my arm to keep me from wiping out. "Careful," he says, his breath warm on my neck. "It's a long way down."

I look past him at the precipitous trail clinging to the eastern slope and feel a lurch in my stomach, but I shake his arm off and continue at a slower pace with Ian and Annika following me, where either of them could easily push me to my death. But I find myself not worried about that. Instead, I'm still fuming about

Annika's verdict on my life. *It's nonsense*, I tell myself. *Pseudo pop psychology*, my father would call it. Annika didn't know the first thing about me or about my mother or what it felt like to watch her lose her mind. What it felt like to come home and find her dead of an overdose—

Lying in my bed, an empty bottle of pills on the night table, eyes wide open and staring at the ceiling as if she wanted one last glimpse of the stars.

The sea and sky before me blur as if obscured by a sudden fog and then switch places as if the world has turned upside down. I take another step—

Into dead air.

The cerulean-blue bay gazes up at me, like the placid eye of a god. It would watch me fall without blinking. Then I feel a warm hand on my arm and the next second I'm lying in the dirt with Annika, my ears ringing.

"What the hell just happened?"

Ian's face appears above us.

"Maia stepped off the path," Annika says. "I pulled her back."

"Yeah," I say, as Ian helps me up. "That's what happened."

Only for a moment, when I felt Annika's hand on my arm, I wasn't sure if she was pulling me back or pushing me over the edge.

CHAPTER TWELVE

We make it down to the cove without any further mishaps. Annika is standing in one of the shallow caves that ring the rocky beach.

"Look at this," she says when we join her, pointing to some marks in the sand. "It looks like there was a boat here that someone dragged out to sea."

"That must be where the boat Sydney took was kept," Ian says. "It would have been easy to sabotage it by boring a few holes in the hull."

"Or Sydney could have damaged it dragging it over those rocks." She points to some jagged rocks down by the water.

"Possibly," Ian concedes, "but why would our Nemesis provide a working escape route?"

Annika shrugs. "There's nothing in these caves. That leaves the grotto." She points out to sea. We all look to the rocky promontory that hugs the cove. Midway along it is a gaping black hole rimmed on top with sharp, jagged rocks. *Like a hungry mouth*, Annika had said the first time we were here. "The opening looks smaller than I remember."

"That's because the tide is just going out," Ian says, looking at his watch. "I'd say we have an hour or so to get in and out."

"Then we'd better get a move on," Annika says, stepping out of her shorts.

I watch as Annika strides into the water, not even flinching at the cold, and dives straight into an oncoming wave. "Fearless as usual," I say, more to myself than Ian.

"No," Ian says. "I think, actually, that she's afraid all the time, and that's why she plunges in without thinking."

"Do you think that's a good thing?" I ask.

He shrugs. "Not always. I think it gets her in a lot of trouble. But then, maybe people like us need people like her to stir us on."

"*To stir the shiftless to toil.*"

"Who are you calling shiftless?" he asks, a smile quirking his lips.

"It's what Hesiod said about the goddess of discord," I say, stripping down to my bathing suit and following Annika before I can lose my nerve. I'm smiling as I plunge into the cold water, thinking that Annika would have loved to have overheard Ian for once not getting one of my classical references.

THE WATER HASN'T warmed up any since I went in earlier to save Sydney. I try to banish the thought of Sydney's drowning as I breaststroke through Annika's wake. Instead, the cold quenching a bit of my anger, I consider what Annika said. Had I really used what I saw between her and Ian as an excuse to go home and lead a safe, boring life that wouldn't expose any cracks in my mind? Because that's what I was most afraid of. I'd been nine when I first realized that my mother wasn't well. Maybe the signs had always been there, like hidden cracks in a pot that only become visible when you pour hot water into it, but I had been so under my mother's spell that I hadn't seen them. To me she was magical, turning the ceiling of my room into the night sky and spinning stories out of thin air. But then she stopped sleeping and would stay awake all night painting. *It always made her worse*, my father told me later. *Painting tapped into something dark inside her and let it out.*

I hadn't understood what he meant until I came to Eris and sat at that olive-wood desk and gave myself over to the inner voices in my head. *To the Muses*, the ancients would say. *A mania*, Socrates called the divine gift of inspiration. I didn't know where those voices came from, only that when I wrote like that I felt as if I'd stepped out of myself and become someone else.

Which made me wonder if I was like my mother.

The thought is accompanied by a frigid current passing over my body. Deep seawater, I tell myself, not the old fear of going crazy.

And yet—

As we approach the jagged entrance to the grotto I'm seized by panic. The cold current feels like it's carrying us into the giant maw, as if the grotto were alive and sucking us into its gullet. The water churns near the entrance, lifting us up closer to the jagged teeth. There are sharp stones below, too, I remember. Argos believed that the entrance to the grotto had been carved by ancient acolytes of a mystery cult to make it appear like a giant hungry mouth. *The experience of entering the grotto*, he said, *was of being swallowed into the belly of the beast.*

When she reaches the opening, Annika surface dives to avoid being impaled on the sharp teeth. I try to turn to tell Ian that we have to dive, but I'm unable to tread water in place. The grotto's current is tugging at me like tentacles, pulling me into its mouth. I have to dive or I'll be dashed against the rock teeth. I take a quick lungful of air and submerge, straining my eyes open in the salty water to watch for the bottom teeth—

But I'm blinded by an explosion of light streaming out of the grotto. It's like a tractor beam from a spaceship, paralyzing my limbs. All I can do is go limp and let it carry me, remembering the explanation Argos had given for the light, that there's a deeper hole below the entrance. As light comes through it, red light is filtered out, leaving only blue light to enter the grotto and turning the water a brilliant unearthly aquamarine.

Like being caught in the gaze of a god, Argos had said.

Like being flayed alive and having your insides served up on a platter, Annika had described it when we came here that one time. *It's like it sees into your very soul and doesn't much like what it finds there.*

I'd wondered then what she had seen of herself hanging suspended in that pitiless light. Was it as bad as what I'd seen in myself? The naked fear that I was as crazy as my mother? When Annika told me later that she had been assaulted and experienced PTSD as a result, I wondered if she had relived the attack when she squeezed through the mouth of the grotto.

Now when I surface next to her, I notice that her eyes are wide and rimmed in red. "Maia!" she gasps with her first breath. She says my name with the same urgency as when she woke me up in the middle of the night with some brilliant idea that couldn't keep till morning. But then Ian surfaces behind us.

"Bloody hell!" he splutters, spitting water. "That's like being swallowed by a sea monster and spit out whole."

"Are you okay?" I ask.

He's blinking seawater out of his eyes, dazed as a newborn calf. "The light," he says. "It's . . ."

The refracted light in the grotto coats everything with a pearly shimmer as if we have all been turned into marble.

"It feels like a dream," he says, following me to the ledge, where Annika's already climbed out. "I can see why the local fishermen think it's haunted," he adds after we're all on the ledge. "You two look like ghosts."

"Remember, Argos thought that there might have been mystery rites enacted here."

Ian nods. "My father described something like it in one of his books—*Pythagoras and the Mysteries*—"

"Okay, you two," Annika interrupts, "we're not here for a history lesson. We're here to find our Nemesis."

She takes out a flashlight from the belt around her waist and trains its beam along the walls of the cave. It's practically useless, though, in the dazzling, prismatic light, which reflects off the water, producing wavy patterns on the grotto walls that make them look as if they're moving, as insubstantial as sheer curtains blowing in a breeze—

There *is* a breeze. A current of air caresses my face, carrying with it a hint of sulfur, and then it swells. The cave fills with a low moan, like the voice of someone keening in grief.

"What the hell is that?" I ask, all the hairs on the back of my neck rising.

"I remember that sound," Annika says. "That's why we didn't stay long last time and why we never came back. Maia was scared of it—"

"*I'm* scared of it!" Ian says. "It sounds like someone's dying."

"It sounds like someone grieving," I say, feeling my eyes sting, not just from the salt water, but from tears as well. "It sounds like a mother grieving for her lost daughter, like Demeter weeping for

Persephone. No wonder the locals thought this was an entrance to Hades."

"It's just the wind," Annika says with a brave attempt at reason. Everything about this place—the light, the sounds, the smell of sulfur—feels unreal and irrational. "It makes that sound moving through tunnels."

"What tunnels?" I say, looking around the large cavern. I don't see any openings—and I don't see any place to hide. Our Nemesis isn't here. Maybe we should leave—"

"Wait," Annika says, laying her hands on the walls and feeling her way around the cavern. "There's an opening here. You just can't see it because of the light."

Ian joins her at the wall but I stay where I am, chafing my arms to bring feeling back into them. I had forgotten how cold this place was—and how terrifying. All I want to do now is leave.

"Hey, guys," I say, looking toward the mouth we swam through, which looks smaller than when we came in. "I think the tide is rising. The opening is closing—" I turn to show them.

But they're gone. Both Annika and Ian have vanished into the rock, leaving me alone in this hellish place.

"Hey!" I scream. My voice echoes hollowly in the domed space, coming back at me in mocking waves. I stumble to the place I last saw them, screaming their names. "Ian! Annika! Stop it! This isn't a game!"

I stretch my hands out in front of me to feel the rock wall, but they pass right through it as if *I* have become a ghost and I can walk through walls. Panic grips my brain like a vise, splitting it in two between what's possible and what's not. I am suddenly sure that if I walk through this rock wall, I will be trapped inside the rock for all eternity. *That's* what the sound is—the cries of all the hapless souls entombed in this stone sarcophagus.

And then, a pair of warm hands takes mine and pulls me forward into a space so bright I have to close my eyes. *I have died*, I tell myself, *and this is the afterlife*.

"Maia," I hear Annika cry, "look! You won't believe this!"

I open my eyes and find myself looking into the blind eyes of a god. Or, rather, goddess. I blink and recognize an archaic kore, much like the one in the museum. She holds a pomegranate in one hand, a poppy in the other, as if she were offering them to me. "What is this?" I say, looking around the cavern. It's lit, I see, from a wide oculus at the top of the high domed ceiling, which lets in a shaft of pure golden sunlight that falls on the kore in front of me and on her sisters gathered around her. I turn in a circle and count a dozen archaic statues, all in pristine condition, their smooth marble faces glowing as if lit from within. There are also bronze Poseidons and fish-tailed Tritons, graceful marble nymphs and great serpentine sea monsters, their ranks crowding the large domed cavern as if they were waiting for a train.

"Are these all . . . *real*?" Annika asks.

For a moment I think she's asking whether we are dreaming, but then Ian answers, "They look authentic to me, but Maia's the expert. What do you say, Maia?"

I'm still standing in front of the kore. Her eyes, deep-carved pits, hold me captive. Her lips, curved in an ancient knowing smile, seem to mock me. *Of course I'm real*, she seems to say, *as real as you are*.

"They're authentic," I say, the curatorial part of my brain snapping to attention. "Sixth-century BCE, I'd say. From the iconography—the pomegranate, the poppy—I'd guess they were part of some kind of mystery rite."

"Hey, look at this," Annika calls from a shadowy edge of the cave. I walk over and find her kneeling by an open crate. "These are packed and ready to go." She lifts a large amphora out of the crate. "Isn't this a lot like that vase your father put together?"

I take the amphora from her gently and move into the light. The baked clay feels cool in my hands, the rounded contours pleasing to touch. I stare down at the black figures painted on the red background. Annika's right. The style is very much like the Wedding Vase, but then, that could just be a coincidence. But as I rotate the vessel in my hands, following the figures, trying to make sense of their gestures, I see that the subject matter is also similar to that of the Wedding Vase.

A wedding procession moves toward an altar at which two armored soldiers stand beside a robed priest. A robed woman wearing a crown presents a young woman whose veil indicates that she is a bride. It is very much like the procession on the Wedding Vase—a mix of mortals and gods and sea creatures. A band of stylized ocean waves and tall-masted ships indicates their proximity to the sea. As I carefully revolve the vase, my breath held, time moves forward. The scene is the same only now the young bride is prone on an altar, and the priest is slitting her throat with a dagger. The armored soldiers turn away and the crowned woman throws back her head and screams in horror, a sound which I hear echoed in the keening wind in the tunnels. My hands turn slick and tremble at the vivid shock of the scene, as if it is happening right in front of me. I nearly drop the vase.

"It's the sacrifice of Iphigenia at Aulis," I say. "When Agamemnon sacrificed his own daughter to gain a favorable wind for the Greek fleet bound for Troy."

"This vase shows the slave girl Briseis being taken from Achilles by Agamemnon," Ian says, examining another amphora.

"Someone is getting stabbed in their bath in this one," Annika says.

"Clytemnestra slaying Agamemnon," I reply.

"They seem to be part of a series," Ian says, "illustrating episodes from the Trojan War and its aftermath. They look like the work of the same painter—"

"They are," I say, staring at the bottom of the amphora. "It has the same potter's and painter's marks as the Wedding Vase. You were right." I wrench my gaze away from the amphora to face Annika, expecting a smug look of vindication, but instead, all I see is pity. "This is where the Wedding Vase came from."

CHAPTER THIRTEEN

Swimming out of the grotto is harder than swimming in. The current is against us and the mouth has narrowed to a thin slit—a tight-lipped sneer that seems to mock our flailing efforts to pass.

"You have to dive and swim straight through," Annika says, demonstrating with hand gestures. "Don't hesitate, don't look back, don't think, just full speed ahead or you'll get impaled on the rocks."

"Great," Ian says. "A gauntlet that favors Annika's life philosophy."

I laugh in spite of—or perhaps because of—how scared I am. Then I take a deep breath and plunge underwater. Annika is right in front of me—an arrow aimed straight at the glowing mouth. She shoots through and vanishes on the other side. I follow, stroking hard toward what looks like an impossibly narrow opening. *Don't think, don't think*, I chant, feeling the pressure of every fear and doubt knocking against my skull, urging me to *Turn around! Look back!* And most insidiously: *What if Annika and Ian want me dead? This would be a perfect place to do away with me.* But I sail straight through into the cold dark sea and then flounder, unable to tell up from down. Something grabs me and I picture, horribly,

Sydney's dead, bloated body pulling me down to the ocean floor. But when I surface, my lungs bursting, Annika's with me, closely followed by Ian.

"There's a bad riptide," Ian sputters, "pulling out to sea. Let's stay close."

He strokes toward the shore and I follow—or try to. The current feels like a muscle, like a giant sea serpent coiling around my body and pulling me into the open ocean. I picture the bronze monsters in the cavern slithering after us to keep us from revealing their hiding place—

Don't think! I command myself. *Swim.*

I put everything into each stroke, focused on the bobbing line of shore, and when I falter Annika loops her arm over my head and buoys me until we get to land, where Ian helps me over the rocks and onto the sand. The three of us lie there panting for a few minutes.

"I think I might have misread the tide table," Ian admits.

Annika barks a hoarse croak. "Detective Pythagoras would be ashamed of you."

I sit up and look at my watch—a cheap plastic model that I bought at the Met last year. It's supposed to be waterproof but it's stopped ticking. Then I look at the sky. "It's getting dark," I say. "How long were we in there?"

"It felt like millennia," Annika says, "especially when you two started in about mystery cults."

"We'd better get going," Ian says, getting to his feet and offering me a hand up.

"And the others will be wondering what happened to us," I say, taking Ian's hand and then offering one to Annika. "We have to tell them about the antiquities."

"Let's not do it right away," Annika says. "I want to see if anyone is suspiciously worried about what we found—and then gauge their reactions when we tell them."

"You think that's our Nemesis's motive?" I ask.

"What else could it be?" she asks, looking squarely at me as if to challenge my suspicions of her and Ian. *Clearly it can't be us*, her eyes say. They could easily have killed me in the grotto, so they must not want me dead. At least not yet.

THE CLIMB UP to the ridge is grueling.

"*Facilis descensus Averno*," Ian mutters under his breath.

"'The road to hell is easy,'" I translate for Annika, and then add the line that comes after it in the *Aeneid*, "'the road back is hard.'"

Annika gives us both the finger.

As we climb, I think about what we found and what it means. Yes, it's likely that the Wedding Vase was part of the same series as the vases in the grotto and, yes, my father had written to Argos about the vase admitting that he was partly to blame. But did that mean he knew the shards came from here when he found them? Maybe it was only later. Maybe . . .

My mind spins, desperately grasping to threads of hope, unable to believe that my father knowingly acquired a looted piece of art. By the time we reach the top, I'm panting and soaked in sweat. Ian and I share the last of our water with Annika, who's drunk all of hers. I look toward the west, where the sun is at the horizon, slipping into the violet-colored sea, and feel suddenly chilled. I don't want to spend another night on this island.

"There are no lights," Ian says, as if commenting on the impending dark.

But then I look down at the villa and see what he means. The whitewashed villa, tinted lilac by the evening light, is unlit.

"They just haven't turned them on yet," Annika says.

"I noticed last night that the terrace lights came on automatically," Ian says. "I asked Eleni about it and she said they were on a timer."

"Someone might have turned them off," I suggest, "to conserve power. Where does Argos get his electricity?" It's not something I'd ever bothered to ask about. Lavyrinthos had always seemed to run on the power of Argos's desires.

"Propane generator," Ian answers as he starts down the path. "Maybe it's run out—but I don't like it. We'd better get back."

The villa seems eerily still as well as dark as we approach it. When we're a few yards away Annika takes from her pocket a hot-pink plastic tube, which I recognize from the one Jenner keeps on her key chain as Mace. Ian opens the back door gingerly and motions for us to stay back, but Annika shoulders past him, holding her Mace spray out in front of her. Halfway down the corridor she stops and holds up a finger. There's a sound coming from the kitchen, a rhythmic chopping. I picture Bill in his chef hat neatly dicing up Eleni and Olivia.

Annika pivots in the doorway SWAT team–style, brandishing the Mace. When she doesn't shriek in horror, I creep behind her and find Bill at the counter calmly chopping cucumbers. "There you are," he says, lifting his head. "I'm glad you're back. Olivia and Eleni have been at it like alley cats since you left and I think Olivia's lost her mind."

"What's happened to the power?" Ian asks.

"Genny ran out of propane," Bill says. "Whoever planned this didn't think very far ahead. 'Fraid we're on a raw diet for dinner."

"What do you mean, Olivia's lost her mind?" I ask.

"She's been scouring the library for something she *says* she saw and blaming Eleni for stealing it—it's not a pretty sight."

"Are they still in the library?" Ian asks.

Bill nods, eyes on the silver blur of his fast-moving knife. "Since you left."

"Alone?" Annika asks.

Bill looks up from his chopping board. "Who else would be with them?"

Ian and Annika exchange a glance and then quickly head to the library.

"Did you find anything?" Bill asks without missing a beat with his knife.

Remembering what Annika had said I reply, "We'll talk about it when we're all together," then follow Ian and Annika to the library. The sound of chopping recedes as I walk down the hallway but then is quickly replaced by angry shouting.

"I'm sure it was here and I saw you looking through those papers so don't tell me you don't know what I'm talking about."

I recognize Olivia's voice but when I reach the library and look past Annika and Ian, who have paused in the doorway, I hardly recognize her. Her white capris are covered with grime, her usually neatly coifed hair is standing on end, and her face is haggard. She's holding a handful of crumpled paper, gesturing toward Eleni, who stands still as a statue in a drift of paper. The library, which had been so neat when we left, has been reduced to a chaos even worse than we found this morning.

"What's going on?" Ian asks.

Olivia turns toward us and flaps her arms up and down, shaking handfuls of paper at us. She looks, bizarrely, like a cheerleader shaking her pom-poms. I bet she was a cheerleader, I think absurdly. "Well, I'm glad you finally decided to come back. While you've been having a day at the beach, I have figured out who is responsible for this mess." She gestures at the scattered papers and I try to picture Eleni strewing them about the room—and can't.

"I came in and found her like this," Eleni tells us. "It seems Ms. Knox has mislaid something—"

"I HAVE NOT MISLAID ANYTHING!" Olivia roars. "I know there was a file here that's gone missing and it disappeared just after she"—Olivia jabs a finger in Eleni's direction—"came in with coffee this morning."

Annika approaches Olivia gingerly. "What was in the file?" she asks. "Maybe *I* moved it."

"It had pictures of statues and vases—it looked like an auction lot. I did some research on auction houses for an art heist book I wrote a few years ago so I know what one looks like! There was something about it that I think may have been important. If I could look at the folder again I'd remember what it was but I can't because SHE"—Olivia rounds on Eleni and jabs her finger toward her again, so close that Eleni flinches—"took it."

Eleni's face has the resigned expression of someone who's familiar with accusations, which I can well imagine a housekeeper would be. I remember once when my parents took me on a vacation to a hotel in New York City and I'd lost my favorite charm bracelet, my mother told me that she'd been a maid once in a hotel and that the guests were always accusing the maids of stealing. *They misplace something and blame the person closest at hand who can't defend herself. Never accuse someone of a theft unless you are one hundred percent certain.* Sure enough, I'd found my bracelet under a soap dish in the bathroom.

"Why would Eleni take anything?" I say. "Isn't it more likely you misplaced it or misremember—"

"My memory is perfectly fine, thank you very much, and I should think it's quite obvious why she would steal the file; it had evidence in it that points to her guilt over killing Argos and sending those invitations!"

"Why would I want to invite you all here so I can wait on you and make your beds and listen to you squabble like children?" Eleni says. "I had enough of you last time."

"See?" Olivia says, nodding her head. "She resents us all. I noticed it last time, always watching us, spying on us. When we were here fifteen years ago, I heard you interrogating that girl Gena until she cried."

"She was crying because you were cruel to her," Eleni says. "You all were—"

"Aha! It's just as I said, she hates us all. And who else knows how this place is run? Who else could have come back here and easily killed Argos and then written those invitations? Who else could have sabotaged the boat Sydney took? Who else—"

"Olivia," Annika says, picking up Olivia's tote bag, which is lying open on the desk, and extracting a prescription bottle from it, "how many of these have you taken?"

Olivia turns and, at the sight of Annika holding her bag and pill bottle, lunges at her. "How dare you—"

Ian steps neatly in between the two of them and puts a restraining arm around Olivia's shoulders. I'm expecting her to thrash and fight but she slumps against him instead, her eyes fluttering. He grabs her more firmly and helps her to a chair. I look at the pill bottle in Annika's hand. "What is that?" I whisper.

"Xanax," Annika says. "I noticed her taking one earlier. I don't blame her—I almost asked her for one myself—but I know from experience that too many of these babies can turn you into a first-class bitch on wheels."

"From experience?" I echo.

"Don't ask," she says, grimacing. Then she turns to Eleni. "Are you okay, Eleni?"

Eleni nods stiffly. She had held herself so regally a moment ago but now her shoulders sag. "If you don't mind, I would like to go now to my room. I'm sure Chef will be able to manage your dinner on his own."

"Of course, Eleni," Annika and I both say in unison.

But Ian surprises me by saying, "Can you stay a little longer, Eleni? There are some things we need to go over and we should all be together."

"Of course," she says, stiffening her shoulders again. "I'll just go and see if Chef needs help and meet you all on the terrace."

"Annika, would you help me get Olivia to her room?" Ian says. "And, Maia, could you get a bottle of water from the kitchen?"

"Sure," I say, starting to move, but Ian looks up and adds:

"Make sure it's an unopened one."

I HURRY TO the kitchen, where I find Eleni and Bill leaning against the counter, their heads together, whispering, an open bottle of retsina between them. I don't blame them. I'd like to ask for a drink myself but right now I have the feeling that "the guests" are not very welcome in the kitchen.

"That was crazy, Eleni," I say, opening the refrigerator and searching for an unopened bottle of water. "I hope you realize that nobody thinks those things. Olivia was just . . . well, it looks like she may have taken too much of her medication."

"What are you looking for?" Bill asks. "Can I help you?"

"Water," I say, "for Olivia—and honestly, I'm parched, too."

"There's more in the cooler," he tells me, pointing toward the walk-in cooler, "although it's not going to stay cool for long if we keep opening the door."

"Oh!" I say, realizing I've been letting all the cold out of the refrigerator and closing it quickly. "I'm so sorry, yes, can you get me a couple of bottles? If it's not a bother?"

"No bother," he says, smiling.

He strolls into the cooler, closing the door behind him. "Eleni," I say, trying again. "I feel terrible—"

"It is not your fault," she says formally. "You were not the one accusing me . . . although I suppose we will all be at each other's throats soon enough. Did you find our . . . what have you been calling him? Our *Nemesis* in the grotto?"

"No," I say. "But we did find—" Too late I remember what Ian said, but if I seem to be holding back on Eleni now, it will only increase her feeling of being mistrusted. "We found a cave filled with statues and pottery—antiquities. It looks like Argos was engaging in illegal antiquities trading." She nods and takes a sip of her wine. "You don't seem surprised."

"Argos thought himself above the law. He took what he wanted," she says so bitterly that I wonder what he took from her.

"I didn't want to believe that . . . I don't know if you remember, but he was a friend of my father's . . ."

"I remember," Eleni says. "I was here the first summer that Argos brought your father. Your mother was here, too."

"Oh!" I say, surprised. I can't remember if she told me last time that she had known my parents. "That must have been after they all met at the American Archeological School in Athens. Argos invited them both here to Eris, which he'd just inherited. My father always said he fell in love with Greece and my mother at the same time—" I stop, ashamed to realize I'm about to cry. That's the last thing Eleni needs—another emotional American burdening her with their drama. "The amphorae appear to be part of a series that includes the one in our museum, which my father assembled from shards. Also, there's a Persephone statue that looks like a match, which I suppose my father eventually knew came from here—but maybe he didn't know at first . . ." I'm rambling and clutching at straws while Eleni stares at me impassively. Why is Bill taking so long?

"Persephone? That is fitting," Eleni says.

"Fitting?" I echo, confused.

"The maiden who was stolen from her mother," she says, taking a long drink of her wine. "Stolen a second time from her country."

"Oh!" I say, startled and not sure what to say to that. Luckily, Bill finally returns with the water and a package of scallops.

"Ceviche!" he says, shaking the package at me.

"Great," I say. "Thanks for the water. I'm going to bring it to Olivia and then I think Ian wants us all to meet on the terrace? If that's okay?" I fumble my way out of the kitchen, gesturing lamely with my water bottles, wincing at how ridiculous I sound. But I can't help it. What Eleni said has rattled me. *Persephone stolen a second time.* As if whoever took the statue was guilty of abduction and rape.

CHAPTER FOURTEEN

I bring the water to Olivia's room, grateful that it's on the first level. I remember how touchy Olivia had been at the implication that she was too old to handle the stairs—as she had been at her publisher's suggestion that her books weren't up-to-date and she was losing her faculties. How frightening it must be for a writer to feel that what they have to say may not be relevant and that they're losing the words to say it! I remember how frustrated my father was after his stroke that he couldn't make himself clear and how agitated he would become, much like Olivia today. No wonder she resorted to anxiety medication and became suspicious of everyone around her.

At least she seems calmer when I come into her room. She's lying in bed, placidly allowing Annika to plump her pillows and smooth the covers over her. Ian's standing at the window looking out to the woods.

"Here's the water," I say, handing the bottle to Annika.

"Is the cap sealed?" Olivia asks, her eyes flicking to me. "Are you sure it hasn't been opened?"

Annika shows her the sealed cap and then twists it off and pours water into a glass in front of her, like a magician demonstrating that there are no tricks up her sleeve. "Olivia's been telling us that some of her pills are missing and she's sure she didn't take them," Annika says, looking across Olivia to me and Ian.

"That woman must have slipped them in my coffee," Olivia says. "I'd never have taken so many. I know the effect they have on me. And I know I had that folder on the desk before lunch and it looked like an auction lot. I bet that woman has been helping Argos sell looted art for years and she decided to kill Argos so she could have all the money for herself and frame one of us for it. That's what you've found in the caves, isn't it? Looted art?"

"Excellent deduction, Detective Moreau," Ian says. "I bet you'll get a great book out of this!"

Olivia looks at Ian slyly. "You don't fool me, Ian Davies. You're here as a spy for your father, aren't you? But you won't steal this idea from me—hand me my notebook." Her hands flutter restlessly over the covers. Ian turns and picks up a leather-bound notebook from the desk beneath the window and passes it to me to give to Olivia. She takes it in both hands and runs her fingertips over the engraved monogram. "I did some research for a book on Nazi art looting . . ." she says dreamily as her eyes flutter and close.

Annika puts one finger to her lips to warn us to be quiet as she gets up. I look over to Ian to find him going through the drawers of the desk.

"What are you doing?" I demand.

"Just making sure she doesn't have any more pills," Ian whispers. "Or that she doesn't have that folder she keeps talking about."

"I'm pretty sure she imagined that folder," Annika adds from the door. "Let's go before she wakes up again."

Ian pauses to search Olivia's suitcase and then joins us. We all let out a breath as he closes the door behind us.

"Thank God," Annika says. "That was worse than getting my five-year-old niece to bed. Poor Olivia. I think she may be in the early stages of Alzheimer's."

"It's possible," Ian says. "She was acting just like my father did at the beginning—furious when he couldn't remember something and terrified that he was losing his faculties—but that doesn't mean she isn't onto something."

"You don't really think she's right that Eleni took the folder?" Annika asks.

"Why would she imagine a lost folder that had something to do with looted art even before we found the statues in the grotto?" Ian asks. "How do we know Eleni's not involved? She was Argos's secretary for decades and it seems a little odd that Argos would have asked her back all these years later if she wasn't still involved in his business dealings—or that she'd come if she didn't have some motive."

"I don't believe Eleni would betray her own country by selling looted art abroad," I say. "And why would she invite us all here?"

"To punish us," Ian says. "We were pretty insufferable—at least, I know *I* was. I was completely oblivious to that girl Gena. I saw her crying once and just thought she was a drama queen. We were all too busy with each other to find out anything about her."

"But why would Eleni care so much about Gena?" Annika asks. "Wouldn't she be just another spoiled American to her?"

"I'm not sure," Ian admits. "Maybe we can see when we tell her about the stolen artifacts in the cave—"

"Um, about that," I say awkwardly. "I kind of told her. It just slipped out and I didn't like the idea of keeping anything from her."

Ian sighs. "Did she seem surprised?"

"No," I admit. "She said Argos thought himself above the law. When I told her that the Persephone in my museum came from here, she said that it meant she'd been abducted *a second time*."

Annika sucks in her breath. "That doesn't sound like something she'd have gone along with."

"She could just be saying that to throw us off," Ian says. "She was, after all, in Greece last week—"

"As were you," Annika points out.

"And you," Ian counters.

"Okay," I say, feeling the tension crackling between them. "We should just go and talk to Eleni and Bill. They're probably waiting for us on the terrace."

"Right," Ian says, walking past us. "We shouldn't leave them alone together too long."

ELENI AND BILL have laid out a buffet for us to help ourselves and seated themselves at the long table, where they're working on a second bottle of retsina. There's a palpable feeling of *us versus them* as we walk onto the terrace. Even the marble goddesses seem to be glaring at us like we're the intruders here. We fill our plates quickly and sit down, Ian seating himself at the far end of the long table directly across from Bill. He doesn't wait for us to finish eating before bringing up our discovery.

"As you probably heard we found a cache of artifacts hidden in a cave," he says. "It looks as if Argos was illegally exporting antiquities—"

"How can you tell that?" Bill asks. "Couldn't there just have been a bunch of statues and vases down there?"

"There are crates of pottery all ready for shipment . . ." I hesitate, feeling queasily disloyal, but brace myself and go on. "They appear to be part of a series that includes one in the museum I work at and that my father claimed he assembled from shards he purchased from reputable dealers. The vase must have come from here, whether my father knew that or not."

"It seems clear to me," Bill says, "that your father was in collusion with Argos. Why shouldn't we believe that you are, too? After all, you're the one here who knows the most about Greek art and has the most to gain from having access to it."

"Maia would never—" Annika begins to defend me, but I hold up my hand.

"That's a fair question. You don't know me well, so there's no reason to trust that I couldn't be involved in buying illegal antiquities. But I wasn't in Greece last week, so I didn't kill Argos."

"Your friend could have," Bill says, looking straight at Annika, then switching his gaze to Ian. "Actually, both of them were here in Greece last week, and as I recall from our last time together, you three were thick as thieves. I always suspected you might have some kind of threesome going on."

I feel myself color and sense Ian tense. Annika just laughs. "If we were getting it on together, why would we have asked you lot here? No offense, Bill, but you're not my type."

"None taken," Bill says with a sulky smile.

"Slinging accusations at each other is getting us nowhere," Ian says. "I suggest we try to stay out of each other's way until the boat comes back for us."

"And how do we know it *is* coming back for us?" Bill asks.

"The captain will want to be paid, won't he, Eleni?" I ask. "If he can't reach Argos—or whoever hired him—by phone or email, he'll have to come back to collect."

Eleni shrugs. "I suppose so . . . unless he's been paid in advance."

"Let's hope not. After all, our Nemesis has to get off this island somehow, too," Ian says, looking down at his food. "In the meantime, I hope you won't mind if I help myself to some of the canned goods in the kitchen. No offense, Bill."

"None taken," Bill says, taking a big bite of cold moussaka. "I suppose I can't interest you in any of this wine, either?" He holds up the bottle.

"Thanks," he says, raising the bottle of Mythos he's just uncapped. "But I think I'll stick with this."

"WELL, THAT WENT well," Annika says after we have repaired to the balcony off my room with cans of tuna and sardines, crackers, and a six-pack of Mythos.

We have quickly become two opposing camps, leaving the first floor and main terrace (and all the fresh food) to Eleni and Bill and a sleeping Olivia, while taking shelter on the bottom floor. Ian's brought his backpack and sleeping bag down and had proposed to sleep in the hall to keep guard, but Annika suggested that there was probably an empty bedroom on the same floor. After trying all the doors—and finding one at the far end locked—we found an unlocked, mostly empty storage room right across from the stairs that Ian declared to be a perfect guardroom.

"I think you're enjoying this," Annika accuses him, when he unpacks a paraffin stove to make us tea. "It brings up all your Boy Scout training."

"Please," Ian said, "I was a Sea Scout."

"Oh, a Sea Scout," I say appreciatively. "Can't you make us a boat out of empty water bottles and twine?"

"Let's hope it doesn't come to that," he says seriously. "In the meantime, let's focus on staying alive." He leans out over the balcony, looking up and down. "I don't think anyone can get to this balcony from outside, but you should lock your window, just to be safe. Annika, maybe you should stay in here."

"I think Bill's put ideas in your head," she says teasingly, but then, more soberly, "My window locks just fine and besides, I think we may be overreacting a little. I mean, Argos could have died accidentally."

"After inviting us all here and challenging us to find the murderer?" I ask.

"Maybe whoever invited us just wanted to scare us," she says. "There haven't been any more deaths since Sydney. The whole thing might be a joke gone wrong. I bet when we wake up tomorrow, the boat will be here and we'll let the Greek police know that we found Argos and the statues and that Sydney drowned himself and then . . ." She looks back and forth between us. "Then things can go back to the way they were . . . only maybe we can all be friends again?"

She looks at me. "I'm sorry about what happened fifteen years ago. I was jealous and angry after my conference with Argos; he told me I'd never be as good as you."

"He told me that I'd always be in my father's shadow," Ian says, "and that if I stayed with you, I'd be in your shadow, too. It's no excuse, but I think he wanted to drive Annika and me together by making us both resent you, Maia. We stopped right away."

I look at the two of them, picturing the scene that's run through my head a thousand times over the years since, but for once, instead of causing me pain, it makes me angry. I can see Argos's hand in all of what happened that night. "I get it," I say. "Argos had a way of getting under your skin. That thing he said about always being in your father's shadow—" Something Ian said earlier suddenly registers. "Wait, you said your father has Alzheimer's. But if that's true, how has he been writing the Detective Pythagoras books? I haven't noticed any drop-off in their quality. In fact, this last one was my favorite."

"Really?" he asks, a blush rising up his face along with a shy smile. "You think so?"

"Oh my God!" Annika says. "You've been writing them!"

Ian turns bright pink, confirming Annika's guess. "I didn't set out to write them. At first, I was just reading them for my father—checking facts, giving him notes—but when his mind started slipping . . . well, it was really painful to watch. I sometimes thought he saw himself as the Pythagoras character. It would have broken his heart not to be able to write them anymore so I fixed them—made sure they still made sense before sending them to his publisher. Then as he got worse, I just started writing them, using his notes sometimes and sometimes just coming up with my own ideas. When I put a new one in my father's hands he smiled with as much pride as if he had written it himself."

"Gee," Annika says, "I seem to remember you saying fifteen years ago that the last thing you wanted to do was write mysteries like your father."

"Have I mentioned that I was a pompous idiot?" Ian asks.

"You have," Annika and I both say in unison.

"I think we all were," I add.

"So," Annika says, "it's really kind of a good thing we were all invited here. I mean, it's terrible about Sydney, *I guess*, but at least

Maia knows we didn't betray her and we can all be friends again."
She looks at us both so hopefully I can't bear to disappoint her.
And after the events of the last twenty-four hours, it seems petty
to hold an old grudge that was just a misunderstanding. "Sure," I
say. "That is if you . . ." I turn to Ian, remembering how angry he'd
been at me for ghosting him all those years ago. Would things
ever go back to the way they were with him?

He holds my gaze for a long moment, all jesting gone from
his face. Then he says, "Once you've been Sea Scouts together,
there's no going back. Friends for life."

I see Annika grinning and for the first time I truly believe what
she and Ian have been telling me. They made a mistake fifteen
years ago, but so had I.

"When I had my conference with Argos he told me that both of
you would betray me because you were jealous of me," I say. "It's
like he orchestrated everything that happened that night."

"And he's been doing it ever since," Ian says. "Even after his
own death."

"I'm tired of being his puppet," I say, lifting my bottle of Mythos.
"Here's to being better than that. *Sto kala mas.*"

"*Sto kala mas,*" they both echo.

We finish our beers and then drink our tea and eat some
crackers, for all the world like British schoolchildren on a holiday adventure. When we say good night Ian waits until Annika
goes to her room and we hear her lock her door. Then he turns
to me, a hopeful look in his eyes. For a moment I think he's
going to ask to stay, but then he taps his knuckles against the
doorjamb and reminds me to lock up. I close the door and lean
against it for a moment, imagining him standing on the other side.
Was it possible . . . ? After all these years . . . ? I wait until I hear

him turn and walk down the hall, his sneakers squeaking on the marble floor, before going to bed. I don't close the window because I want to feel the sea breeze on my face and, as Ian said, no one could get in through the high balcony. I fall asleep to the sound of the waves lapping against the dock, moonlight pouring through the window like a god entering the room as light.

It's only just as I'm drifting off that I wonder if the reason Ian didn't ask to stay was because he wasn't entirely sure *I* am not Nemesis.

CHAPTER FIFTEEN

I'm not sure what wakes me—the creak of the floorboard or a shadow blocking the moonlight. When I open my eyes, a dark shape stands over me, rimmed by a silver aura like the moon-god I had fallen asleep imagining. Maybe I'm still asleep—then the shadow leans over me and covers my mouth, blocking off air as well as light. I struggle, making all the noise I can to wake up Ian or Annika.

"Shh, Maia, it's me, don't scream."

Annika?

When I stop struggling, she takes her hand away.

"There's something I have to tell you," she says.

"How did you get in?"

"I have a key . . . never mind about that, I'll explain everything, but first you have to promise not to scream."

"Why would I scream?" I ask, beginning to feel the creep of fear. Why does Annika have a key? What is she doing here in the middle of the night? What does she have to tell me that she couldn't tell me in front of Ian? I sit up, trying to clear my head, and reach to turn on the lamp, but then I remember there's no electricity. Annika is sitting on the side of my bed. With her back to the moonlit window, I can't see her face. I have a feeling that's how she wants it.

"I wanted to tell you sooner, but I wasn't sure if I could trust you."

"You weren't sure if you could trust me?" I repeat, affronted.

"Well, your father was friends with Argos."

I'm about to tell her that she has a lot of nerve throwing that in my face when I hear a sound which I first take for the pounding of my heart, but then realize is a footstep outside the door.

"But I wanted to tell you now—"

"Shh." I grab her hand to shush her. "Did you hear that?"

I point toward the door. We both wait, listening to the silence. Even the usual sounds of water lapping at the dock and the dry rattle of wind through the olive trees are gone. The night seems to be holding its breath—

And then it comes again. A footstep right outside my door.

"It could be Ian," Annika whispers, "patrolling."

I replay in my mind the squeak of Ian's sneakers I listened to earlier. "Those don't sound like Ian's shoes," I say.

I creep out of bed and press my ear against the door. No sound comes from the other side, which means that whoever is out there has paused outside my door. Could it be Ian? He might have changed his shoes. He might have come back—

The doorknob turns.

Annika is at my side so suddenly I nearly cry out. Did she lock the door after she came in?

Why does she have a key?

The knob turns once, clockwise. The wood of the door presses against my cheek, as if it were breathing, and then subsides. The doorknob turns back counterclockwise. There is a moment of silence in which I brace for an explosion of splinters—a forced entry—but then the footsteps resume, a soft padding that moves briskly down the hall and then fades.

"They're gone," I whisper to Annika.

"For now," she says, her hand on the doorknob.

"What are you doing?"

"Finding out who just tried to break into your room," she says. *As if she hadn't just done the same thing.* She opens the door slowly and then looks outside. Moonlight spills from my open door in a wedge into the dark hall. It's impossible to see anything past it. The intruder could be hiding in the shadows at either end of the hall.

"Come on," she says. "Let's see if Ian is still in his room." I follow her to Ian's room, where she takes out a key and starts to open the door.

"Are you crazy? He might charge you if he hears you breaking in!"

"Yeah, you're right. Here, hold this—" She gives me her flashlight and takes out her Mace spray.

"You can't *Mace* Ian!" I push past her and rap my knuckles on the door. "Ian?" I whisper. "Are you in there? We're coming in and watch out for Annika; she's got Mace."

Annika pushes the door open and I aim the flashlight at the empty sleeping bag on the floor, then quickly scan the rest of the room. It's equally empty. "So it was probably Ian," I say.

"Why would he try your door . . . unless"—Annika looks at me, a smile crooking her mouth—"you had an assignation."

"No," I say quickly, glad that because I'm holding the flashlight she can't see me blushing. "But maybe he just wanted to check that my door was locked. Maybe he heard you unlocking my door—why do you have a key, Annika?"

"Never mind that now," she says. "Let's go find Ian." She heads out into the hall and I follow her up the stairs, sweeping the flashlight into corners for intruders. I nearly scream when the light lands on a leering face before I realize it's just one of the Gorgon masks. On the second floor, Annika stops at each room to check for anyone hiding. Sydney's room is empty, of course, but books and clothes are strewn all over the floor and bed.

"I wouldn't have pegged Sydney for such a slob," Annika says.

"No, but I wouldn't have thought he was foolish enough to row out to sea in a leaky boat, either. I wonder why he was so scared?"

"Guilty conscience," Annika says.

"About what?"

"All the mean reviews he wrote over the years. He probably figured there were lots of aggrieved writers out for revenge." She picks up a book from a pile on his desk and holds it under the flashlight beam. "*The Talented Mr. Ripley*," Annika reads the title. "Figures he'd like Patricia Highsmith."

We close the door and continue to the first floor. As we're coming up the stairs we hear someone stirring in Eleni's room. Annika motions for me to turn off the flashlight. There's enough moonlight on this floor coming in from the archway to the terrace that we can see without it. We walk slowly until we reach Eleni's door. Someone is definitely moving around inside.

"It's probably just Eleni," I whisper to Annika.

"Rearranging the furniture at three a.m.?" she asks skeptically. She takes out her key and starts to unlock the door, but I knock before she can. The last thing Eleni needs after all the suspicions aimed at her earlier tonight is to have one of us break into her room. "Eleni?" I whisper. "Everything all right?"

The sound stops but no one answers. Impatient, Annika unlocks the door and swings it open, Mace ready—

Ian stands in the middle of the floor holding a folder.

"What the hell, Ian?" Annika says. "What are you doing in Eleni's room? And where's Eleni? What have you done with her?"

"What are you doing with a key?" he counters. "And what are you two—"

A scream cuts short his question.

"That sounds like Eleni," Annika says, racing toward it. I turn to follow but Ian grabs my arm.

"What's Annika doing with a key?" he demands.

I don't have time to answer even if I knew what to tell him. I shake him off and run after Annika. As I pass his room, Bill's door opens and the chef appears, in a T-shirt and boxers, hair standing up around his head bandage, brandishing a heavy metal meat tenderizer. "What the . . ." he sputters.

"It's coming from Olivia's room," I say as I run past him.

Olivia's door stands open. Inside Eleni is standing by Olivia's bed, a hand clasped over her mouth, moaning now instead of screaming. Annika is leaning over the bed, blocking my view. I ease around Eleni and join Annika at the bedside. The room is full of moonlight and—I notice—a long mournful sound. I think it must be coming from Olivia but when I get closer, I see it can't be. Olivia's face is frozen in the moonlight, her eyes open wide and staring, sightless and glazed as glass.

Like my mother when I found her.

And still the mournful sound fills the room. It's coming from the woods outside her window—*Athene noctua*, the little owl, singing a dirge for poor Olivia.

ONCE AGAIN, WE gather on the terrace, huddled around a flickering firepit that Bill has lit to keep us warm and give us some light. He also brings out a bottle of ouzo, which he makes an elaborate show of unsealing and opening. I think we'd all drink it no matter what.

"It could be an overdose," Bill suggests, filling our glasses.

"I searched her room for any more pills," Ian says. "And why would Olivia deliberately take an overdose?"

"She could have hidden a bottle somewhere you didn't find," I say. "And then taken more without remembering what she'd already taken. My father would lose track of his pills. I had to be very careful to monitor his medication."

"What were you doing in her room, Eleni?" Ian asks.

Eleni glares at him. "I was checking on her. I got up and heard the owls. I remembered that the sound of them bothered her last night and I thought I'd go check to see if she was all right and if she needed anything. When I opened the door—" She shudders. "I saw her face and knew she was gone."

It sounds like a convincing explanation to me but Ian narrows his eyes, looking for all the world like Detective Pythagoras. "You were gone when I reached your room and I was in there for at least fifteen minutes. That's a lot of time to walk to Olivia's room and find her dead. Why did it take you fifteen minutes to scream?"

"I didn't harm her," Eleni says angrily without explaining the discrepancy in time. "Why would I?"

"She accused you of stealing that folder," Ian says.

"The poor woman was addled—"

"And in fact," Ian goes on, "I found this in your room." He holds up a dark green folder, the same one I'd seen him looking through in Eleni's room.

"How dare you go into my room and look through my things!" Eleni shrieks, lunging for the folder in Ian's hand. It's such a quick transformation from Eleni's usual calm and dignified demeanor that all of us are taken by surprise. Except for Ian, who holds the folder out of Eleni's reach.

"Yeah, *mate*," Bill says. "You have a lot of nerve."

"Was it the file Olivia was looking for?" Annika asks in a small voice.

"As a matter of fact," Ian says, opening up the folder, "no. But it's another file that had gone missing—Gena's file."

"Gena's file?" I glance over at Eleni, who has gone very still, her face as frozen as those of the marble statues guarding the terrace. The most terrible of the goddesses, I think: Nemesis. "Why do you have Gena's file in your room, Eleni?"

She turns her head slowly toward me—like an owl, I think, and for a moment I imagine Eleni turning into one of the little Athena owls and flying away. "Why do you care? You didn't bother yourself with her welfare when you were here."

"I . . . I didn't realize that she needed any help from me," I say. "I tried to talk to her once or twice and she seemed very shy . . ."

"And when she came to you to talk about Argos? Did she seem shy then?"

"She didn't—" I begin. But then I remember. It was in the last weeks of the summer. I was completely absorbed in the book I was writing except for the evenings, which I spent with Ian and Annika. I was startled when someone knocked on my door. The "house rules" stipulated quiet hours between nine and five so it was unusual for anyone to interrupt when you were writing in your room. Even Annika obeyed those rules. I immediately thought that it must be an emergency—that Argos had received a call about my father.

My heart was pounding when I opened the door. I was surprised to find Gena and I wondered if Argos had sent her with a message.

What is it? I said, perhaps a bit brusquely.

Oh! She seemed immediately sorry to have knocked. *I . . . I didn't mean to interrupt your writing. I wondered if you had a moment to talk.*

I must have glanced regretfully back over my shoulder toward my desk, which was strewn with papers, because when I looked back, she was bright pink and stammering. *Never mind . . . I'm sorry I bothered you . . .*

"She fled before she told me what she wanted to talk about," I say.

"And you never asked her again what it was?"

"No," I say, thinking back. By the time I sat back down at my desk I'd forgotten all about Gena. "I guess I thought if it was important she'd bring it up again."

"You can't blame Maia for—" Annika begins, but Eleni rounds on her before she can finish.

"And you with your interrogations about how she got into the residency, as if she were some kind of imposter!"

"I really didn't mean anything by it," Annika says, but Eleni has already turned toward Ian.

Before she can say anything, though, Ian says, "Yes, I failed her, too. She asked me one day what it was like having a famous father who was a writer. Did it make it hard to be a writer myself?

Did I worry about living up to his legacy? Did my father encourage me? Honestly, it was all a bit too close to the bone for me. I think I dismissed her with some trite advice about exorcising the paternal demons. I told her that coming to Eris against my father's wishes had so angered him that I felt like it had freed me from that anxiety of influence." Ian laughs derisively at himself. "That was idiotic, of course. I hadn't freed myself at all. If anything, acting out against my father had just locked me into a power struggle with him that made me more dependent on him than ever. Is that what happened to Gena?"

Eleni nods. "She took your advice and wrote the book about Argos, which made him so angry that he disowned her."

"Disowned her?" I echo. "Wait . . . are you saying—"

"*That's* how she got in," Annika says. "Gena was Argos's daughter."

Eleni lets out a wail that raises every hair on my body. The sound is like something rent from the bowels of the earth. The anguished cry at the end of a Greek tragedy, the keening of Demeter grieving for Persephone.

"And yours," I say, like the chorus supplying the coda to Eleni's cry. "Gena was your daughter."

CHAPTER SIXTEEN

"Oh, Eleni," I say, "I'm so sorry. Why didn't you tell us? Why didn't Gena tell us fifteen years ago?"

"She didn't want anyone here to know. She didn't want you all to think she was being treated differently because she was Argos's daughter or mine. I thought it was because she was ashamed of me and didn't want anyone to know she was the secretary's daughter—a secretary who'd made the foolish mistake of getting pregnant with her employer's child and then stayed on working for him even after he refused to make our child legitimate."

"Argos wouldn't marry you?" Annika asks.

Eleni laughs. "Argos marry a poor fisherman's daughter? No, I was good enough for a dalliance. It was the summer your father and mother were here." She looks at me, then at Ian. "And your father. I was only eighteen, hired straight out of the convent school, where I'd learned English, typing, and shorthand, to be Argos's secretary. How lucky I thought I was! To spend my summer on a beautiful island, surrounded by such cultured and educated people!" She looks around the terrace as if it were peopled by a throng of scholars. "There were a dozen students from the American Archeological School in Athens, including your mother, Maia. Mostly all girls, which I thought a marvel at the time, that

American girls were allowed to leave their homes and travel to a foreign country to study art and learn such impractical skills as Latin and ancient Greek. It didn't occur to me that Argos liked to surround himself with pretty young women who were in awe of his learning and wealth. I was in awe of him, too, but even more, I was in awe of those American girls with their straight, white teeth and loud voices and strong opinions. Your mother, Maia, was so beautiful. And kind. She talked to me as if I were one of them and encouraged me to go to university. She even tried to warn me about Argos."

"Why?" Annika asked.

"She saw how I worshipped him and how he could take advantage of that. But I didn't listen to her. I thought she might want him for herself."

"But she was with my father," I say automatically. "He always said that they fell in love that summer."

Eleni smiles indulgently at me. "I am sure *he* fell in love—and perhaps she did, too, in time—but it was difficult to look anywhere but at Argos when he was in a room. He had a charisma to him that was hard to resist. I know I couldn't. I have no one to blame but myself for what happened."

"You were very young," I say, thinking of my mother, who was only a few years older when she was here. "And inexperienced."

"And foolish," Eleni says. "When I told Argos I was pregnant I actually thought he would offer to marry me. He laughed when I suggested it. *Do you think Zeus married Leda? Or Danaë?*"

"What an asshole," Ian says.

"He certainly had a bit of a god complex," Bill adds.

"He *did* offer to support *the child,* as he referred to her, and he was happy to keep me on as his secretary. *I have no quar-*

rel with your work, he said. What choice did I have? I would be out on the streets on my own. Secretly, I hoped that when our child was born, he might feel differently. Perhaps if it had been a boy—a son he could pass his business on to—it would have been different. He seemed pleased with Gena, but he did not hide his disappointment that she wasn't a boy. He was true to his word, though, and paid for her support, including the most expensive private schools and allowing her to live with me here in the summer. I hoped that he would grow fond of her—that he might come to love her—but I'm not sure he was capable of real love. Yes, he petted and indulged her and laughed at her antics but he would grow quickly bored and displeased if she crossed him, which didn't stop her from desperately trying to please him. But no matter how she twisted herself to anticipate his moods, they changed too quickly. He was a mercurial god that she could not placate because, as I came to see, he only loved what he saw of himself in her. He never loved her for herself. My poor girl! I should have taken her far away from him and never let him have such influence over her. By the time he sent her away to college abroad it was too late; she was dependent on his approval. I didn't like the idea of her going so far away but Argos said I mustn't hinder her opportunities." She smiles bitterly. "I imagine that's what Agamemnon said when he told Clytemnestra to bring their daughter Iphigenia to Aulis to be married."

"Gena—" I say.

"Yes," Eleni says, "*Iphigenia*. That was the name Argos chose for her. I thought it was ill-omened to be named for the daughter who was sacrificed by her father, but I gave into Argos's wishes because I needed his help to raise her. My parents had disowned me when I got pregnant with my employer's child. I thought that at least she would get to live my dream of going to an American university. And she seemed to bloom there. At first, she studied classics and archeology, to please her father, of course. But when she saw that Argos had become more interested in artists and writers—it was about that time that he turned Eris into an artists' colony—she changed her major to creative writing. She thought he would be proud but when she came home on holiday and she showed him a few of her poems and stories, he told her that she had neither the talent nor disposition to be a writer or artist of any kind. She was heartbroken—" Eleni's voice falters at the memory of her daughter's pain. Ian moves to refill her glass but she waves the bottle away, as if she doesn't deserve to alleviate her own suffering when she hadn't been able to do that for her own daughter.

"I actually thought it might be the best thing, that she would be better off without such unrealistic hopes. I'd seen quite a bit of you lot by then"—her eyes rove coldly over the three of us—"and I had come to see it wasn't such a good life. And of course, by then I'd heard of what became of your mother, Maia."

I startle at the mention of my mother and have a sudden vivid image of her standing at an easel, her clothes and face paint-splattered, her hair wild. And then I picture her stilled, cold as marble, by death. The only time I ever saw her look peaceful.

"I don't know how much that had to do with being an artist," I say. "My mother had other demons."

Eleni nods. "Yes, I'm sure she did. Some of those demons, I believe, she met here. At any rate, she couldn't have stopped painting even if she tried, no more than Gena could stop writing. She told me it was the only time she felt *real*. And she hoped, I think, to finally impress Argos. And she did. She applied to the residency under an assumed name—Gena Wilson—and Argos read her stories and admitted her. When she told me, she was triumphant! I was afraid that Argos would be angry at her deception but instead he was impressed—or at least that's what he *said*. I have always suspected that he was angry at being fooled by his own daughter—a mere girl!—and he was only biding his time before delivering his punishment for deceiving him. He suggested she attend the residency under her assumed name and tell no one that she was his daughter or mine. *Let us see*, he told her, if you can hold your own among real artists."

"Us?" Ian repeats incredulously. "As if we were somehow paragons to live up to?"

"She thought you were," Eleni responds. "Especially you, Maia. She thought you were just the kind of American girl she wanted to be. She wanted so badly to be friends."

"And I was too busy with Annika and Ian to even notice her. I am so sorry, Eleni."

She shrugs. "You were young and youth is cruel. It was Argos who was most at fault. The way he pitted you against each other with his games and contests, the way he encouraged Gena and then at the end—"

Eleni draws in a shaky breath and moves closer to the fire. The flames make her face look haggard, as if she has aged decades in the telling of this story. She looks like an ancient bard recounting the exploits of mythic beings or one of the chorus, who comes on in the beginning of a tragedy to tell of a great man—Agamemnon, Oedipus, Theseus—and his downfall.

"Or perhaps, as you suggested to her, Mr. Davies, she thought she would exorcise her demons and free herself of her father. She was so proud of what she'd written here. She thought it would please Argos. She drew from the classical mythology she knew he loved, set her story on an island, and told the tale of her name-sake, Iphigenia, daughter of Agamemnon and Clytemnestra, the girl sacrificed by her father to gain a favorable wind. And it *was* good! But she made the mistake of portraying her Agamemnon too much like Argos—with all his grandeur and charm, but with his flaws and failings as well. When she gave it to me to read, I begged her to wait before showing it to him, to give herself some time to reread it and reflect. She agreed. Then on the last night when Argos called her in for her conference, he had a copy of her manuscript on his desk. I thought at the time that it must have been Olivia who had given it to him. She had spent a lot of time with Argos that summer, flirting with him. I suspected they might have been having an affair."

"That must have angered you," Ian guesses.

She gives Ian a disdainful look. "You think I killed Olivia because she was sleeping with Argos? She would have been one in a long line of mistresses Argos paraded in front of me over the years. I had long ceased to care."

"But if she stole Gena's manuscript," Annika says, "and gave it to Argos . . ."

"Yes," Eleni concedes, "that would have angered me. But I did not know for sure who it was and I know now that it was that man Sydney Norton because we found the report he wrote about it. So, I'd have no reason to blame Olivia for it now. But on that night, all I knew was that Argos summoned Gena and me to the library and said she had betrayed his trust in her with a piece of maudlin fantasy. He cut her off—disinherited her—and told her she should leave in the morning and never set foot on the island again."

"What a bastard!" Annika cries.

"Yes . . . and then he did something even worse . . ." She pauses, a tremor going through her so strong that for a moment I think that there must be an earthquake shaking the villa. "He told me I could stay."

"Oh, but . . ." Annika begins, her face confused.

We all are, I think. I know it's not what I was expecting.

Eleni's lips draw back from her teeth in a rictus of pain. "Don't you see? He wanted to divide us so she would be left with nothing at all . . . and I played right into his hands. While she looked at me, waiting, no doubt, for me to say that of course I wouldn't stay, of course I would stand with my daughter against her monster of a father, I was thinking, *But then she will have nothing! If I stay, I can still help her and perhaps I can convince Argos to change his mind.* And so . . ." She takes a long, rattling breath like someone drowning. "I said, yes, I would stay. When I turned to Gena, she looked at me as if *I* were the monster. She told Argos that he would be sorry, that she knew things about him that would destroy him."

"What did she mean?"

"Antiquities looting," Eleni answers. "He took pots and statues from the island and sold them abroad. She threatened to expose him. Argos only laughed and said no one would believe her, she had no proof. *I'll get proof,* she said, and then she left without a second glance at me. I tried to follow her, but Argos detained me with some trifling chore. By the time I was able to leave I could not find her. I searched the whole villa. I was afraid . . . I went up to the ridge and climbed down to the east cove, terrified . . ."

I remember Eleni telling us about the dangers of swimming in the east cove and the haunted look on her face.

"You thought she'd drowned herself in the grotto," Annika says. "But she didn't."

Eleni shakes her head and takes another shuddering breath. "When I got back to the villa it was dawn and I saw Argos's yacht motoring out of the harbor. When I came to the terrace I found you"—she turns to Ian and Annika—"and I asked you who had left and you told me that Maia and Gena had both gone on the first boat to catch an early train."

"That's right," I say. "Gena was on the boat with me, but she barely said a word. She spent the passage down below being sick. I thought . . . well, we'd all had a lot to drink the night before. But she was alive. What happened after?"

Eleni shakes her head. "I never heard from her again. A few weeks later the police came and said they'd found her suitcase in a cheap hotel in Athens with signs of drug use. But they never found her."

The tears now fall freely and silently down her face. "I begged Argos to spend his money to find her but he said that we were better off without her. That she would only cause trouble. It was then that I suspected."

"You can't think—" I begin.

"That Argos killed his own daughter—his own flesh and blood?" she asks fiercely. "I would not put it past him."

We are all silent for a long time. Finally, Ian says, "I think I can speak for all of us when I say that none of us blames you for seeking revenge on Argos and the rest of us. I'm only sorry we can't all kill the bastard over again."

Eleni laughs—a sound as surprising as if one of the statues had made it. "Do you think I care enough about any of you to bother with you? As for Argos—yes, when I received the summons to come here, I thought, I will go and kill him. Just as Clytemnestra avenged her daughter by striking down Agamemnon in his bath. But one of you took that away from me, too. Argos was dead when I got here. I am not your Nemesis."

CHAPTER SEVENTEEN

"Eleni," Ian says after a moment's silence. "I think we can all agree that after what Argos did to you and your daughter, you'd be completely justified in whatever you did." He looks around our little circle and we all nod.

"I'd've strung him up," Bill says. "Bastard got what he deserved."

"And Sydney was an accident, right?" Annika says. "No one could blame you for that. We'll all say that when we got here Argos was dead and Sydney freaked out and drowned trying to row away."

"By the time the police get here they're unlikely to be able to tell whether Argos died before the invitations were sent," Ian says.

"And Oliva Knox?" Eleni asks. "How will you explain her death?"

"Accidental overdose," Ian says. "The situation got to her and she took too many antianxiety meds."

"Or suicide," Bill suggests. "She must have been terrified she was losing her mind."

Eleni looks around the circle. "You all think you're so good at this, plotting deaths, coming up with excuses, catching the murderer. But you're all wrong. I didn't send those invitations or push Argos to his death or punch holes in the rowboat Sydney Norton took or give Olivia Knox a fatal overdose—and if *I* didn't do it, one of you *did* and I will not take the blame." She glares at each of us, daring us to refute her.

Or maybe to confess.

When no one says anything, Eleni nods as if we have confirmed her worst suspicions about us. "Now I am very tired. I would like to go to my room and lie down. You are welcome to lock me in. I want only to be left alone."

Ian looks around the circle again but no one objects. "I guess that's all right, then," he says. "If you all agree."

"I'll get you some bottled water and bread, Eleni," Bill offers.

"Prisoner's rations," Eleni says with a grim smile. "Just the water, Bill. *Efcharisto.*"

"*Parakola,*" he replies and goes off to the kitchen.

Ian and I walk Eleni to her room while Annika stays behind on the terrace. It feels all wrong, as if we are escorting a prisoner to the gas chamber. Who are we to judge Eleni? When we reach her room and she turns to us, her face shows me that she has convicted herself of far worse crimes than the ones that have been committed over the last two days.

"I don't think you should be alone," I say, apprehension seizing me. "Let me stay with you. Ian can lock us both in. I'd like to sit with you, in quiet, if you like—or if you'd be willing, you could tell me more about what you remember about my mother when she was here."

"You are very much like her," she says, touching my face, "but I hope you are stronger."

Then she turns and walks into her room. She sits on the edge of her narrow, neatly made bed. There's an antique Byzantine saint's icon on the wall above the plain brass headboard and a framed photograph on the night table. Gena, I guess. The room resembles a nun's cell. Or a prisoner's.

Bill appears with two bottles of mineral water, a clean glass, and a package of biscuits and lays them on the bureau, which is bare save for a brush and an embroidered cloth smoothed neatly over the surface.

"Oh," she says, taking something from her pocket, "you'll need this." She hands Bill a key. "That's the master key. It opens all the doors in the house."

Bill looks at the key and then tosses it to Ian. "You keep it, mate, guard duty is above my pay grade."

"Is this the only master key?" Ian asks, looking at the key in his palm.

"Argos had two made," Eleni says, "but when I arrived there was only one, hanging from a peg in the kitchen. The second one should have been in his desk drawer but I didn't find it there." She glares at Ian. "Do you want to search me?"

Ian blanches. "That's not necessary. I don't think you mean us any harm, Eleni, even if we deserve it. I want you to know I'm sorry I didn't do more for Gena. It's no excuse, but that last night . . ." He looks at me and I know what he's thinking. After I'd seen him and Annika on the balcony, I left him a letter in his room telling him I didn't want to see him again. He spent the rest of the night camped outside my door begging me to tell him what he'd done wrong. We'd both been oblivious to what was happening to Gena. Now he looks away toward the window where, I notice, the sky is just beginning to lighten. A long mournful cry comes from the woods—the little owl of Athena—and Ian lets that be the last word. He turns and walks out of the room. Bill follows and I turn, too, but before I leave, Eleni murmurs something. I turn back to see if she has some final message for me. She's lying down, her eyes closed, her lips moving, murmuring words in Greek. My modern Greek is not that good but I recognize the words *mother* and *protect*. She's praying, I think, turning to leave, asking for the Holy Mother's protection. Only as I get to the door do the words rearrange themselves in my head and I realize what she really said: *At least your mother protected you.*

BILL SAYS HE'S going to get some sleep. I'm exhausted but I know that if I close my eyes I'll see Olivia's deathly pale face and staring eyes.

Or my mother's.

Instead, I walk toward the terrace to find Annika, but as I'm passing the library I see that she's in there bending over a pile of papers on the floor and straightening the mess Olivia made yesterday.

"Annika," I say, "I need to talk to you. What did you come to my room to tell me and where did you get that key?"

Annika looks up and I see that she's been crying. She looks more vulnerable than I've ever seen her. We've all been stricken by Eleni's story.

"What key?"

Ian comes in behind me.

Annika's eyes flicker from me to Ian and a veil falls over that vulnerability. She digs her hand in her jeans pocket and tosses Ian the key. "I found it in Argos's desk yesterday and thought it might come in handy. You keep it now since you've appointed yourself jailor. What were you doing lurking around the villa in the middle of the night and searching Eleni's room, by the way?"

"I heard someone moving around upstairs and I went to investigate," he says. "I saw Eleni's door open . . ." He looks embarrassed. "I just wanted to see if she had that file Olivia was so upset about."

"Well, congrats, Master Sea Scout, you caught our Nemesis."

I look from one to the other and wonder. The camaraderie of last night when we were all Sea Scouts together has vanished. Annika seems pissed off at Ian. Granted, his exposure of Eleni seems cruel in retrospect, but none of us look too good in light of Eleni's story. What's clear to me is Annika isn't going to tell me what she came to my room to confess with Ian in here. I need an excuse to get her alone.

"So, what are we looking for?" Ian asks, scanning the chaos of files and papers.

"I thought Maia might want to see if there's anything here about her mother," Annika says, handing me a stack of papers and widening her eyes at me—a signal, I'm pretty sure, that she wants to get rid of Ian.

But Ian has other ideas. He sits down cross-legged on the floor in the middle of the scattered papers and begins sorting through them. "Good idea," he says. "Let's look for proof of Argos's illegal looting operation while we're at it. The least we can do for Gena is to finish what she started."

WE SPEND THE entire day searching through the library, taking turns napping on the couch, drinking the tea Ian makes on his paraffin stove, and snacking on Nutella and crackers that Annika has "liberated" from the kitchen. We go through all the filing cabinets, replacing the residency files that had been taken out and searching through the ones that had been left inside. We look through Argos's desk, knocking on the wood for false bottoms and secret compartments. We take every book down from the bookcase, rifling the pages for loose papers and checking for hollowed-out cavities. We've lifted the framed prints from the walls and looked for safes.

"There doesn't seem to be anything but the files of all the writers and artists who ever came to this godforsaken island," Ian says after we've searched for hours, "and I'm sick to death of reading about their accomplishments and aspirations."

"It makes sense that Argos wouldn't have left evidence of illegal activities just lying around in his filing cabinets," I say, "but I was hoping that there would at least be something about the summer my mother and father were here. My father said that Argos got the idea of starting an artists' residency when he figured out that there weren't any significant archeological finds on the island—"

"But that was a lie," Ian points out. "He must have found those statues and pottery in the cave somewhere—and there should be a record of a dig." He stands up and looks around the room. "He must have a safe," Ian says, exasperated. "A man in his position would."

"But he'd have it in some really clever place," Annika says. "He had this villa built from the ground up, right? He'd have been sure to install secret hiding places."

"That's a good point," Ian says. "Have we come across a plan of the villa anywhere?"

"I haven't seen one—" I begin, but then I realize that I have. Opposite Argos's desk hangs the architect's rendering of Lavyrinthos—Argos's *opus*, according to my father. I take it down and lay it on the coffee table so we can study it together. *Lavyrinthos* is inscribed in classical block letters. There's a watercolor sketch of the exterior of the villa as seen from the water and a cross section of the lower levels excavated from the cliffside.

"You can really tell it was meant to look like a labyrinth from this drawing," Ian says.

"What an ego!" Annika exclaims. "He saw himself as King Minos."

"More like the Minotaur," I say. "Devouring youths sent as tribute. That's what we were—all these artists and writers that Argos brought to his island over the years and then spurred into competition—he enjoyed watching us vie for his favor just as he enjoyed watching his own daughter try to please him. He really was a monster!"

Annika is tracing a pattern of the hallways on the lower levels. "You know, it's really *not* a labyrinth. There's only one way to get to the center."

"That's how ancient labyrinths were depicted," Ian says. "See here in the corner of the drawing, there's a little pattern—" He points to the corner of the print where there's a simple line drawing of a labyrinth. "That's the classical seven-course unicursal labyrinth."

Annika snorts. "Oh, the *classical seven-course unicursal labyrinth, Detective Pythagoras*," she mocks. "That's a pretty fancy way of describing something that could come off a diner placemat. Besides, there aren't seven courses here." She taps the glass over the floor plan. "There are only three courses, barely an appetizer, main, and dessert."

"Even Argos must have recognized some limits," Ian says. "Excavating three stories down into the rock cliffside must have cost a fortune—and he must have had an archeologist do a survey and sign off on all the work to make sure there weren't any significant ancient artifacts where he was digging."

"After all we've learned about Argos," Annika says, "I don't see him worrying too much about a survey. He could easily have bribed an archeologist to sign off."

"We could track down this architectural firm," I say, pointing to the corner of the print where the name of the firm is partly obscured by the frame. "I mean, after we get out of here."

"I can't read it," Ian says, squinting at the name. "Let's take this out of the frame."

I turn the frame over and we each work at unbending the metal prongs that hold the back in place. When it's loose, Ian lifts the cardboard backing off. As he does, something falls to the floor. I lean over and pick it up. It's an eight-by-ten photograph, a group shot of half a dozen people posing in front of an excavation pit. I look closer at the faces of the people—and my heart contracts in recognition. There is my mother, in a T-shirt and jeans, a smattering of freckles across her sunburned nose, long hair in braids, young and smiling. She's standing between my father—also impossibly young-looking in khakis and work shirt, not at all the stuffy professor I had grown up with—and Argos, his shaven head gleaming in the sun, grinning behind dark glasses. He's looking at my mother with a covetous gaze that makes my skin prickle, perhaps because she seems wholly unaware of it.

Eleni had said that it was hard to look anywhere but at Argos when he was in a room, but my mother and father only had eyes for each other.

"That's my father," Ian says, pointing at a young, slightly built man kneeling in the front row of the group. He's pointing to something in the ground.

"These must be the other students from the American Archeological School," Annika says. "Eleni is right, Argos liked them young and pretty. Oh, and here's Eleni. Look at how beautiful she was! Like a young Melina Mercouri!"

The young Eleni is, indeed, heartbreakingly beautiful in this photograph—before Argos destroyed her life and she watched her own daughter spiral into a destructive obsession—but I'm looking instead at the ground at Clive Davies's feet. It's an excavation pit, crisscrossed with string marking coordinates as for an archeological dig. There's something in the dirt, a half-buried amphora—

I peer closer. "Can you hand me that magnifying glass on the desk?" I ask.

Ian hands it to me and I hold it over the amphora until a winged figures comes into focus. I'd know her anywhere because I've seen her every day for the last fifteen years I've worked in the Museum of Ancient Artifacts. It's Eris, the goddess of discord, lobbing her apple into the wedding party of Peleus and Thetis. Here is the Wedding Vase, supposedly assembled from shards purchased from reputable dealers, lying intact, half buried at my father's feet. Not only is this incontrovertible proof that my father knew that the Wedding Vase came from here, he knew that it was intact when it was found.

CHAPTER EIGHTEEN

That's proof that Argos was engaged in antiquities looting, right?" Annika says.

"It's not enough," Ian says. "This photograph could have been taken anywhere."

"But we have the statues and pottery in the grotto, too," Annika says.

"But no proof of where they came from," I say. I look closer at the photograph and point at the smudged horizon line behind the group. "That looks like the ridge behind the villa, but it's too blurry to be sure. If it is, then the statues and the Wedding Vase were found when Argos was excavating for the extension of the villa. I'd like to know what archeologist signed off on its construction after that!"

"Someone easily bribed," Ian says. "Look, there's something drawn on the back of the blueprint."

Annika and I both lean over to examine it, but our shadows obscure the faint pencil lines. Without electric lamps the light in the library has grown dim. We've been in here all day and now the light is failing. When we bring the blueprint out onto the terrace for better light, we see that the sun is setting over the sea.

"Ah, there you all are," Bill says, coming out with a tray of cheese and olives. "I thought the three of you might have been added to the growing list of casualties. What have you got now—a treasure map?"

"A blueprint of the villa," Ian says, smoothing the paper out on the long table, reverse side up. Annika picks up a few lumps of marble and seashells from the rock garden and uses them as weights to keep it from flying away in the quickening breeze. "There's a pencil drawing on the reverse side that we want to look at more closely."

Bill peers at it over Ian's shoulder. "Looks like one of those games you used to get on diner placemats," he says. "I hope you're not suggesting my food is comparable to diner fare—not that there's anything wrong with a good diner."

"Bill," Annika says reprovingly, "I'll have you know that this is a seven-times cursed classical labyrinth."

"*Cursed* is right," Bill says. "I wouldn't want to get lost in that thing. Where's it supposed to be?"

"Here, I think," Ian says.

The drawing is a rough sketch of the villa, its three floors following the plan of a labyrinth. What distinguishes it from the blueprint on the other side, though, are the levels beneath the lowest floor, which coil down into the rock core of the cliff. At the center is a drawing of a bull's head—the Minotaur.

"I haven't come across anything like that, mate," Bill says.

"It could just be a fantasy," I say. "Argos was obsessed with the idea of labyrinths. What was that thing he used to say about them?"

"*We must all walk the labyrinth,*" Ian quotes, "*to find our true self.*"

"And *The minotaur more than justifies the existence of the labyrinth*," I add.

"I think that's Borges," Ian says.

"I think that's bullshit," Bill says, "*literally*. I bet Argos liked to think his villa was perched on top of a maze and he was the prize bull sitting on top of it all."

"What if it is?" I say, feeling a tingling that starts in my toes and seems to travel up to the crown of my head, as if something is vibrating far below me. I look down at my feet, half expecting the ground to open up beneath me—a yawning chasm with a hungry mouth at the bottom ready to swallow us all—and find my eye traveling the lines of the marble paving.

"It's a labyrinth," I say, pointing to the pattern of black and white marble.

"It's the same pattern as the floors inside," Annika says. "I remember when I had too much to drink the floors always made me dizzy."

"Yeah, so what?" Bill says. "We know he liked the design. It's on everything—the plates, the silverware, the plaques on the doors. Eleni said that he believed the pattern dispelled bad luck."

"Eleni," I say, suddenly recalling the apprehensive feeling I'd had this morning. "Have you checked on Eleni today?" I ask Bill.

"I thought she'd had enough of us lot," he says, "and needed some sleep, which is how I spent my day."

"Can I have the key?" I ask Ian. That tingling apprehension climbing up my spine, I walk from the terrace into the villa, aware now of the lines of the labyrinth beneath my feet. We've all been walking its pattern since we set foot on the island—no, since even before we got to the island: ever since we got those invitations with the sign of the labyrinth. Here it is again, inscribed on a bronze plaque on Eleni's door. I rap my knuckles against the door, but already I'm sliding the key into the lock and calling Eleni's name, my call as plaintive as the little owl we'd heard this morning. How could we have left her alone all day? According to the pattern—

I open the door and Eleni sits up in bed.

"Oh, thank God, I thought—"

"That I had made an end of myself?" she asks, crossing herself. "I don't doubt it's what your Nemesis wanted. I found this under my pillow." She holds up an amber prescription pill bottle, *Alprazolam* typed on the label along with Olivia Knox's name.

"How—?"

"Someone thought I just needed a little push. And, God forgive me, I have thought about doing just that every day since my Gena disappeared. But I have been lying here thinking about Gena—" Her eyes travel to the photograph on the night table. It's a picture taken, I think, the summer we were all here. Gena is sitting on the terrace framed by the marble columns overlooking the sea, her face bathed in golden light, beaming at the camera—beaming at her mother, who had taken the picture, I imagine. There's something stubborn in her expression. *See, Mom, I do belong here.* "I don't believe she would leave me wondering about her fate all these years. I know in my heart that she's dead and I think that she's somewhere here on the island."

"I think so, too," I say, placing a tentative hand on Eleni's shoulder. "And I think I know where."

ELENI DOESN'T NEED any coaxing to come out on the terrace. By mutual consent we agree not to mention the bottle of pills she found under her pillow. If it means that Nemesis is still among us,

I don't want to alert them that we know. She's changed out of her uniform and put on a pair of white slacks and a red gauze blouse that makes her look younger and somehow fiercer. Three pairs of eyes look up when we step out onto the terrace and I scan them for surprise. They *all* look surprised, but whether because Eleni is willing to join us or because she's still alive, I can't tell.

Do I really suspect that Ian or Annika is the Nemesis? I'd sooner believe it of Bill, but I know that Bill wasn't in Greece until a few days ago, while both Ian and Annika were. Plus, Annika had the master key. But what motive did she have to kill Argos? Ian, who hated Argos, had more, and how well do I really know him after all these years?

I can feel my brain racing down the labyrinthine path of suspicion and doubt. It's what *it* wants, I think, as if the labyrinth has a will of its own.

I try to focus instead on the drawing of the labyrinth spread out on the table. Eleni, however, has picked up the photograph I left beside it. "I remember when this was taken," she says. "How young we all were!"

"Do you remember when they found this amphora?" I ask.

"Yes, of course," she answers. "They were all so excited—your father most of all. *A find of world-class significance*, he said."

I can hear my father's professorial voice in her imitation. What I can't imagine is my father not going public with this find, and allowing the artifacts discovered here to pass into private hands rather than to the public world of scholarship.

"Where was this?" I ask.

Eleni looks around the terrace and points to the ground. "Here," she says. "Right in front of the old farmhouse that Argos had torn down to make way for his new villa."

"But how could Argos keep building on this site?" Ian asks. "Wasn't there a state archeological survey done?"

Eleni nods and taps the face of a young man in the picture. "He was the state archeologist—a young, impressionable man new to the job. I'm sure he was paid well to say whatever Argos told him to say."

"Do you remember," I ask, "what else they found during the construction of the villa and how deep they dug?" I trace my finger along the lines coiling deep into the cliff. "Did they find a labyrinth?"

She stares at the pattern so long I think that she, too, has been drawn into its snare. She shakes her head as if clearing her ears of water. "Argos sent me back to Athens early that summer to ready his winter apartment, he said, and to escort the students back to the American school. He said they weren't needed anymore. The amphora, he told us, had been a fluke—an import buried by eighteenth-century pirates. He was bringing in a construction crew to finish the villa. It would be easier with fewer people staying on the island. The only ones from this group to remain were your father and mother, Maia, and your father, Ian. When I came back the next summer the villa was completed. I was surprised at first by the design—that instead of building *up* he had built *down*, and that two floors had been added below the level of the terrace—but Argos said he wanted to *keep a low profile*."

Bill snorts. "Like he was a humble environmentalist."

I look around the terrace at the black-and-white-patterned marble stretching to the edge of the cliff to touch the horizon of sea and sky, a few elegant columns framing the view, and then turn to look at the low, whitewashed building nestled into the wooded slope of the ridge. At first glance it is, if not humble, then elegant in its simplicity. "Keeping a low profile could also be a way of evading the attention of the authorities," I point out. "Having the additional floors below the terrace makes the villa seem smaller at first sight."

"And hides whatever they dug up here," Ian says, studying the pencil drawing. "This plan looks familiar . . ."

"It should," I say. "It's like the hidden labyrinth in your father's last Detective Pythagoras—"

"In *Ian's* last Detective Pythagoras," Annika corrects and then, at Bill's confused look, adds, "Oops, sorry, Ian, I didn't mean to give away your secret."

"*You've* been writing those books?" Bill asks. "Kudos, mate, those are solid. I read the last one. Did you think of that hidden labyrinth stuff yourself?"

"No," Ian admits. "I found a sketch of it in my dad's old notebooks. I figured he'd been working out an idea for a book he never got around to writing. I showed it to him on one of his more lucid days, but it got him so agitated I was sorry I had. *Stay out of the labyrinth,* he told me. *Once you've walked it, you're never free of it. The labyrinth gets inside you.*" Ian pauses, his jaw tightening to control the emotion that has come over him. "He kept tracing the pattern with his finger even after I took the drawing away. I had the terrible feeling that it's what's inside his brain. It occurred to me that's what it's like for him now—like he's trapped inside a labyrinth in his mind."

I wince and reach my hand out to touch his, but Eleni reaches him first. "I remember he was a kind man, your father. Maybe too kind to withstand Argos's influence."

"Do you think," Annika asks, "that he drew that plan of the

hidden labyrinth because he'd seen it here, because Argos had it built that summer?"

"That would have been quite the engineering feat for even a man as rich as Argos," Bill says.

"He might not have had to build it," I say, staring at the drawing. "He might have found it."

"You mean they came across an ancient labyrinth built into the cliff?" Ian asks. "That would have been an astonishing find."

"It would have been," I say, "a career-making discovery." I recall the way my father used to talk about the great archeologists— Heinrich Schliemann, Arthur Evans, Carl Blegen—with longing in his voice, and I wonder again how he could have let such a find remain in the dark.

Below where I stand now.

I look down again at the black and white pattern on the marble floor. Beneath the chair at the head of the table—where Argos always sat—is the center of the labyrinth. *Of course it is.* I get up, holding the blueprint in my hands, and start walking the pattern outward.

"What are you doing?" Annika asks.

"Walking the labyrinth," I say. The pattern takes me on seven loops around the terrace before depositing me at the arched entrance into the villa. The hallway is paved in a black and white geometric pattern, the border made of miniature labyrinths and a diamond pattern down the middle. It always seemed quite busy to me, and now, after completing the circuit on the terrace, dizzying. I close my eyes but the pattern is still there.

The labyrinth gets inside you.

I shudder at the thought and open my eyes—and see the diamond pattern anew. "They're arrows," I say, striding forward. I complete the circuit of the first floor and then descend to the second, and then the third, noticing how each level is a circuit in the labyrinth. I pass my room and come to the end of the hall, where the arrows stop. The last door at the end of the hallway is closed and locked. There's a silver plaque on it with the design of the labyrinth etched into it. I try to remember if I've ever seen this door open, but I can't.

"What's in here?" I ask Eleni, who, along with Annika, Ian, and Bill, has followed me.

"I don't know," Eleni answers. "It was always locked."

I still have the master key in my pocket. I take it out and fit it into the lock. I turn it, but nothing happens. "It's the one door in the villa that the master key doesn't open?" I ask. "There must be something inside Argos didn't want anyone to see. Where would that key be?" I turn to ask Eleni, but it's Annika who answers.

"Try this one," she says, handing me a key and then shrugging when I stare at her. "I found it in Argos's desk."

I turn it over in my hand and see that the labyrinth pattern is etched into the head. I slip the key in and turn it—the lock clicks and the door opens when I push forward. A gust of warm, moist air wafts out as if it had been trapped inside waiting to be released. It smells like salt and sulfur, like—

"It smells like the grotto," Annika says. "And listen . . ."

A low, keening moan rises and echoes as if it is coming from far, far below us. It sounds like a monster trapped in the rock, like the Minotaur.

"It sounds like the wind in the grotto," Ian says, aiming his flashlight into the darkness, revealing a long tunnel carved out of stone. "It must go all the way down to the sea. You've found the labyrinth."

CHAPTER NINETEEN

All this time—the whole summer we were here and these last two days—we were sleeping down the hall from *this*?" Annika says.

I shudder at the thought. It's like opening your bedroom closet and finding a portal to hell. Because that's what this feels like—not an archeological curiosity like the catacombs of Paris or the buried cities of Pompeii and Herculaneum, but a doorway to hell.

"They must have found the entrance to this passage when they were excavating for the villa," Ian says. I can hear in the tightness of his voice that he is struggling to maintain a scholarly objectivity. "I think you were right, Maia, when you said the Persephone statue in the grotto suggested that this might have been the site of an ancient mystery rite."

"What kind of mystery rite are we talking about?" Bill asks. "Some kind of old Greek version of mystery dinner theater? Because I've done a couple of those and let me tell you, they can get pretty scary. Some Florida retiree doesn't get his Death by Chocolate Mousse and there's hell to pay!"

"The ancient mystery rites weren't quite dinner theater," I say, glad that Bill's humor has given me a chance to dive into scholar mode. "Although they were a performance of a sort. They were a reenactment of the abduction of Persephone to the underworld by Hades, her mother Demeter's grief-stricken search for her, and her return to the world of the living."

"Even I know this story," Annika says. "Demeter lets the whole world fry while she searches for her daughter. But she gets her back, right?"

"Zeus sends Hermes to bring her back but because Persephone has eaten six pomegranate seeds, she has to remain in the underworld for six months of the year. The mystery rites reenacted the journey down to the underworld to rescue Persephone. The initiates were supposed to experience the terror of death and the knowledge that comes from that terror."

"So, like a literal trip to hell," Annika says.

"And back," Ian says. "The return is the important part. The idea was that once you've faced your own death you can live an enlightened life."

"She would of been a good woman if it had been somebody there to shoot her every minute of her life," Annika says.

I turn to her, surprised. "Look who's quoting now!"

"Quoting Flannery O'Connor is *not* the same as spouting Latin and Greek all day," she answers, staring at the passage. "And this place doesn't feel like a dress rehearsal for death."

"It feels," Eleni says, *"evil."*

"So we shut the door, lock it, and throw away the key?" Bill suggests.

It sounds like the most sensible thing to do. The air wafting out of the passage is warm and fetid, like the breath of a corpse-eating monster hungry for more. In the minutes we have stood here the shadows have only grown darker and closer, as if the darkness was creeping out of the passage and stealing over us, looking for a way into each of our hearts.

Once you've walked the labyrinth, the labyrinth is inside you.

Is this what had gotten inside my mother? Had something happened to her here that fractured her mind? Something so bad my father kept this place a secret?

"I think she's in there," Eleni says.

I turn and stare at Eleni, sure that she has somehow read my mind and is talking about my mother. But then I see the expression on her face and know it's not my mother she's talking about.

"Gena," she says. "When she left the library the last night, she said she was going to find evidence that would prove Argos was engaging in antiquities looting. I think she came here."

"But how would she have known about this place?" Annika asks.

"She spent every summer here," Eleni says, "and she was always roaming about while I worked. She must have seen Argos go through this door at some point. The last thing she said to him was that she was going to show the world what he really was. I think she went in here"—her voice catches on a sob—"and that she never came out. I think this is where she died."

I open my mouth to point out that even if Gena did go down into the labyrinth, she can't still be there since I saw her leave the island. When I look into Eleni's eyes, though, I see a hunger to know what happened to her daughter. That same hunger is in Ian's eyes.

"I have to go," he says. "I have to know what my father saw in there."

I nod. "And I need to know what happened to my mother in there," I say. Then, turning to Eleni, I continue, "I'll go for you."

I GO BACK to my room to change into warmer and sturdier clothes (with a bathing suit underneath in case we do end up in the grotto) while Ian looks for a rope and lanterns. Annika follows me back to my room. "I don't think you should go in there," she says. "You have no idea what you'll find. There could be rockslides and bottomless pits and . . . bats."

I laugh at her last suggestion, recalling Annika's phobia. "I'm not scared of bats," I tell her.

"You *should* be! I heard of a woman who got trapped in a cave in Greece with them and she lost her mind. She lived the rest of her life in a convent."

"Annika," I say firmly, "that's the plot of that Sidney Sheldon novel we found lying around the villa fifteen years ago and took turns reading." I put both hands on her arms and look into her eyes. She looks genuinely terrified. "What are you really afraid of? That Ian is the Nemesis and he'll kill me—or that it's Bill and he'll kill you and Eleni while we're gone?"

"No," she says. "I know it's not Bill or Ian because . . . it's me."

"What?"

She sinks onto my bed, drops her head in her hands, and sobs. I sit down next to her and wait for the sobs to subside, handing her tissues from a box on the night table. When she's gotten herself under control she starts talking, keeping her eyes on a middle spot in the distance instead of looking at me.

"I came here two weeks ago to talk to Argos," she says.

"You what? Why?"

She looks embarrassed. "I'd lost my contract with Paulson Pratchett right after he bought the company. I thought he must have had something to do with it and that he could get them to give me my contract back if he wanted to."

"Annika," I say, "what made you think he would do that?"

"I don't know!" she wails. "I was desperate. And at first he led me on. He told me, yes, he'd love for me to visit him on the island. He'd been following my career with great interest. But when I got here all he did was ask me about you and Ian."

"What did he ask you?"

"Was I still in touch with you both because we'd all been so close. Did I know if you and Ian were still writing, had I read the latest Detective Pythagoras book, what had you told me about your mother. He even asked if you had sent me."

"Why on earth would he think that?"

"I don't know. To tell you the truth he seemed . . . *crazy*. He started ranting about the Furies coming home to roost and Nemesis finding him at last. He asked me if *I* was Nemesis come to seek revenge because I'd been . . ." She stops and swallows hard, looking down at her hands.

"What?"

"Because I'd been raped, too," she says, lifting her eyes to meet mine. "And when I asked him how he knew that he said because you had told him what happened to me in college."

"I never—" I begin, but then I remember our conference on the last night. When he told me that there was something missing in Annika, I said that she couldn't help how she was because of what had happened to her in college. "I didn't say you were raped," I tell her. "I told him something bad had happened to you in college and he guessed."

I can tell by how skittish she is around me.

"I'm so sorry, Annika. I didn't mean to betray your trust."

She smiles wryly. "It was Argos," she says. "He brought out the worst in all of us. When he said you'd told him, I was furious—at you, at him, at myself for letting him get to me. I pushed him. He hit his head on the corner of the altar but he didn't die right away. He had time to laugh at me and tell me . . ."

"What?" I ask.

"That he would still have the last word."

"What did he mean by that?"

"I didn't know! I went back to the villa—I was going to call the police, I swear!—but when I went to the library to radio the boat I started to worry about how I was going to explain to the Greek police what I was doing here and what had happened to Argos and I was afraid of what it would look like. I thought that was what he had meant by having the last word. He knew I'd be convicted of his murder. So I fled. The boat was waiting for me down at the dock and I went back to Skiathos."

"But the invitations—"

"Mine came a few days later—not to my apartment in New York but to the hotel in Skiathos, even though I hadn't told him where I was staying! He must have sent them out before I got to the island but for a moment I thought—" She looks at me, a haunted cast in her eyes. "I thought, Maybe he isn't dead. Maybe he can't die—he's immortal like a Greek god."

"Oh, Annika," I say, imagining her terror.

"I couldn't come back here alone. I had to find out if you and Ian were going to be here, too. I'm sorry. I should never have let you come."

"It's okay," I say, "you didn't know what would happen."

"You have to believe I had nothing to do with Sydney's or Olivia's deaths. I didn't destroy the phone or the radio or sabotage the rowboat—Sydney must have damaged it dragging it across the rocks."

She looks so upset I can't help but reassure her. "I believe you," I say. "Those could have been accidents. It wasn't your fault that Argos had sent the invitations or that he taunted you like that—what an asshole! He pushed the wrong person too far and she pushed back."

"Or the *right* person," she says, her hand turning cold in mine.

"What do you mean?" I ask.

"I've had the dreadful feeling since we've come here that he planned it all—even down to me killing him—and that we've been playing his game all along."

I MEET IAN at the door to the labyrinth. He looks like he's going spelunking. He's got headlamps for both of us, a backpack full of water, extra batteries, and a long, coiled rope. I've got the blueprint with its penciled map.

"If you're not back in an hour we're coming down there for you," Bill says.

"How will we know where to find them?" Eleni asks. "There could be branching paths in there." She looks balefully toward the dark gaping hole. I imagine she's thinking of her daughter walking into that darkness. "A person might wander in there forever."

It's a terrible thought. The wailing that comes up from the tunnels sounds like the cries of lost souls. *What if it is?*

"Here," Annika says, clasping my hand. She ties a string bracelet around my wrist, like the friendship bracelets we made on the beach fifteen years ago. For luck, I think, noticing she's threaded a blue *mati* and a tiny shell onto it. But then I notice that the bracelet is attached to a ball of twine, which Annika holds in her hand. "Ariadne's clue, right?" she says, looking proud of herself for remembering this bit of classical mythology. But then she adds, "I've never understood why it's called that—it's just a ball of string."

"It's where the word *clue* comes from," I say. "From the ball of thread Ariadne gave Theseus so he could find his way out of the labyrinth after he'd slain the Minotaur. It came to mean *something that guides you*."

"Thank you, Professor Etymology," Annika says with a smirk. And then she hugs me. "Be careful," she whispers in my ear, "and remember what I told you."

We've all been playing Argos's game all along, she'd said. It's an awful thought to accompany us into the dark, that I'm following the path laid down by a dead man, but then that's what the mystery rites were all about—following a dead person down into the underworld. Eleni must have the same thought because she reaches out and presses something cold and metal into my hand.

"We had matching ones," she tells me as I look down and see the gold bracelet adorned with a *mati* charm. "Take mine with you—and if you find one like it, you'll know it's her." I squeeze her hand back and put her bracelet in my pocket. Then I turn to follow Ian into the dark.

THE PASSAGE SLOPES downward for several yards before the first turn. Ian is standing there aiming his flashlight at the wall. "Look at this," he says.

I follow the beam and am startled to find a face looking back at me, eyes wide with fear, mouth open in a silent scream. The paint is faded and cracked, the image barely visible, and yet the raw emotion of fear is palpable.

"An initiate," Ian says, tracing the line of her white cloak with his flashlight. "I think we're supposed to feel as if we're part of the throng of the dead descending to the underworld and experiencing their fear." He delivers this speech with scholarly confidence but as he sweeps his flashlight beam across a host of terrified faces, I notice that his hand is shaking.

"Well, it's successful," I say. I glance back to the door of the villa. Already its light looks dim and faraway. I give a little tug on the string and Annika tugs back. Ian's looking toward the door, frowning.

"I don't like leaving Annika and Eleni alone with Bill," he says in a low voice as if afraid Bill might overhear him. He might, I think; who knows how sound travels in these tunnels?

"If you're worried that Bill's the Nemesis I think I can put your mind to rest."

"I know—he wasn't in Greece."

"Not just that." I'm not sure Annika would like me sharing what she told me but Ian deserves to have his fears allayed, so I tell him everything.

"I'd be angry at her for not doing the sensible thing and going right away to the authorities but if she had we wouldn't have both come here and I wouldn't have had a chance to explain what happened fifteen years ago to you." He glances shyly at me.

"I'm glad about that part, too," I say, returning his smile. "But it's unnerving to think Argos had already sent out the invitations before he died. Why would he suddenly invite us all here?"

"I've been thinking about that," Ian says, "and I'm afraid it might be my fault."

"Your fault?"

"You said that he asked whether Annika had read the latest Pythagoras?"

"Yes, but—"

"I sent the latest Detective Pythagoras to Argos three weeks ago. It's what my father had done and I didn't want Argos to know my father has Alzheimer's. Argos always sent back an email acknowledging that he had received my father's latest book and congratulating him on its publication—but this time he wrote back, *I thought we had an agreement never to talk about the labyrinth.*"

"What did he mean?"

"I had no idea, but now I think Argos was angry that I wrote about the labyrinth. I used my father's notes, which I thought were just ideas for a book, but now I see that they were descriptions of this place. Argos must have thought that using them was some kind of veiled threat."

"Did you answer Argos's email?"

"I didn't know what to say. I tried talking to my father about it but he got agitated. He said . . ." Ian hesitates and I imagine that whatever his father told him about the labyrinth is not something he wants to repeat here. But that's not the reason he doesn't want to tell me. "He said that Elizabeth lost her way in the labyrinth and never came back."

"But she did," I say, my voice wobbling as if I didn't quite believe it. "Of course my mother came back. I wouldn't be here if she hadn't."

"I told him that. I thought he might have misremembered what happened, but he was adamant. *Elizabeth found the monster at the heart of the labyrinth,* he said, *and once you've seen the monster it's in you forever.*"

CHAPTER TWENTY

That's—" I begin.

"Awful, I know. I'm sorry. I didn't want to tell you. If you want to go back . . ." he says, looking toward the dim light of the doorway.

"No," I reply, "we'd just be in the same situation as before. We have to make sure no one is hiding here. If my mother found something here that made her lose her mind, I want to know what it is. If Argos didn't want your father—or mine—to talk about the labyrinth it must mean that he hid something here he didn't want anyone to know about. I'm tired of playing his game. I feel like my whole life has been a lie, that someone's been pulling the strings—" I hold up my twine-bound wrist to demonstrate and laugh. "I need to know the truth and I have a feeling it's down here."

"Okay," he says, aiming his flashlight down the long sloping corridor. "There's no one I'd rather go to hell with. And so you know—I grabbed this while I was gearing up." He withdraws a long dagger from his back jeans pocket. It gleams bronze in the light of our headlamps and I make out the word *NEMESIS* engraved on the blade.

"Argos's letter opener. Fitting. Remember how he would toy with it during our conferences?"

"I was always afraid he was going to hurl it at me for my crap prose. *Write like a man*, he once said, aiming the blade right at my jugular, *or you'll end up penning cozies like your father*. I guess he was right."

"I love those books," I say. "Especially these last couple. Pythagoras has become humbler and more fallible since he went into exile. I should have known you were writing them. I heard your voice when I was reading." I turn to Ian. "In the last one he finds out that the king has killed his queen because she had fallen in love with his trusted advisor. Was that in your father's original notes?"

"Some of it," Ian says. "Along with a plan of the labyrinth, my father had drawn a triangle. Of course, there were often triangles because of the Pythagorean theorem, but on this one he had written three names—the King, the Queen, the Consul—so I gathered he planned to write about a love triangle between those characters. Also . . ." He glances sideways at me. "I was thinking about the three of us—you, me, and Annika—and wondering how you got the idea that I'd wanted to be with Annika instead of you."

"I told you—I overheard you on the balcony—and I saw you kiss!"

"Yeah, I know, only . . . what do you remember about our last night on the island?"

"You mean before overhearing you and Annika? It's all a little blurry. We drank a lot at dinner. Argos got out his *private reserve*."

"That stuff! He called it *Artemisia absinthium*, 'the green nymph,' and hinted that in addition to the traditional wormwood, there was something a little extra in it. I think the little extra might have been opium."

"I wouldn't be surprised. I remember feeling quite euphoric."

I see us all on the terrace, gathered for our last night together. Argos dressed in a white linen tunic that made him look like a priest, Annika and myself in blue and white gauze dresses we'd bought in Skiathos. *The goddesses have alit,* Argos said when we came onto the terrace together. And then he'd looked over at Gena in her usual jeans and hoodie and said something . . .

"Do you remember what he said to Gena when we first came onto the terrace?" I ask.

"I wasn't paying attention to Gena," he says. "I was looking at you. You really did look like a goddess that night."

"I think that was the opium," I say, feeling the heat rise in my face. I close my eyes to summon the scene and watch Argos turn toward Gena, his lips twisting into a cruel sneer—

"*And so have their handmaids.* That's what he said to his own daughter. Poor Gena. She deflated like a punctured balloon. Then he told the story of Scylla, the daughter of King Nisus, who betrays her father to the invading King Minos."

"By cutting a purple lock of hair that gave him power," Ian adds. "Remember how Argos went on about the perfidy of women?"

"And how Minos was betrayed in turn by his daughter Ariadne, who helped Theseus slay the Minotaur? I remember wondering why he was going on about daughters betraying their fathers."

"I thought he might be talking about you," Ian says.

"Me? But I'm not—"

"Figuratively. You were his friend's daughter and his favorite of us. I wondered if he was afraid of you betraying him."

"But why—"

"I didn't know then, but when Annika told me about the antiquities looting, I thought he might have been afraid of you finding out. What did he say to you at your conference?"

I think back, remembering how very conscious of how drunk I was and afraid of making a fool of myself, but when he began by telling me how pleased he was with my progress over the summer, I relaxed. *You have bloomed in the Mediterranean sun like an asphodel.*

"He compared me to an asphodel and I'm afraid I might have giggled," I say. "It seemed funny that he chose that flower."

"Because it's associated with the underworld?"

"Because of the asphodel meadow where we . . . you know . . ."

"Ah," he says, smiling. "Did you think he had spied on us?"

"I think I believed he was all-seeing, like a god, because he said next . . ." I reach back in my memory for the exact words, picturing Argos in his white tunic, the lamplight catching his bald skull and the flash of that bronze knife in his hand, like a priest about to sacrifice the fatted calf. Me, in other words. "He put his hand on my manuscript and said: *I can see from this you have experienced loss, because of what happened to your mother, and I've watched you experience love this summer.* And then he said something very strange . . ."

I again think back to that night. I've relived the moment on my balcony overhearing Annika and Ian a thousand times, but the rest of the night has always been blurry, a result, no doubt, of the intoxicating qualities of Argos's *private reserve.* I remember, though, that when I'd heard Annika and Ian, I hadn't been entirely surprised. I'd even thought, Argos was right.

"He said, *You won't be a real writer until you've experienced the heartbreak of betrayal and I'm afraid that moment may come sooner than you expect. When it does, my dear, don't give into despair. I achieved my greatest accomplishments after experiencing the greatest betrayal. It is the thirst for revenge that will spur you on to the great work I know you have inside you."*

"What a load of crap!" Ian says.

"Do you think? When I saw you and Annika from the balcony, I thought that he'd been right. That he'd foreseen it."

"Maybe he'd done more than foresee it," Ian says. While we've been talking, we've been steadily looping down into the rock, accompanied by the throng of dead painted on the walls and the keen of the wind through the tunnels. Now a veiled priestess looks at me, her mouth open in a round O of surprise.

"What do you mean?" I ask.

"When you came out you were all lit up. You told me and Annika you needed to go to your room to write and you'd see us later, remember?"

"I remember that Olivia said something like *When the muse calls . . .* A little snarkily, I thought."

"Very snarkily," he says. "After you left and Argos had called Annika into the library for her conference, Olivia turned to me and said, *Better be careful, young man, or you'll end up playing Zelda to Maia's Scott.*"

"Ew. She must have been really drunk."

"She was knocking back shots of that private reserve like a sailor. I sat with her as first you, then Annika, and then Gena were called. *All the pretty young things,* she said. When Gena was called in, Olivia turned to Annika and said, *I'd love to be a fly on the wall for this one to know why he's so hard on her.* Then she winked and excused herself to *powder her nose.* Annika watched her go and then checked that Bill and Sydney weren't paying attention—they'd been huddled together on the edge of the terrace all night in some kind of bro drinking match—and then she put her finger to her mouth to signal to me to be quiet and scampered up the ladder to the roof above the library."

"Where we used to go stargazing," I say.

"And where you could overhear what people said in the library. Olivia had given her the idea to hear what Argos said to Gena. It must have been something awful because when Gena came out she looked like she'd been crying and ran into the kitchen."

"To find Eleni," I say.

"Probably. I remember feeling like I was watching a bedroom farce with all the comings and goings—maybe because I was pretty high by that time. Argos called me in next. I knew that Annika was still on the roof listening and I felt kind of embarrassed at first, but then I was glad that I had a witness to all the crap Argos said to me. He said some stuff about Annika, too, which I knew was going to piss her off."

"What stuff?" I ask, curious in spite of myself to know what Argos really thought about Annika.

"He predicted she'd be very successful but that her success would trap her into writing the same book over and over again just as Sisyphus was condemned to roll the same boulder up a hill for all eternity."

I feel like I've been trapped into writing the same book over and over again like that stupid guy with the rock.

"She said that Argos had been right. His words got under her skin."

"He was good at that," Ian says, wincing. "I hear that thing he said about me ending up writing cozies like my father every time I sit down at my desk. I was pretty blown away by the time I got out of there. I just wanted to get drunk and go find you—but when I came out onto the terrace Eleni and Gena were there. Apparently, Argos had asked to see Gena again and she was crying. I asked if everything was all right but she just glared at me like *I* had done something to her. She and Eleni went into the library—Bill and Sydney had gone off somewhere, to get high, I thought—and then Annika came down from the roof. She dragged me down the stairs and onto the balcony of the Muses' grotto and told me that Gena had accused Argos of selling looted antiquities and that your father was involved. Annika thought we should tell you—"

"And you said it would kill me."

"I can see why you thought we were talking about an affair."

"The part that made me think you were having an affair was when you kissed," I say.

He winces. "I don't even know how it happened—I swear it had never happened before! As soon as we stumbled into the grotto, we both pulled away. Annika even laughed. *This is exactly what Argos wants*, she said, *to tear us all apart*. We went back to the terrace. Annika wanted to talk to Gena, but we couldn't find her. Bill was back, waiting for Sydney to come out of his conference, and he said that Gena had stormed off somewhere. He thought she might have gone up on the ridge so we went up there but we couldn't find her. Then when I went back to my room, I found the note you left telling me you never wanted to see or talk to me again. When I went to your room you wouldn't talk to me and you left on the first boat in the morning without even saying good-bye. But Gena was on that boat with you, right? So she did leave the island."

"Yes," I say, recalling how awful she looked. "She was sick the whole way over—I thought because of drinking too much the night before, but she must have been devastated by her father disowning her. Maybe she went back to the island to confront Argos when the boat went back to take the rest of you to Volos. Did you see it dock?"

"No. Annika and I were looking all over for you and then Annika went into the library and had a big scene with Argos, demanding to know what he'd said to you that made you leave so suddenly. Then she told me to get ready so we could get to the train station and catch up with you—but Argos told the captain to wait until after lunch to take the next *load* over. If Gena came back, I didn't see her."

"Maybe she did take the train to Athens and . . . disappear. If my own father had disowned me like that, I'd be destroyed." I remember when I came home from Greece, heartbroken and angry, I thought my father would gloat and tell me that he'd been right. Instead, he'd made me cups of tea and covered me with afghans when I fell asleep on the couch and generally treated me like an invalid, until he had his stroke and it was my turn to take care of him.

"Argos wasn't anything like your father," Ian says, as if reading my thoughts. "He was a manipulative bastard. I think he *knew* Annika was listening on the roof and he said those things to get under her skin—to *provoke* her. He knew she'd have to tell someone about what she'd heard and it wouldn't be you because you'd gone to your room."

"Argos couldn't have known she'd tell you on the balcony beneath my window," I say. "But he had planted the idea that I was going to be betrayed. And he told me that he thought Annika would be successful, too, only without the part about her being cursed to repeat herself. He said I mustn't mind too much if she eclipsed me—*stars that shine the brightest burn out soonest*, he said—which I guess wasn't very nice to her, but at the time I just thought about her being a bright star and me being a dim one—"

I find suddenly that my vision is blurry and I have to stop and lean against the wall. "Are you all right?" Ian asks.

"I was such an idiot!" I wail, adding my voice to the multitude in the labyrinth. "I let Argos poison me against both of you. He manipulated me—and all of us. It's exactly what my father said about him—*Argos likes to play games with human beings as his chess pieces*. And he's still doing it. He's got us wandering this labyrinth like rats in a maze."

I look around at the faces painted on the walls—the rolling eyes and mouths open in terror. "There's something about this mystery rite that's not . . . *right*. The initiates are supposed to be led toward knowledge. These poor women look like cattle being herded to the slaughter—and do you notice they're only women? Have you ever heard of a mystery rite with only female initiates? And where are the initiates coming back from the great revelation?" I sweep my flashlight over the walls on both sides but find only one-way traffic going down into the depths and feel a prickling of unease. "How do they come back?" I whisper, as if I'm afraid of being overheard. "If this is the road to hell it's supposed to be easy—and it is. We haven't had to choose between different paths, it's all been one loop down. But then what's to stop us from just turning around and heading back the other way?"

Ian turns in a slow circle, shining his flashlight on the faces of the—*initiates*? I'm no longer sure that's what they are. They're beginning to look more like—

"They're not initiates," he says. "They're sacrifices. That's why they don't come back."

He walks a few steps forward toward the woman with the surprised look on her face. As I watch him, a long desperate shriek splits the air like a warning. *It's just the wind*, I tell myself, but then I notice something. The sound seems to be coming from below us, as if there is a deep cavity just beyond where Ian is walking.

"Ian," I call, "be careful—"

But my words are drowned out by a deeper shriek as Ian vanishes before my eyes.

CHAPTER TWENTY-ONE

an!"

I scream out his name and rush forward, the cries of the labyrinth echoing mine until Ian's voice cuts through them all.

"Stop! Don't come any closer—there's a pit."

I manage to skid to a halt, sand and gravel sliding under my feet. I drop to my knees and shine my flashlight over the ground until there's no more ground to see.

"Are you okay?" I call, inching forward carefully on my hands and knees to the lip of a deep pit. I shine my flashlight down and find Ian's bloodstained face, terrible as the painted faces of the damned, looking up at me.

"Just some scrapes and bruises," he says, with a lightness belied by a wince of pain as he tries to stand. "And I may have sprained my ankle. Shine your flashlight on the ground so I can find my flashlight and rope."

"Good thing you brought the rope," I say, trying to keep the panic out of my voice—and head. The air I felt just before Ian fell is still stirring restlessly around me. It feels like dozens of icy fingers plucking at my clothes, grazing my skin. I can feel the frightened eyes of all the painted figures—*sacrificial lambs being led to slaughter*—watching us. Ian finds his flashlight and scans the bottom of the pit until he spots the coil of rope.

"Yeah, good thing," he says, picking up the rope with difficulty and grimacing with pain. His right arm is hanging at an odd angle. "I think I may have dislocated my shoulder as well."

He aims his flashlight at me and I'm blinded for a moment.

"Sorry," he says, moving the beam along the edge of the pit. I can see now that it spans almost the whole width of the passage, leaving only a narrow, foot-wide ledge on the left-hand side, and extends a good ten feet to the far side, which is lower than the side closer to me. It's too wide to jump across.

I look back down at Ian and see that he's trying to swing his injured arm. "I'm afraid my cricket days might be over," he jokes, switching the rope to his left hand. He makes an experimental toss but the rope falls several feet short of the top.

"I think the other side isn't as high," I say, "and there's that mound of dirt that you could stand on. I think there's enough room for me to walk across if I stay close to the wall—"

"Absolutely not," he says. "It's not safe. If you fall in here, you could hurt yourself badly—worse than I have—and then who's going to come save us?"

"Annika," I say, holding up my wrist with its twine bracelet. The thought of Annika on the other side of the twine gives me a little burst of confidence. "Besides, if we get you back up on this side we've still got to get across."

"I'm not sure we should keep going. There could be more cave-ins like this one—or worse ones. This looks like it was dug deliberately. I'm lucky there weren't sharpened stakes in here—oh, shit—"

"What?" I shine my flashlight down into the pit to see what

new hazard he's found. He's crouched by the mound of dirt on the far side, brushing loose soil away from something that gleams white in the beam of my flashlight. A toppled statue, perhaps, or—

The dirt slides away, revealing a skull.

"One of the sacrifices," I say, looking up at the painted faces on the wall. The keening in the tunnel swells as if they are mourning one of their own.

"I've been thinking about that," Ian says.

He sounds so much like the classics nerd I met—and fell in love with—fifteen years ago that I nearly laugh at the incongruity. Here he is trapped in a subterranean pit with a skeleton and he's theorizing while excavating. He's kneeling in front of the dirt mound, gently brushing soil away from the bones.

"I think our first theory that this was the site of a mystery rite is off. Think about the original labyrinth of Crete. What do we know about it?"

"Okay, Detective Pythagoras," I say, humoring him. He's clearly trying to keep me from panicking—a technique my father often used when I woke up from a nightmare in the middle of the night—and from trying to get across to the other side. "King Minos had the brilliant craftsman Daedalus construct the labyrinth to house the Minotaur."

"Who was?" he prompts.

Clearly I'm not going to be allowed to give the SparkNotes version of the myth.

"The son of his wife Pasiphaä, who conceived an unnatural passion for a bull as punishment for King Minos reneging on a sacrifice to Poseidon—notice how it's always the women made to pay for the sins of their menfolk." I go on to recount how in order to feed the Minotaur, Minos exacted a tribute from Athens of ten young women and ten young men who would be sent into the labyrinth to meet their doom.

I pause there. It's not a very nice story to recount down here in the dark. I look up at the painted figures on the wall and feel their panic and hear in the wind both the bellow of the Minotaur and the death cries of its victims. I look closer at the women and girls huddled together and notice for the first time that their ankles are shackled.

"They're slaves," I say.

"I think so," Ian agrees. "Remember what you said to me on the boat the first time we sailed to the island?"

"That we were entering the land of myth?"

"Yes, and that we were traveling the route the Greeks took to Troy—"

"And the route they took back, bearing the plunder of war—the gold of Troy and its women who were taken as slaves. But these paintings can't be that old," I say uncertainly, although an electric prickling along my skin suggests otherwise. *You can feel it*, my father once said to me, *when you're in the presence of great antiquity*.

"Maybe not," Ian says. "We'd have to test the paint. But they've been preserved by being underground—think of the murals at Knossos. Those date from the thirteenth century BCE, around the time of the Trojan War. But even if these aren't that old, the rite might be. The memory of the slaves brought here and sacrificed could have lasted for centuries."

"It's too awful," I say.

"Yes," he agrees, "and so is this."

I look down, aiming my flashlight at him. He's holding up something in his hand that glints gold in the light. "Is it—"

"A gold bracelet with a blue *mati* and the initial *I*—"

"For Iphigenia," I say, feeling the air sucked out of me. It's one thing to ponder the sacrifice of three-thousand-year-old victims; it's another to picture shy, awkward Gena lying here in this god-forsaken pit. "Poor Eleni."

"She thought she was here."

"But I saw Gena on the boat—and her suitcase was found in Athens . . ."

"Maybe someone wanted it to look like she left and made it to Athens. At least now Eleni will know what happened to her and she'll be able to bury her."

"It's just too awful to think of her lying here all these years . . ." *While we went on living oblivious to what happened to her.* "What do you think she was doing down here?"

"Looking for something, I would guess. Proof that Argos was selling looted antiquities. There's a camera here as well. If the film's still good, we can get it developed."

"Do you think she fell and then was just stuck here?" It's horrible to think of Gena all alone down here in the dark while we were all right above her, playing out our little dramas.

"No," Ian says, "she didn't just fall." He holds up something else that glints with a dull metallic gleam. It takes me only a second to realize it's a bullet.

"She was shot?" As terrible as the alternative is—Gena slowly dying in the pit—the solid fact of the bullet induces a new tremor of fear. Someone followed Gena down here and shot her in cold blood, left her body, and then took her suitcase to Athens to make it look like she had left the island and died on the streets. The pure evil of it makes my skin itch.

"She came down here looking for proof that Argos was trading in antiquities," I say, getting to my feet. "We have to find what she was looking for."

"What are you doing?"

"I'm going across. It's low enough on the other side for you to toss the rope and it will be easier to get you up on that side. There's plenty of room here for me to cross."

I brace one hand on the wall for balance and slide one foot onto the narrow ledge, testing its stability. It holds, so I slide my other foot forward.

"I wish you wouldn't, Maia."

"If wishes were horses . . ." I say, walking heel to toe as if on a balance beam.

"There's something else here," Ian says.

"Don't distract me," I tell him. My next step causes a mini avalanche of dirt that sifts down to the pit. I halt for a moment to catch my balance, frozen halfway across the pit.

"Shit," Ian says.

"It's okay, just a little landslide. The rest of the way looks stable."

"I think I know who shot Gena," he says.

My next step loosens a cascade of dirt and rubble. I leap across the rest of the way, landing on the other side in a crouch, my heart pounding. "What?" I gasp. "How do you know?"

"There's something here—a silver cuff link, just like the ones that pretentious ass Sydney wore, and it even has his initials—"

"Thank you," a voice comes from behind me. "I wondered what happened to that."

I turn around to find Sydney Norton, very much alive and aiming a gun at my head.

CHAPTER TWENTY-TWO

I feel like Odysseus running into his helmsman Palinurus in the underworld, only then the shock had been that Palinurus was dead. For a moment I consider the possibility that we really are in the underworld and Sydney *is* dead—a ghost with a Classical Society tote bag hanging from his shoulder. Then he takes a step forward and presses the steel muzzle of the gun against my forehead and the burning cold of it convinces me he's no ghost. But how?

"I saw you drown," I say accusingly.

"Did you?" he asks. "I think you saw what you wanted to see—poor Sydney thrashing around like he couldn't swim. Did you like my classical callout? Of course I'd gotten the reference right away and thought it added a piquant touch to my supposed panic. I didn't think Ian would try to knock me out, though." He rubs a bruise on his forehead and aims his voice toward the pit. "That's quite a right hook you have on you, man. I nearly did drown after that."

"You were going to take Maia down with you," Ian shouts up. "If you'd like to get even, give me a hand up. I'll be happy to give you a fair fight on dry land."

"I've always preferred using my brains to my fists," Sydney replies. "Besides, the gun rather makes a fistfight superfluous." He takes a step toward the edge of the pit but I block his way, afraid he means to shoot Ian.

"How did you survive in the water?" I ask, guessing that Sydney will enjoy bragging.

"I swam to the grotto, of course. What? You think you and Annika were the only ones to explore the grotto last time? I know it quite well—better than you, in fact. It was easy to make it look like I'd drowned and swim underwater through its mouth."

"And you've been hiding on the island ever since?" I ask.

He laughs. "Don't be ridiculous. I had a boat in there. I took it to the mainland for supplies and then came back to see how you were all faring."

"And how did you have a boat there—"

"He's been helping Argos in his illegal trading," Ian says.

"Bingo," Sydney says.

"Since when?"

"Since we were all here together fifteen years ago. At my final conference, Argos offered me a way of *subsidizing* my career."

"But why? You're a respected writer."

He laughs. "Do you know what even the best journals pay for my work? Practically nothing. There are barely any outlets left for serious criticism. And I wasn't willing to put out commercial dreck like you lot."

"Selling looted art is better?"

He shrugs. "Why shouldn't the discerning have access to beautiful things? Haven't you enjoyed the choice pieces Argos gave your father for your little museum? Oh yes, I know all about the deal your father had with Argos, so don't play all high and mighty with me. Argos offered me a way to make a good living without compromising my aesthetic ideals. We'd come to a mutually beneficial arrangement before that hysterical girl tried to ruin it."

"You followed Gena in here and shot her," Ian says. "Did Argos know you killed his daughter?"

"I didn't know she was his daughter until after. He'd asked me to escort her off the island, but she made a fuss and got into the labyrinth, so . . ." He waves his gun toward the pit as if shooting Gena was a minor detail he'd had to take care of. "And then I did take her off the island, in a manner of speaking."

"It was you on the boat!" I say, recalling the slight figure in a hoodie and sunglasses, hair covered by a bandanna, being sick down below—just as Sydney was sick on the yacht coming over this time. "You pretended to be Gena so everyone would think she had left. But the suitcase . . ."

"I stowed it at the train station and then hid on the boat going back to the island. I left the island later that day as myself."

"Still sick, as I recall," I hear Ian mutter down below.

"I retrieved Gena's suitcase and took it to Athens, where I abandoned it at a dodgy hotel near the train station along with some drug paraphernalia. It was really quite entertaining! I felt like a character in a Patricia Highsmith novel. That's when I realized that I much preferred *living* a mystery to writing one."

"As if you could write one," Ian mutters again. "It sounds like a lame excuse not to write."

A muscle twitches on Sydney's face and I see that Ian's barbs have hit a nerve. But why is he trying to antagonize a man with a gun? As Sydney steps closer to the edge of the pit, leaning forward to wave the gun at Ian, I guess why. It wouldn't take much to push Sydney into the pit. I edge closer—and Sydney rears back and aims the gun at me. "Not so fast, dollface."

I start to laugh at the comically hard-boiled language but a swift stinging cuff to my forehead with the gun kills the impulse. I cry out instead and fall to my knees.

"Maia, are you okay?" Ian calls. "Did he hurt you?"

"I'm fine," I say, wiping a sticky trickle of blood away from my eyes. "For a critic Sydney doesn't take criticism very well."

"None of this is my doing," Sydney rails. "I didn't kill Argos. I got an invitation just like the rest of you. When I tried to reach Argos, he didn't respond."

"You must have been worried he was cutting you out of your lucrative illegal trading," Ian says.

"I was worried," he says, "that he might be bringing in someone else—like you, Maia. When I saw your friend Annika posting all over social media, tagging you two, I thought Argos might have lost his mind and recruited you three. I had to come check it out. When I found out Argos was dead, I realized I had to get off the island. I wasn't going to end up part of some Golden Age mystery plot."

"You saw an opportunity, didn't you?" Ian says. "To steal the antiquities for yourself."

"Why not?" he asks, shrugging. "I've put a lot of work into the operation for a measly cut. I was just going to come back with a bigger boat and clear out the inventory, but then you three had to go exploring in the grotto, forcing us to come up with a plausible scenario for all of your deaths."

I feel a chill not just at his casual reference to our impending deaths but at the plural pronoun. "Us?" I repeat.

"I may have the brains to plan this on my own, but do you think I could manage the logistics without some help? That's flattering, but not very practical. Bill isn't very bright—and his books are abominable—but at least he knows his place and how to follow orders."

"He destroyed the phone and radio the first night," I hear Ian say from the pit. "And he killed Olivia, didn't he?"

"He did that on his own," Sydney says. "I told Bill to make sure that there wasn't anything in the library that could link us to the antiquities smuggling, but she found a folder with details of our operation in Geneva—"

"Which made her suspicious of Bill when he said he'd been in Geneva," I say.

"Exactly. It wasn't difficult to help her along with an overdose of her own Xanax. By now he's subdued Annika and Eleni."

He looks down at the twine around my wrist and gives it a good yank. It falls loosely to the ground. "You might want to wind that up so you don't trip over it."

I do as he says, somehow hoping that Annika will appear at the end of the thread, but all I find is a drop of blood staining the twine, which I stick into my pocket. "What has he done to them?" I demand.

"Nothing much yet." Sydney pulls a bulky phone out of his canvas bag. "I haven't gotten a recent update since there's no reception down here, but the last time we talked, he was sticking to the plan."

"And what is the plan?" I ask, enraged on top of everything else that duplicitous Bill has had a phone all along.

"I'll fill you in along the way," he says, motioning with his gun for me to precede him down the sloping path. I don't move. Once

I move Ian will be an easy target. He must guess the reason for my hesitation.

"Don't worry, I'm not going to shoot your boyfriend right now. Too risky getting close to the edge of that nasty pit with you ready to push me in. Do you hear that, Ian?" he shouts down into the pit. "Your girlfriend has earned you a stay of execution. You may curse her for it later if I decide to leave you here to die slowly in the dark."

"Don't you dare hurt her," Ian growls.

"Or what? You'll devise some fiendish geometrical demise for me? Oh yes, Bill told me the big secret that you've been writing your father's books for him. I thought I'd detected a change of style. Frankly, I liked your father's work better. You've made Pythagoras too chatty—speaking of which, time to end this little expositional interlude. Maia and I have someplace to be." He nudges me with the muzzle of the gun.

"I'll be back for you," I tell Ian. I think of all the time I've wasted these last fifteen years. What can I possibly say to make up for that lost time?

He must be thinking the same thing. "I'll be here waiting for you," he says.

CHAPTER TWENTY-THREE

We walk in silence for a few moments, giving me some much-needed time to sort through all the revelations of the last few minutes. I picture Sydney in his disguise of hoodie, bandanna, and sunglasses and berate myself for not recognizing him—but then I'd barely paid attention to Gena or Sydney that summer, so enthralled had I been with Ian and Annika and the book I was writing. Gena and Sydney—and Bill and Olivia and Eleni—had been bit players in my personal drama. That last morning, after overhearing Annika and Ian on the balcony, I was especially sunk in my own pity party. I was already sitting on the dock waiting for the boat by sunrise. Gena—or, rather, Sydney dressed as Gena—had slouched onto the boat at the last minute before we left and immediately gone down below as if she—*he*—knew they were going to be sick. Yet on the boat trip to the island, Gena hadn't been sick at all. If I'd thought about that I might have gone down to check on her. And if I'd done that, I might have at least uncovered Sydney's disguise. Instead, I sulked behind my sunglasses, hiding bloodshot eyes, and spent the voyage staring moodily out to sea, as disenchanted with the landscape as one of those Trojan women carried away from their homeland.

I glance at the painted figures on the wall and notice that

there's been a change in their demeanor. The women no longer roll their eyes and thrash their arms and open their mouths to cry out their misfortune. Instead they bow their heads and gaze downward as if they have become resigned to their fate. I refuse to go as docilely to mine.

But what can I do or say? Sydney has shown no sign of remorse for killing Gena; the only taunt that reached him was when Ian impugned his ability to write a novel. Perhaps I can appeal to his intellectual vanity.

"Haven't you ever thought about what you're keeping from the world here?" I ask. "Think of the prestige that would come to the person, the scholar, who discovered this and wrote about it."

"Argos didn't want his private island turned into a theme park. Have you been to Pompeii or the Acropolis lately? Mobbed by tourists with their selfie sticks, passing through on their way to the gift shop. Can you see these faces on a refrigerator magnet?"

We've reached an arched doorway, framed by two draped and veiled figures. I peer closer and see that the faces behind the veil are skeletal. What *is* this place? My mind reels with all the possible interpretations—mystery rite, death cult, orgiastic brotherhood—a labyrinth of choices to explore. Although up until now there have been no choices—just one downward spiral. But when I step through the arched door all that changes.

We're in a huge round chamber with a high vaulted ceiling, so high that when I shine my flashlight upward the beam dissolves into the dark as if swallowed by it. When I track my beam around the circumference of the chamber, I find more veiled statues standing sentinel between archways, each one a vessel of darkness. I count twelve—thirteen including the door we came through.

"What is this place?" I ask.

"Argos called it the omphalos, that's—"

"The naval of the world," I quickly supply, damned if I'm going to let Sydney Norton mansplain Greek cosmology to me. "And the Greeks thought the omphalos was in Delphi."

"Not these Greeks apparently," Sydney says smugly. "But we don't have time for that. I didn't bring you here to chat about mythology, although I do need your expertise."

"For what?" I ask eagerly. If Sydney needs something from me, maybe I have some bargaining power.

Sydney swings his flashlight around the chamber, pausing on each archway. The light, though, doesn't penetrate the dark inside those arches at all. "Each one of these leads to a maze. This is where the real labyrinth begins. I've tried going into them but they're impossible to navigate—there are so many branching paths; the tunnels go on for miles and some of them have been blocked by cave-ins. You could get lost in there forever."

I steal a glance at Sydney and see that look on his face again, the same one he got when Ian taunted him for not being able to write a novel—pique at being bested, humiliated at the failure of his intellect. I remember my father paraphrasing Socrates—*the wise man knows he knows nothing*—but Sydney is rendered helpless and pissed off in the face of his limitations.

"What are you looking for in there?" I ask. "Don't you have enough looted art?"

"Argos told me there was something hidden down here. It was the most valuable find but he told me I would never be able to find it. I think he enjoyed telling me that because he knew I would try. There was only one person who had been able to find it but it had driven her mad."

I feel a prickling on the back of my neck. Before I can ask who he means, he takes an envelope out of his shirt breast pocket and from it, a photograph. When I look down, I see a picture I think I've seen before. It's a portrait of a dark-haired, dark-eyed woman arrayed in spectacular golden jewelry—a braided headdress circles her brow and then hangs down in a gold cascade on either side of her face, joined by long tasseled earrings. A heavy breastplate worked in an intricate pattern lies on her chest beneath her crossed hands, which are stacked with gold rings and bracelets. She is practically *armored* in gold. I realize where I've seen something like it before—it looks just like the famous photograph of Sofia Schliemann, wife of the archeologist who discovered Troy (and an archeologist in her own right). He had audaciously photographed her in the gold jewelry they had excavated at Troy—the so-called Treasure of Priam—after smuggling it out of Turkey. But this isn't Sofia Schliemann. I look closer and recognize my mother's face.

"How do you have this?" I demand, furious that Sydney had anything to do with my mother.

"I saw it on Argos's desk once and when I asked about it, he said it was your mother. He told me that she had found the treasure— *the lost gold of Troy,* he called it—and willingly posed in it. But then she'd gone nuts and said it was cursed and had to be returned to the labyrinth. When I asked Argos why he hadn't gone look-ing for it he told me he believed that it *was* cursed. *Look at what happened to poor Elizabeth,* he said, *it drove her mad and she took her own life. Besides, I don't think anyone but a madwoman could find it. Sometimes it takes the disordered mind of an artist to make sense of the irrational.* There's a letter from your father, too"—he holds up the envelope—"that goes into more detail. I'll be happy to show it to you once you've located the gold." He puts the enve-lope back in his breast pocket and pats it.

"What do you mean?" I ask. "Why do you think I can find it?"

"Argos believed that your mother had instilled in you her madness and had taught you the path of the labyrinth. So somewhere in there"—he taps the side of my forehead with the muzzle of the gun—"is the treasure map to where the gold is hidden. I'll give you ten minutes to think about where it is before I shoot you."

"That's absurd," I say. "My mother never spoke of this place. And even if she had, I was only nine when she died. Do you think she drew me a map and I memorized it?"

"I think you remember everything about your mother. Don't forget, I read your book, *The Professor's Daughter*. It should have been called *The Madwoman's Daughter*."

I take a step forward, aiming to smack the supercilious look off his face, until he aims the gun at me. "Easy, Maia, don't be so sensitive. It was my favorite part of the book. *I followed my mother's ravings as if they were a road map through her tortured mind that would lead us both out into the light.* That's all I want you to do now."

As disconcerting as it is to hear myself quoted by a gun-wielding critic, the line sparks something in me. It takes me back to those nights my mother would come into my room and lie beside me in my bed, telling me stories about the constellations—

"Turn off your flashlight," I say.

"So you can rush me in the dark?" he asks incredulously.

"Just do it if you want me to find the treasure."

He glares at me stubbornly for a moment but when I don't back down, he lets out an exaggerated sigh and thumbs off his flashlight. We're plunged into darkness. This *would* be a good time to rush him, I think, but then I feel the cold sting of the gun at my temple and give up that idea. Instead, I look up and wait—

As I would when my mother turned off my bedside lamp, a

moment I always dreaded because it meant she would soon be gone and I would be alone in the dark. *Whenever you're afraid of the dark*, she would say, *just wait. There's always a glimmer of light even in our darkest moments.*

And then, as if by magic, as if she had summoned them, the stars she had painted on my ceiling would appear.

As they do now. Pinpricks of light emerge far above us on the domed ceiling. Beside me, Sydney gasps. "How'd you know—?"

"Shut up," I say, tired of his voice. I'm listening now to my mother's.

Do you see Orion? You can always start with Orion's Belt because it's the easiest constellation to spot in the sky.

The three stars of Orion's Belt emerge out of the dark as if summoned by my mother's voice. The stars are painted on the domed ceiling in luminescent paint. *There he is*, my mother whispers in my ear, *aiming his bow and arrow at Taurus, and just beyond Taurus is Aries, the ram, and Cygnus, the swan. Zeus, come as a swan to ravish Leda, and there's Delphinus carrying Amphitrite to Poseidon, leaping through the current of the Milky Way, riding it past Ara, the altar, and Chiron, the centaur, who holds a slain beast to sacrifice upon it. Virgo, the maiden, whom some believe is Persephone, the stolen daughter, stands above him, and the Great Bear runs to hide in the dark from Orion.*

My mother's voice carries me all around the domed ceiling, which is painted just as she had painted my childhood bedroom's ceiling. She must have gotten the idea here, but why would she want to re-create this place where, according to Argos, she had lost her mind? Had she been trying to make sense of it? I wonder as I stare up at the three bright stars of Orion's Belt, *the easiest constellation to spot in the sky.*

That's so his prey can see him.

A chill goes through me as I recall her words, words so strange I'd tried to block them out all these years. But now it's as if she's standing beside me in the dark, whispering the old stories to me, her breath acrid as spent matches.

There are the Pleiades running from Orion. He pursued them so relentlessly that they had to become stars and yet still he pursues them across the night sky. No matter how they run they always come round in a circle. Just as Europa is carried away by the bull and Amphitrite was carried away by the dolphin and Helle rode the ram over the Hellespont.

They were all women who were pursued and abducted by the gods.

Raped by the gods.

There's Zeus in the shape of a swan come to ravish Leda. There's Callisto, who became a bear after she was raped by Zeus. The sky is full of predators and their victims and the creatures who carried them off at the gods' bidding. That's what my mother saw when she looked up and that's what she painted on my ceiling, as if she was trying to warn me. And yet I've ended up here anyway.

I follow the stars around and around the ceiling until I feel as if the room is spinning, looking for a story that is not about chase and deception. My eyes come to rest at last on the four stars of Ara, the altar. They're painted just above the archway directly across from the one we came through. *This is where Peleus and Thetis were married,* I hear my mother saying, her voice coming to me on a sulfurous breath that seems to be wafting from the open archway. *That's where it all started.*

Later, when I was older and had listened to my father's lecture on the Wedding Vase a dozen times, I thought she had been talking about the cause of the Trojan War—Eris tossing that apple into the party, which led to the fight between the goddesses, and Aphrodite giving Helen to Paris, so that the Greeks had to sail to Troy to get her back, and Agamemnon had to sacrifice his own daughter to gain a favorable wind for the ships, and then Clytemnestra slaughtered him when he came home, and her son Orestes had to kill her in turn, et cetera, et cetera, all the way down a chain of disaster like some horrible cosmic Rube Goldberg machine. Now I wonder if she'd been trying to understand what happened to her in the labyrinth that unhinged her mind. To trace back her madness to its root cause. I walk toward the open doorway below the constellation of the altar. There's definitely a reek of sulfur coming from there. Are there vents under the floor as there are underneath the altar at Delphi, where the oracle was said to have sat above a crack in the earth that leaked intoxicating fumes?

Is that what had driven my mother mad—a bad trip on ancient psychedelics?

That's where it all started, my mother's voice tells me.

If I follow my mother's voice into this place, will it drive me mad, too?

"Is this it?" Sydney hisses. I'd almost forgotten he's here. "Because I don't think that can be the right way. I tried it once and it just went around in circles."

There's an edge in his voice I haven't heard before. Something about this path in the labyrinth scares him. *Good. Let's see who bolts first.*

"This is the way," I tell him with absolute certainty. "Follow me."

CHAPTER TWENTY-FOUR

Sydney wants to turn on his flashlight but I tell him no; I need to be able to see the luminescent markings on the walls and ceilings. In the dark, the glowing paint makes the narrow passage look like a crime scene that's been dusted by luminol. I suppose it is a crime scene. Women were taken from their homes and raped and made slaves, an ancient form of trafficking.

Don't you find all these stories triggering, Jenner once asked me after I told her the story of Daphne and Apollo, *with the gods always chasing and raping women?*

The question shouldn't have surprised me. In recent years there's been more attention to the way ancient depictions of sexual assault in classical art are handled in the classroom. I've even attended a few seminars on the subject at classics conferences that argue that ignoring the context of that art normalizes violence against women. But the answer that spilled out of my mouth was the one my father had always given—that the stories of the gods pursuing women and having sex with them was an expression of the union between the mortal and the divine. It had made me sound like an apologist for a sexual predator. Now, walking in this place where women were brought as slaves to be sacrificed, the horror of those stories is made real. The women, outlined in lu-

minescent paint, have become a ghostly procession. Their names
are tattooed on their arms—Briseis, Cassandra, Andromache—
the women of Troy taken by their conquerors as slaves. Among
them are the women taken by the gods—Persephone, carrying the
pomegranate that seals her half-year servitude in the underworld;
Europa, riding her bull; Amphitrite on her dolphin; Leda with her
swan. The constellations they became glimmer above us on the
vaulted ceiling. When we come to the first turning and two archways, I stop and study those stars. How am I supposed to know
which stars mark the right path? I look back and forth between
the two arches for so long that Sydney gets agitated.

"Which one?" he demands, jamming the gun into my ribs, as if
that will help me concentrate.

Above one of the arches I spot the familiar stars of Orion—*the
easiest ones to spot*, my mother said. Does that mean it's the right
way to go? But then I hear her voice saying, *That's so his prey can
see him.*

No, I think, that can't be the way.

I look at the stars painted over the other arch—seven stars in
a familiar pattern. Of course it's familiar; it's the star pattern on
my mother's ring, which my father gave me—the Seven Sisters
pursued so relentlessly by Orion that Zeus took pity on them and
turned them into stars. *And yet still he pursues them*, I hear my
mother's voice saying.

"This way," I say, choosing the path of the Pleiades.

Sydney follows me, relentless as Orion. "How can you tell?" he
asks.

"It's the women painted on the walls," I say, not wanting to
give away the star code to him. "See, here's Cassandra"—I pick
a slave woman at random, standing beside an archway marked

with the Pleiades—"the prophet who foresees the Trojan War and her own death just as she shows us the right path to take." I go on, spinning mythological nonsense out of thin air at each turning. "Here's Ariadne with her ball of thread to point the way." The figure I indicate is actually Persephone holding a pomegranate but I don't give Sydney long enough to study her too closely. Besides, all the figures are beginning to look a little blurry, the effect, I suspect, of the fumes wafting up through the cracks in the stone floor. I am beginning to feel lightheaded and the figures as we pass them seem to stir at our progress, their drapery rustling with a soft susurration as of women whispering.

Perhaps they *are* whispering, passing on the news of our arrival from one to the other. *Hurry,* I think I can hear them say, *flee the hunter as we did, and perhaps some god will take pity on you and transform you into a tree, a spring, or a star.*

Is that the only way to escape, I'd like to ask them, *to change into something else?* I think of my mother, both the smiling girl in the group portrait we found and the haunted woman I grew up with. What happened to her that caused that change? And why did she paint those stars on my ceiling and teach me a map to find my way through these passages?

If in fact she had.

As we go deeper and deeper into the maze, turning again and again, I wonder what will happen if I don't find the gold treasure. Will Sydney lose patience and shoot me? Even if I do find the treasure, won't he do that anyway?

Hurry! Flee! the women urge me on. *Stay one step ahead of the hunter, that's all any of us can do.*

Their whispering has become louder and more urgent.

"What's that sound?" Sydney asks.

I turn around to ask him if he can hear the women, too, but the words die in my throat when I see him. He's become one of the labyrinth's ghosts, shimmering with the same eerie ectoplasm as the figures on the walls. His eyes are wide dark pits in his sickly green face. He looks like the corroded bronze Gorgon mask up in the villa. He looks equally horrified at my face. *"You!"* he says. "You're on fire!"

I hold my hand up and see that my skin is indeed kindling a yellowish green. I think of Argos's green nymph when he gave us his *private reserve*. Is that what we've become? Then I look up at the ceiling and feel something touching my face, soft as a powder puff. "It's the phosphorescent paint," I tell Sydney with more confidence than I feel. "It's sifting down from the ceiling and sticking to our skin."

"And that sound?"

I listen more closely to what I'd taken for women whispering and realize that it's the sound of water. "There must be an underground spring," I say. "I think that's where we're heading. Come on," I say, as if he's become my companion instead of my captor. Maybe, I think as I take the next turn, not even bothering to give Sydney any explanation for my choice, I can turn him into something else rather than having to change myself.

We take three more turns, the sound of water becoming louder, until we reach a wider arch. There's just one; no choice here, this is the only way. Whatever my mother was leading me to lies beyond that arch. Is it the thing that had made her lose her mind? Maybe I've already followed her into madness. I've inhaled the subterranean fumes and absorbed the phosphorescent paint through my skin into my bloodstream.

But if this is madness, I think, as I step through the arch, yet there is method in it.

Or, as Argos said, *Sometimes it takes the disordered mind of an artist to make sense of the irrational.*

Somehow, I've gotten us here.

I step through the arch into a round chamber so full of aqueous light that I feel as if I have plunged underwater. There is a pool of green water at the center, ringed by verdigris-tinted women, their scaled hands linked, slick viridescent skin glowing, mossy pointy teeth bared as if they're about to feast on their prey. Perhaps Sydney and I are their main course. I walk toward the first green-tinged woman and touch one of her webbed fingers. *Marble,* I tell myself, *covered in some kind of bioluminescent algae.* When I raise my gaze to her face, though, I feel as if I am looking into the eyes of an ancient being who's been turned to stone, its cells replaced one by one with microscopic ectoplasm secreted like a shell around its core, where the creature still lives, looking out at me from across the millennia.

For a moment I see my mother's eyes gazing back at me, steady and calm.

But then I blink and I'm looking at marble and stone. The eyes are inset with agate and she wears a gold crown with her name etched into it. *Thetis*, the sea nymph given to the mortal Peleus. I look around at the circle of statues that ring the pool. One wears a cape of swan feathers, another has the horns of a bull—Leda and Europa. One wears a bearskin and another holds a pomegranate—Callisto and Persephone. I count seven with stars on their foreheads—the Pleiades. All of them are women who were pursued or taken by the gods, or, in Thetis's case, given by the gods to a mortal man, and all of them are adorned with gold jewelry.

Behind me I hear Sydney chirping away: "This is it! This is it! This is the gold treasure. They're wearing it!"

I turn and see him flitting from statue to statue, stripping them of their earrings and rings, diadems and breastplates, stashing them in his canvas tote. All the jewelry my mother wore in that photograph. She brought it all back here. Why? Did she really think the gold was cursed?

I turn in a circle, looking at each of the strange statues. I've never seen anything quite like them. They are each recognizable as a figure from mythology, but they are in some intermediary state of metamorphosis, as if they have taken on the qualities of their captor. Standing at the head of the spring is a regal woman bigger than all of them, who holds an upraised dagger in her left hand. I wipe the green algae from it, noticing that it's loose in her hand, and read the word inscribed on it.

NEMESIS.

"What are you doing here?" I ask her.

"Never mind that one," Sydney says, busily gathering up the gold from the statues—so busy, I notice, that he's stuck his gun in his pants pocket. "She doesn't have anything valuable on her."

No, she's not wearing any jewelry, nor does she seem to fit with the rest of the statues. She's not a slave or a victim—

Although, I suddenly recall, there is one myth about Nemesis, a less common tradition, that she, not Leda, was raped by Zeus as a swan and gave birth to Helen. I look at her more closely and notice that she *is* wearing one piece of jewelry—a small gold earring hanging from her right ear. I slide it off and wipe the green algae

from it to see the design inscribed on it. Seven stars. It's identical
to the ring I wear, which my father told me was made from an
earring. It's as if my mother left it here for me.

"What's that?" Sydney, as alert to the shiny bauble as a magpie,
is suddenly right behind me.

I look into the eyes of Nemesis and think about Gena, shot
and left to die in a pit where Ian now waits for me, and reach for
the dagger.

"I think this is gold," I say, sliding the dagger out of Nemesis's
marble hand.

"I doubt it," Sydney says prissily. "A dagger would be more likely
made of bronze and it's not in the photo—"

Before he can finish correcting me, I've spun around and
slashed Sydney's smug, supercilious face with the dagger.

"You bitch!" he screams, clutching his bleeding cheek and
reaching for his gun. I slash at him again but he steps back too
quickly—so quickly he doesn't realize how close he is to the pool.
He teeters on the edge, pinwheeling his arms for balance. I step
forward to push him—and notice the envelope with my mother's
picture sticking out of his breast pocket. I pluck it out—and he
grabs my wrist, hanging on to me to keep from falling. Instead
of leaning back I step forward and slice at his wrist with my
dagger. He lets go of my hand and falls backward into the pool,
splashing green, viscous water everywhere. Without waiting to
see what happens to him, I run—around the pool and out of the
chamber—back into the labyrinth.

CHAPTER TWENTY-FIVE

I run through the dark, guided by the luminescent stars, the ghostly women urging me on. *Hurry! Flee!* I've struck at my pursuer but I haven't killed him. He can still climb out of that pool and follow me. He's resurrected himself before, faking his drowning and returning to the island to kill all of us and steal Argos's stolen treasure. Even now, Bill could have already killed Eleni and Annika. I might be too late to save them, but I have to try. First, though, I have to get to Ian, help him out of that pit, and hope that we can get across it before Sydney catches up to us. My only hope is that he gets lost in the labyrinth since I didn't tell him how to follow the stars.

The stars guide me back to the large chamber. I walk straight across because I remember that the archway we came though was directly across from the one marked by the altar constellation. Only there *isn't* an archway directly across. I find myself standing between two arches. Did I misremember?

Did the archways move?

Ice water floods my veins, a surge of pure fear that freezes me in place. Am I even in the same chamber I came through before? What if the star path I followed didn't work going back? After all, I was looking at the reverse side of each arch on the

way back. What if it was a trick to strand me in the labyrinth—
another sacrifice to whatever hellish gods were worshipped here?
I am so frozen that I might stand here forever, slowly becoming a
statue—*Girl, Undecided*. I look from one arch to the next, studying the pattern of the stars over each, but they swim before my
eyes, swelling into supernovas and bursting so violently I have to
close my eyes and press my hands over them, but the stars are still
there, exploding inside my head.

Am I having a stroke?

I open my eyes and stare at the two arches through a kaleido-
scope of shifting pyrotechnics—and then my vision clears and
resolves on something lying on the floor in one of the archways.
I walk toward it cautiously, afraid it's another hallucination, and
kneel down to touch something rough and prickly. It's Annika's
ball of twine. It must have fallen out of my pocket by sheer accident. But here it is, doing its job by showing me the arch I came
through. I start to put it back in my pocket but then I have another idea. I leave it lying in the second arch in the hope that it
will mislead Sydney.

The path back up is steep and dark, lit only by the glowing
stars painted on the ceiling and the traces of luminescence on
my own skin and clothes. This, too, I imagine, is a lesson of the
mysteries: we make our own light. The same women who accompanied me on the way down are still somewhere in the dark, but
now I can only make out the luminescent paint above their heads
and see that there is an aerial host of women with wings and
snakes in their hair flying upward.

The Furies.

Night's other daughters who exact revenge for wrongdoings.

Hundreds of them are streaming up from the underworld to right the wrongs done to all the women who were sacrificed in this place. The shrieks of the wind in the tunnels are now their blood-thirsty cries demanding vengeance. I can feel them thrumming in my blood, urging me on, making me grip the dagger of Nemesis harder in my hand.

At last, I see a glow ahead that I guess is from Ian's flashlight. I get down on my hands and knees and crawl carefully toward the pit and peer cautiously over the edge, praying that Ian is still alive. He's there, sitting cross-legged at the bottom in a circle of weak light, intently drawing triangles in the dirt.

"Practicing Pythagoras's theorem?" I ask.

He looks up and all the blood drains from his face. He looks as sickly pale as the statues in the green pool and for a moment I'm afraid I've come too late; he's metamorphosized into stone and algae. Then he squints at me and says my name.

"Maia?"

"Who else were you expecting?" I ask, trying to keep my voice light, but it comes out with a tremor as if I'm no longer sure who I've become. Ian's laugh brings me back to myself.

"Honestly, I thought you were a ghost," he says. "You look like you're covered in ectoplasm."

I look down and notice the luminescence clinging to the hand still holding the dagger of Nemesis. I'll have to let it go to help Ian out of the pit. As I slide it into my pocket, I feel the spell of the subterranean green pool loosen. I join in with Ian's laughter as he tosses the rope up to me and I lower one end down to him. I feel almost human again.

When I get Ian back up, I tell him about the green pool and

what I did to Sydney there. "I wounded him but he was still alive. If he found his way out of the labyrinth, he could be on his way up here right now."

"Let's hurry then," Ian says. "Once we get across the pit we can destroy the ledge so he can't follow us this way."

I look at the narrow ledge with dread. It had crumbled when I came across it before and looks even narrower now.

"I'll go first," Ian says. "And I'll tie the rope around my waist. If I fall down, we'll just have to climb up on the other side."

He winces as he begins tying the rope, so I do it for him, wishing I could do something further to make his arm more comfortable, but there isn't time. He's already inching onto the ledge, dragging his sprained ankle behind him. It's excruciating to watch, but I keep my eyes on him as if my will could keep him upright. When he makes it across, he tells me to tie my end of the rope around my waist and he grips his end with his good hand.

"If you fall, I've got you," he says.

I look across the pit at him. His face is serious and intent, that of the boy I fell in love with.

"I know," I tell him. Then I walk across the pit, sure-footed and resolute, the blade of Nemesis cold and reassuring against my leg.

On the way up I tell Ian about the photograph of my mother and the letter from my father to Argos.

"You still have the letter?" he asks.

I pat the pocket where the paper crinkles. "Yes, but there's no time to read it now."

"No," he agrees. He's silent for a moment during which I guess we are both wondering the same thing: Will there ever be enough time to absorb what happened to my mother here? As we reach the door to the villa, I reflect that if Bill is waiting on the other side with a gun, I may never learn what's in the letter.

But there's no one on the other side of the door or anywhere else on the bottom floor. We check the rooms on the next floor, but there's no sign of Annika, Eleni, or Bill. The villa is eerily silent as we walk up the stairs; the only face we meet is that of the Gorgon, who has no power to frighten me anymore now that I feel like I've become one.

We search the library and kitchen but find no sign of anyone. The villa feels empty, as if some vital essence has been sapped out of it. As if all the women painted on the walls below in the labyrinth—Persephone, Europa, Leda, Thetis, the Pleiades, all the women pursued and taken by men—have climbed out of the labyrinth and ascended into the stars above us. Is that where Eleni and Annika have gone, too?

"Maia!" Ian calls from the terrace. "Come here!"

I step out onto the terrace into the jasmine-scented night air, hoping against hope that we'll find Eleni and Annika—perhaps bound but alive. But the only women on the terrace are the statues—the daughters of Night standing guard over the empty wreckage. The long table and several chairs have been knocked over and broken glass and crockery litter the floor. Annika and Eleni didn't go without a fight.

"Where has Bill taken them?" I ask, my dread mounting. "They didn't have a boat."

"Sydney had one," Ian says. "He said he came back to the island in one. Maybe he brought it to the dock after we went down to the labyrinth."

"No, Sydney was waiting for us on the other side of the pit. He had to have been there before we started down."

I look back around the terrace, turning twice, searching for some sign in the shadows. My eyes snag on the seat of a chair at the head of the table, the one where Argos sat, and notice that the cushion is lopsided as if something was left beneath it. I cross quickly and lift the cushion and find Annika's bracelet, the one I made for her fifteen years ago. She must have slipped it off her wrist and hidden it here for me to find. But why? A farewell? I pick up the bracelet and run my fingers over the intricate knots that Annika taught me that summer, which she had learned from years of sleepaway camps while I had spent my summers on digs with my father. We'd collected shells on the east cove beach and woven them into friendship bracelets—

Whenever I look at this, I'll remember sitting here with you on this beach.

"I think I know where they've gone," I say, slipping the bracelet around my wrist and pulling the slipknot tight. "Come on."

I LEAD THE way from the back of the villa up the steep ridge path, my heart pounding with each step—*let them be there, let them be there*. I don't think I will be able to bear losing Annika, too. How could I have been so petty all these years, pushing her away because of one kiss? Why had I believed the worst of Ian and Annika without at least confronting them and asking them to explain themselves?

Because Argos encouraged you to, a voice whispers in my ear. *Because this island makes you believe the worst thing you can imagine.*

Which is no excuse, I tell myself.

I'm breathing so hard when I get to the top of the ridge that my vision swims for a moment, the stars wheeling over the east cove as if time has sped up—*too late, too late, too late*, my pounding heart sings. Ian grabs my arm to steady me and points down into the cove.

"There—running lights—that's a boat."

It takes me a moment to focus on the lights he means. The cove seems full of light, the stars' reflections turning the water into another starry heaven. But then I make out between the sky and the sea a new constellation, a triangle formed by a red, white, and green light within which another light moves back and forth like a firefly. Ian hands me his binoculars and the moving light comes into focus as a flashlight. I catch Bill's face in its glare and then a seated figure—Eleni. It looks like her hands are tied. There's no sign of Annika.

"Look—" Ian points to a spot a few yards from the boat where another light is moving. I train the binoculars on it and make out a lantern at the prow of an inflatable dinghy motoring toward the looming black cliff face. The lantern is held by a woman leaning into the wind, red hair streaming behind her. Annika. A dark shape crouches in the back of the boat. Can it be—? Annika half turns to say something to the person steering the boat and her lantern light lands on the grossly distorted features of Sydney Norton. His face is still green with algae and half covered by a crude bandage.

"How did he get out past us?" I cry.

"The labyrinth must connect to the tunnels behind the grotto," Ian says.

Which means he never followed me. He found his way to the grotto and the cove, where he must have left his boat and where Bill was waiting for him.

"They're heading into the grotto," Ian says.

"They must want the rest of the antiquities," I say, "but how does he expect to get them out?"

"He's trying to steer the dinghy *into* the grotto," Ian says, "which is crazy. The tide is too low. He'll puncture the bottom of the boat on the lower rocks."

"Or impale Annika on the upper rocks. Come on—" I hand Ian the binoculars. "We have to get down there."

I scramble down the steep rocky path as fast as I can go, skidding the last stretch on the seat of my pants. Ian is right beside me, his binoculars trained on the mouth of the grotto as soon as we hit the beach.

"He's trying to get through," he says.

I grab the binoculars from him and aim them toward the bobbing light on the cliff face. It looks as if the grotto's mouth is swallowing the rubber dinghy. I catch a glimpse of Annika's terrified eyes and Sydney's grimly determined face, as stony as the rocky jaws he's steering through. I open my mouth to shout even though I know they'd never hear me over the chop of the waves, but Ian grabs my arm and points at the motorboat. Bill is standing at the prow, training his own binoculars on the floundering dinghy.

"Our only chance of saving Eleni is if Bill doesn't know we're here," he says. "I'm going to swim out to the boat and come up behind him."

"What about Annika?" I hiss back.

"Look," he says, pointing toward the cliff, "they're making it."

He's right. I train the binoculars in their direction just in time to see the dinghy vanish into the cave mouth. A flicker of light from inside indicates they made it through intact.

"They'll never be able to move the statues in that. They must be going for the pottery, which will take some time to load up,"

Ian says. "I'm going to swim out to the boat and take care of Bill. When Sydney and Annika come out, we'll be waiting—"

"*If* they're able to get out with that boat," I say. "The tide is coming in. It will be even more dangerous getting out—especially if the boat is weighed down by pottery. Sydney will get them both killed. I have to swim into the grotto and stop him."

"Are you crazy? How will you even see to get through the mouth of the grotto? Without the sun reflecting on the water, you'll be swimming blind."

"There's the lantern inside the cave," I say, already shucking off my shoes and peeling off my sweater. "And look at the water."

He glances at the surface of the cove, which is shimmering with light. What I'd taken as the reflection of starlight is biolumi-nescence. The water is *literally* alive with light.

"There's enough light in the water to guide me into the grotto," I say, meeting his gaze defiantly. The truth is I have no idea what the weird refraction inside the grotto will do with thousands of glowing plankton, but I'm not going to let him talk me out of go-ing. He must see the determination in my eyes and understand.

I strip off my shirt and jeans, down to my bathing suit. I fold and stack my clothes on the beach, checking that the envelope with my mother's photograph and father's letter are still in my pants pocket, and weigh it all down with a large stone. Then I take out the Nemesis dagger and use my belt to secure it around my waist.

CHAPTER TWENTY-SIX

We enter the water together to minimize the sound we make but then Ian strikes out for the boat—awkwardly sidestroking with his good arm—aiming to board it from the stern, and I swim toward the mouth of the cave. I realize, though, that Bill will see me if I go straight to the grotto, so instead I swim toward the cliff, planning to stay in its shadow until Ian overpowers Bill.

The water feels cold at first but after a few strokes I get used to the temperature. A warm current must have moved into the cove, carrying with it this luminescent plankton. Each stroke I take stirs the glowing creatures to life. Blue-green ribbons stream off my fingertips and swirl in my wake, forming new constellations with every stroke. I picture Argos seated at the head of the long table like a king on his throne, only like Cassiopeia he hangs upside down, sowing discord and disruption on his journey through the heavens; the Disruptor, he might be called. I imagine my mother bedecked and weighed down by molten gold, Gena revolving around her father and Eleni desperately trying to save her; Sydney a hunter pursuing her through the labyrinth; Annika, Ian, and I forming a triangle. All of our stories revolve around me, entering the cycle of stories that have played out in these islands for millennia. Deception, Abduction, Betrayal.

From as early as I can remember, my mother told me stories—
fairy tales and myths about the stars. I see now that they were
all her story. I suppose she told them as myths because I was too
young to understand—or maybe because she had been too young
to understand when these things happened to her and she was telling the stories to me to figure them out herself.

By the time I reach the shadow of the cliff I'm worn out from
spinning this celestial universe to life. My fingertips tingle and
my limbs feel heavy. Treading water in the darkness beneath the
cliff I can see that my body is glowing with an unearthly gleam. I
imagine the tiny creatures breeding on my skin, knitting together
a nacreous carapace. If I sink here the shell will become limestone and then marble and centuries from now divers will find
my body and take me for a statue—*Drowned Nereid*, perhaps, or
if they find the Nemesis dagger, they might think I was one of
Night's forgotten daughters.

I taste salt on my lips and feel myself sinking—then I hear
a soft *oof* and turn toward the boat. Ian is struggling with Bill
while Eleni moans through her gag. Now is my chance to enter
the grotto, but I can't even make out the opening. I grope along
the cliff face, the sharp rocks cutting my hands although I barely
feel it; my bioluminescent friends have numbed my skin. My fingertips graze the pointed teeth of the grotto's mouth and then I
feel the pull of the current sucking me down—

To be swallowed whole.

I hope you choke on me, I think as I take a deep breath and go
under.

I'm TOSSED AROUND in the current like a piece of flotsam and spat
out into the grotto, so turned around I don't know which way is

up. Light pulsates all around me like stars exploding into life. I feel as if I might be one of them, the air in my lungs on fire and pressing against my rib cage until I burst. I stop thrashing and look around me, imagining the stars I'll form when I shatter, the shapes they'll make, the stories they'll tell. Then I feel myself rising, buoyed by the tiny plankton teeming on my skin. I slip from water to air so seamlessly I barely make a ripple, which is lucky because I'm right behind the back of the dinghy where Sydney is sitting. He likely wouldn't have heard me anyway because he's yelling at Annika, who is standing on the ledge holding a nylon sack. "Just put the pots in there. And remember if you try to run, I'll kill Eleni and leave your friends to die in the labyrinth."

"How do I even know you left them alive?" Annika asks.

"Do you want to take the chance they're not?" Sydney asks, waving the gun at her. "Or maybe you don't really care what happens to them. You always did look out for yourself, Annika. You have an admirable survival instinct; use it now to get those pots before I shoot you."

Annika looks like she has something else to say but then her eyes shift to the right and widen. She's seen me. I shake my head back and forth, hoping she won't give me away. She recovers quickly with a smile. "You're right, Sydney. I've looked out for myself just like you have—and I can tell you that you're crazy if you think you're getting out of here in that boat. The tide's coming in. You found a way through the labyrinth, right? Wouldn't it be smarter to bring the pottery up through the labyrinth into the villa and then down to the dock? If I toss them all in this bag they'll break."

"It doesn't matter if they break," he says impatiently. "We can sell the shards just as easily as the intact pots—easier, in fact.

There's less suspicion around shards and once a buyer has part of a pot they'll pay more for the remaining pieces. Now quit delaying and go get the pots before it's too late to get through the opening."

He starts to turn toward the grotto's mouth—in my direction—but Annika stops him by asking, "Are you afraid that if you go up through the labyrinth Bill will leave without you? I notice you didn't leave that bag on the boat. What's in it, anyway?"

She's pointing to a canvas bag, which I recognize as the Classical Society tote he put the gold jewelry in. Sydney responds by clutching it closer to his side. "Never mind what's in here. Get going before I blow your head off."

"Okay," she says, "but at least give me the lantern."

"And leave me in the dark?" Sydney asks.

"There's plenty of light in here," she says, "unless you're afraid that the sea monster of the grotto will drag you down to her lair." Annika's eyes flick to me and I guess she's sketching out a plan for me to rise out of the water and grab Sydney in the dark, but Sydney foils the plan by tossing a small, pocket-sized flashlight toward Annika.

"There. That will be enough light for you. Now, get going."

Annika turns on the flashlight and aims it into Sydney's eyes, making him turn away from it. I use the moment to slide my dagger into the bottom of the dinghy, pressing with all my might to make a puncture. I see Annika smile and then turn away, wiggling her fingers in a backward wave. "I'll be right back. Watch out for sea monsters."

When she's gone, I pull the blade out. The dinghy lists slightly toward me, but not enough for Sydney to notice. If I can damage it enough without him noticing and then capsize it suddenly, I'll have the best chance of overpowering him and getting the gun.

The best way to do that, I figure, is to let the air out evenly on all sides without him hearing me moving. I take a deep breath and let myself sink several feet before swimming under the dinghy and coming up on the other side. I must come up too fast, though, because I feel Sydney's weight shift toward me and catch the reflection of his lantern as he holds it out over the water—a few feet away from me, thankfully. I quickly stab the boat and then sink back down beneath the hull. I swim toward the front of the craft and this time slide the dagger into the rubber before surfacing. He must hear the hiss of the air coming out because once again I feel his weight shift toward the prow. I swim beneath the boat and surface behind it. From there I see Annika coming back into the grotto, lugging a now full sack.

"Here you go," she says, swinging the sack into the dinghy.

"Careful," Sydney snaps, shifting the sack in the dinghy to balance its weight.

"I thought you said it didn't matter if they were broken—was that how Argos sold the Wedding Vase to Maia's father, piece by piece?" Annika asks, her eyes slanting toward me. She's giving me time, I see, prodding Sydney to talk while I let more air out of the dinghy. I slide the dagger into the back of it and hear a corresponding sigh come from Sydney.

"Argos said it was easy to control Professor Gold and that we didn't need to worry about him. The shards of the Wedding Vase were just a reminder for him to keep his mouth shut."

As he laughs, I stab the dagger hard into the rubber, thinking of my father forced to collaborate in the looting of antiquities, but I still don't understand what Argos could have been holding over him to make him do so.

"What did he have on him?" Annika asks, as if she knows what I'm thinking.

Sydney snorts. "Still trying to torture your so-called friend, Annika? Get me the rest of the pots and I'll tell you. It had to do with the crazy wife—Maia's mother."

"But then how did Argos continue to control Professor Gold after she died?" Annika asks, slanting her eyes toward me as I aim the dagger into the now sagging boat. "Why didn't Professor Gold expose Argos then?"

My hand stills mid-strike to hear how he answers. What is Annika up to now? The dinghy is clearly sinking. One tug and Sydney will lose his balance and I'll be able to drag him into the water.

"I wondered the same thing," Sydney says. "Argos said that if I was so worried about Professor Gold it wouldn't be difficult to arrange a heart attack for the old man. And it wasn't. All it took was an extra dose of digitalis in his coffee."

"Wait," Annika says, her eyes automatically shifting toward me. "You killed Professor Gold?"

"Let's say I helped him along. I was at a classics conference on a panel, 'Classics and Contemporary Fiction'—"

"Maia was on that panel," Annika says.

"Yes, she was. Afterward I introduced myself to Professor Gold as a friend of his daughter's—he was putty in my hands as I heaped praise on his daughter's book, such a proud father! He quite happily drank the coffee I bought him. I was long gone by the time he collapsed—"

Recalling the moment I saw my father falling to the floor, I decide I've had enough. I yank the rim of the dinghy down and grab Sydney's arm. He lets out a high-pitched yelp and tries to aim the gun at me but Annika leaps into the dinghy and lunges at him. The gun goes off, ricocheting off the walls of the grotto and reverberating throughout the passages of the labyrinth like some long-lost echo of the volcanic eruption that made the island. Annika wrestles the gun away from Sydney but in the struggle they both spill into the water. For a moment, it's hard to make out who is who in the roiling water. I see sparks of gold and realize it's the gold jewelry floating down to the bottom of the grotto. One of the figures in the water snaps his head toward the flash of gold and lunges for it. I grab Annika and pull her away and swim toward a patch of light—the surface, I think, but then I feel the pull of the current and realize we're headed for the mouth of the grotto. Only right now it looks more like a half-closed blue eye than a mouth. The tide has risen and drowned the opening. The only way out is to swim underwater through the passage into the cove. I look back once and see that Sydney's gotten the cord from the pottery sack tangled around his wrist and it's pulling him down to the bottom of the grotto. It looks, for a moment, as if some creature has wrapped its tentacles around him to drag him to its lair and feast on his bones.

Then Annika is pulling me through the opening, into the cove, and up to the surface. I try to tread water but my limbs are too heavy. I look around and find the boat but it looks small and far away. The current is pulling us in the other direction.

The sea monster that took Sydney is hungry for more human flesh—

Annika's arm slides over my head and clamps around my neck. I feel myself being pulled, but not under. I'm gliding along the surface, looking up at a sky full of stars that are growing dim.

Perhaps I'm dying, I think. Or maybe I am looking down at their reflection in the sea and I'm drowning. Or maybe I'm lying in my childhood bedroom and the paint my mother used is finally fading.

I make out for one last time Orion aiming his bow at the bull who carries Europa away from her home and warns the Seven Sisters to flee the hunter. They've almost gotten away but there's no place to go now but the sea. They are diving into the water off the edge of the horizon, safe for another turn of the wheel. I close my eyes and see my mother's face above me. *Follow them home,* she says.

When I open my eyes, hers have faded into the blue sky, tinged pink, the last stars winking out above me, the feel of sand beneath me, Annika beside me, her hand clasped in mine.

CHAPTER TWENTY-SEVEN

The climb back is a blur. Somehow Annika gets me up to the ridge and back down to the villa. My limbs feel leaden, as if I am undergoing a metamorphosis from shell to limestone to marble. When we reach the villa, I hear voices on the terrace and for a moment I imagine we are back to the first night of our arrival and Sydney and Olivia are trading barbs over cocktails—or further back and Argos is spurring me and Annika on to compete against each other—or even further and my mother and father are celebrating their good fortune at coming to such a beautiful place and beginning to fall in love. I want to rush onto the terrace and grab my mother's hand and get her off this cursed island before it's too late.

Annika leaves me at the back door for a few minutes to see what is going on. Then she comes back and steers me to my room, explaining that Ian and Eleni have Bill restrained and they've used the radio on Sydney's boat to call the police, who will be here soon. She leads me to the shower, stripping sodden clothes from my chilled flesh. I feel as if I'm shedding my skin, sloughing off layers of myself under the hot water until nothing remains but a husk, which Annika tucks under the covers. Maybe once I've shed the layers that have grown over me there will be nothing left.

I wake up to the sound of wailing. I am back in the labyrinth among the women being herded to the slaughter. I open my eyes to a room tinted orange as hellfire. Is this how my mother felt, I wonder, that she dwelled in hell? Only slowly do I recognize my room at Lavyrinthos. I've slept all day and now the sun is setting. I'm not in the labyrinth. I'm not in hell.

But someone is still wailing.

I dress quickly and open my door to a scene out of a Greek tragedy. White-robed figures are walking slowly down the hall carrying a draped bier. It could be the funeral procession on a Greek vase, complete with mourners following the bier raising their arms and wailing in grief. It's Eleni, I realize, with Annika beside her, supporting her with an arm around her bowed shoulders. Ian is following them. When he sees me, he takes my arm and we fall in behind them.

"The forensics team has been down with Gena all day," he tells me in hushed tones. "Eleni insisted on sitting beside the pit until they could bring her up."

I glance at his ashen face and grimy clothes—the same he was wearing last night. He's cradling his right arm and limping; clearly no one has seen to his injuries yet. "And you've been sitting beside her," I say.

"I was the one who found Gena," he says simply. "I took Eleni to her." He turns to me, his eyes glaringly white in his dirt-streaked face. "I couldn't leave her to sit there alone."

"No," I say, "of course you couldn't. Where will they take her now?"

"To a forensics lab in Volos," he says. "They've already taken Argos's and Olivia's bodies on an earlier boat."

"Good," I say, "I wouldn't want Gena to have to be on the same boat with Argos."

On the terrace the forensics officers pause to talk to a rather urbane-looking gray-haired man in a navy suit in hurried, whispered Greek. Eleni, hearing them, raises her head and draws herself up very tall, transforming instantly from a broken, grieving old woman into something that resembles a goddess. She cuts through their argument with a few simple words, which even I, with my limited knowledge of modern Greek, understand.

I am going with her.

The plainclothes officer nods to her and then to the forensics team, who begin the long walk down the stairs to the dock. As Eleni turns to follow them, she sees me and holds out her hand. I hurry over to her, words of grief and contrition tumbling in my head, but she silences all of them with a look.

"Thank you for finding my daughter," she says, squeezing my hand. "No one should have to stay in that awful place for eternity. She's free of it now—and of Argos—as I am and I hope you will be, too."

She turns and leaves, following her daughter down the stairs to the dock before I can ask what she means. Annika and Ian come to stand on either side of me and together we watch as Eleni and Gena board the boat and motor out of the harbor, west toward the setting sun, where it seems to catch fire—a funeral pyre for Iphigenia.

When we turn away the officer is waiting for me.

"Your friends convinced me to let you sleep but we need your testimony as soon as possible," he says in careful English. He snaps his fingers and a younger man in uniform steps forward to escort me into the library.

"Give her something to eat," Annika calls after us.

"Get one of those doctors to look at Ian's arm and ankle," I counter as I follow the officer into the library.

I'm given hot coffee and semolina biscuits and asked to recount everything that's happened since I arrived on the island three nights ago. Has it really only been that long? I feel as if several lifetimes have passed since we arrived. Certainly, the story I tell could fill a three-act Greek tragedy, which is what it feels like as the junior officer takes it down without expression or comment, as placid as an ancient scribe, complete with the anagnorisis of recognizing Sydney as the villain of the piece. I expect the stoic scribe to at least comment on that—*didn't you guess?*—but the only question he asks at the end is about my father.

"Was Professor Gold aware of the illegal trade in antiquities?"

I open my mouth to reply but nothing comes out. I think of what Sydney told Annika. I realize that Annika wanted me to know that my father was forced into collusion with Argos, that it wasn't his fault. Still the answer is yes, he knew that the Wedding Vase came illegally, shard by shard, from Argos. My father's legacy—

But then I realize that my father's legacy isn't the Wedding Vase; it's his love for my mother. Everything he did, he did to protect her, even if it failed in the end. The rest of it doesn't matter.

"Yes," I tell the officer, "I believe now that he did know and that he went along with it to protect my mother—I'm still not sure why; Argos had something he held over him—but that's no excuse.

There are antiquities that have been stolen from your country and I'd like to work with your government to restore them—starting with the Wedding Vase."

He looks surprised at my easy admission—I've finally gotten a rise out of him—and I use the moment to get up. "If it's all right, I'd like to continue this in the morning. I'm tired and I'd like to see my friends."

He nods, businesslike again. "That is enough for now. We will speak again in the morning when we make arrangements for your removal to the mainland . . ." He goes on in an official manner but I'm no longer paying attention. I pretend to yawn and make my escape to the terrace, where I find Ian, who's wearing a sling on his arm and an Ace bandage on his ankle now, and Annika putting out plates of cheese and bread and salad.

"There's not much left," Annika says.

"What happened to Bill?" I ask, sitting down and filling my plate.

"They've arrested him and taken him to Volos," Annika says. "You should have heard him singing like a canary, pinning everything on Sydney since he's not here."

I look up, the bread and cheese turning to a lump in my throat as I picture Sydney drifting down through the silty green water of the grotto. "They haven't found him?" I ask after swallowing.

"No," Ian says. "They're bringing divers tomorrow to search the grotto. Eleni doesn't think they'll ever find him. She said that the ones who drown in the grotto are never found; they sink down into the underworld."

"Good," Annika says, wrapping her shawl around my shoulders because I'm shivering. "I hope he rots in hell. He deserves it after all he's done. He killed Gena—"

"And my father," I add, shivering as I recall that moment at the conference seeing Sydney talking to my father. "I just wish I knew what Argos was holding over my father that made him go along with selling illegal antiquities."

"Maybe there's something here," Ian says, handing me the envelope with my mother's photograph. "I went back to the beach to get it."

I look up at him gratefully—and then to Annika. "I owe you both an apology—"

"We were in the wrong," they both say at the same time, which makes me laugh.

"I should have confronted you and given you both a chance to explain," I say.

"If I'd come straight to you with what I learned that night, none of this would have happened. I should have trusted that you'd be strong enough to confront your father—and that could have saved him, too . . ." Annika's voice trembles and I see she's on the verge of tears. I reach over to squeeze her hand, bare of the bracelet I made for her fifteen years ago, which is still on my wrist. "We have to make new bracelets before we leave," I say.

"I'll go get the twine," Annika says, "but first"—she points to the letter—"I think it's time you read that."

I look down at the letter with a feeling of dread. Do I really want to know a secret so awful Argos was able to use it as blackmail? Can I bear it? I look back up at Annika and Ian, both of them watching me with the steadfast patience of those statues in the subterranean cave. *Yes, with them here to face it with me, I can.*

I open the envelope and look first at the photograph of my mother—so young and beautiful, decked out like a queen in

ancient gold, her eyes clear and untroubled; a look I never saw
on her. *What happened to you?* I wonder. Then I open the letter,
which is in my father's familiar handwriting, and begin to read.

Dear Argos,

You've made your terms clear so I will not go over them again
here. Elizabeth and I have discussed it and although the onus
of blame lies with you, we will agree to your terms for the sake
of our daughter, Maia, and your pledge to renounce all claim to
her. I want you to understand, once and for all that I do not
recognize the legitimacy of that claim. You took advantage of
a young woman whom you had plied with drugs and led into that
hellish place. I blame myself for not realizing the depths of your
depravity and protecting her. I do not blame Elizabeth (as much
as she blames herself). I have told her that I would happily take
you to court for your assault on her. For raping her. But she is
convinced that you would wield your power and fortune against
us and, most frightening of all try to lay claim to Maia. I fear
that Elizabeth's mental state—already frail after the trauma of
the drugs you gave her, your assault on her, and then her time
lost in the labyrinth—would not withstand that outcome. I have
spoken with Clive Davies, as well and he too agrees never to tell
the world about what we found on Eris—the labyrinth, the
evidence of a secret cult, and the ancient treasures you have
claimed as your own and kept from the world—on the condition
that you never attempt to contact our daughter.
    Because she is <u>our daughter</u>.
    From the moment I first held her in my arms I knew that. I do

not care about your claim of blood; I have the greater claim of love.

As for the shard of the amphora you have sent, I would tell you to desist in sending more, but I know too well your perverse fondness for games. You already have my compliance; you mean only to shame me by sending these broken pieces to remind me of what damage you have done. I can't make you stop. In the end, all I can do is endeavor to take what is broken and make of the pieces something whole.

Yrs,
Julius Gold

I hand the last page to Annika and Ian and look up at them. Both of their faces are as damp as mine. Annika looks stricken. "I always wondered if your mother had been assaulted. When you told me about her claustrophobia, paranoia, and anxiety—I thought it sounded familiar."

"Her mental health problems weren't caused by her painting," Ian says. "They came from being raped."

"And from having to hide it," I say, feeling the weight of the secret both my parents had lived under. "I think she must have been trying to work through what happened to her when she painted. What I don't understand is why they were so afraid. Surely, no court in the world would give a rapist rights over a child—"

"With all Argos's power and money?" Ian asks. "I don't blame your parents for being afraid. They must not have been willing to take the risk of losing you."

Annika nods. "You realize this means that you're—"

"Don't say it," I stop her. "I'm not *anything* of his."

"No, you're nothing like him," Ian agrees. "That bastard. No wonder my father kept silent; he would never have let Argos take you from his friend."

"So your father knew—" I begin. Then I think of what Eleni said before she left—that she hoped I would be free of Argos and the labyrinth. "And Eleni knew."

Ian nods. "While we were waiting for the forensics team to bring up Gena, she told me that she guessed that Argos assaulted your mother because your father and mother never came back to the island. When she saw you fifteen years ago she guessed that you were Argos's daughter, but she didn't say anything because she was afraid you'd come to claim your inheritance."

"My inheritance!" I scoff. "I want nothing of Argos's!"

"Are you sure?" Ian asks. "Think of what you could do with this island—the classical study center it could be—"

"And artists' colony," Annika adds. "One that doesn't pit its guests against each other, of course."

I shake my head. I don't want it. And yet . . . as the wind picks up I hear the voices of the women in the labyrinth.

Tell our stories, they whisper.

Annika and Ian must hear their siren call as well because as we drink ouzo and braid bracelets from twine and seashells, we talk about the women who were brought here.

"I think," I tell them, recalling the statues around the green pool and the luminescent Furies flying back up through the labyrinth, "that the rites were first a sacrifice—like at the labyrinth in Minos's palace on Crete—but that at some point the women who were brought here to be sacrificed gained control and changed them."

"Like Discord throwing the apple into the wedding of Peleus and Thetis," Ian says. "Causing chaos and upending the status quo."

"And Nemesis exacting revenge for the women who were sacrificed," I say.

"So, in other words," Annika says, "this place is like a monument to badass Amazons."

"Exactly," Ian and I say at the same time.

The stars come out above us to listen, the salt air stealing across the terrace and sharpening our words, the lap of waves and the cry of the little *Athene noctua* our chorus, singing a refrain that has echoed on this island for millennia. We stay up all night and only part near dawn, Annika stealing away first, leaving Ian and me alone on the terrace.

"Do you think you'll keep up the Detective Pythagoras books?" I ask in the awkward silence that follows her departure.

"I might write one last one," he says, "for my father—*Pythagoras's Last Case*—but then I think it's time to move on. What about you?"

I shake my head. "I don't know. I feel like I've spent the last fifteen years stuck, frozen in place, but now—"

A breeze stirs at my back, blowing my hair in my face, and we both raise our hands at the same time to push it back. He touches my cheek and I graze his hand and we're suddenly inches apart, as if the wind had nudged us closer together. As his lips touch mine, I feel the curve of his smile and picture the boy I fell in love with fifteen years ago, but as the kiss deepens, I sense the man that he's become since then.

By mutual consent we walk from the terrace, hand in hand, up the path to the ridge, where we stand looking down at the cove. The sky on the horizon is tinged violet, hinting at the coming dawn but still dark enough that the morning stars are visible. I think of the women who came here, stolen from their home and brutally sacrificed. But somehow over the years—the centuries, perhaps—the women gained control and changed the rites to tell the story of Demeter searching for her daughter, of Clytemnestra mourning hers, and the Furies avenging their deaths. I think of Eleni trying to shield her daughter from Argos's influence and my father trying to protect me and my mother. I think of my mother struggling with her madness to teach me a way out of the labyrinth and of my father assembling pieces of the Wedding Vase even though he knew those pieces were stolen. I remember his final words to Argos.

In the end, all I can do is take what is broken and make of its pieces something whole.

I think of Annika and me braiding friendship bracelets on the beach and touch the shells threaded through the twine of my new bracelet and count, one by one, the seven stars poised on the horizon. In the water, their reflections seem to spill out of the grotto, as if the Seven Sisters, led by Maia, the eldest, are finally escaping from the underworld, skimming across the sea, and ascending into the sky. Free at last.

ACKNOWLEDGMENTS

Thanks, as always, to my agent, Robin Rue, and her assistant, Beth Miller, and everyone at Writers House for their ongoing support and encouragement. Thank you to my editor, Tessa James, for traveling the labyrinth with me, and to all the people at William Morrow whose hard work brings books into the world.

I began this book at one writing residency and finished it at another. Thank you to Rosemary Dunn of the Eastern Frontier Educational Foundation on Norton Island, Maine, and to Jennie Lee of the Essere Residency in Tuscany, Italy, for your vision and generosity in creating spaces in which artists and writers can flourish. I'm grateful, too, to all the wonderful artists and writers at Norton Island and Essere for being far nicer and better behaved than the residents of my fictional Eris Island.

I am lucky to have friends and family who support me in this strange writing life. Thank you, Gary Feinberg, Andrea Massar, and Nancy Johnson, for reading early drafts. Thanks to Scott Silverman for all your insights into the stars. Thank you, Lee, for all the trips to Greece and for inspiring Detective Pythagoras. And thank you, Nora, Jeremy, and Maggie, for all the joy and laughter you bring to my life.

ABOUT THE AUTHOR

CAROL GOODMAN's rich and prolific career includes novels such as *The Widow's House* and *The Night Visitor*, winners of the 2018 and 2020 Mary Higgins Clark Awards. Her books have been translated into sixteen languages. She lives in the Hudson Valley.

Discover more from
CAROL GOODMAN

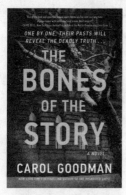

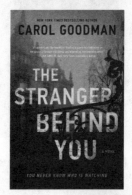

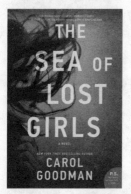

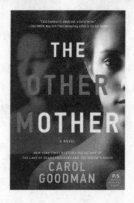

DISCOVER GREAT AUTHORS, EXCLUSIVE OFFERS, AND MORE AT HC.COM.